She petted him on the head again and slowly opened her legs, exposing his reward: the yawning pink of her shaved pussy. 'Such a good boy!' she cooed. 'You get a treat! Get on all fours now, Jimmy! Come on, boy!'

James dropped to his feet and scrambled in between Becky's legs. The stripper raised her left leg and rested the stiletto heel of her metallic-red shoes on James's shoulder. Her foot slid further down his back as he crawled forward and assumed a position of subservient pussy worship.

'Still want to leave?' She giggled.

The tip of his tongue reached out for his prize. She tasted like melting candy.

'Suck on my pussy,' she demanded. 'I want you to suck my pussy, Jimmy.' Becky lifted the bottle and poured an avalanche of sparkling wine over her lower stomach. The champagne thoroughly soaked James's head. He began to slurp and suck on the mixture of lollipop, champagne, pussy juice and body rub.

'Yeah, good boy.' Becky laughed, 'Suck on my pussy and drink up, honey. It'll make you feel good.' She pushed her pussy into his face, straddling his head with her legs. 'Almost forgot, song is nearly over, lover. Show me how much you love eating cunt.'

LONGING FOR TOYS

Virginia Crowley

This book is a work of fiction.
In real life, make sure you practise safe, sane and
consensual sex.

First published in 2007 by
Nexus
Thames Wharf Studios
Rainville Rd
London W6 9HA

A catalogue record for this book is available from the British
Library.

www.nexus-books.com

Typeset by TW Typesetting, Plymouth, Devon

The paper used in this book is a natural, recyclable product made
from wood grown in sustainable forests. The manufacturing
process conforms to the regulations of the country of origin.

ISBN 978 0 352 34138 9

Distributed in the USA by Holtzbrinck Publishers, LLC,
175 Fifth Avenue, New York, NY 10010, USA

Penguin Random House is committed to a sustainable future for
our business, our readers and our planet. This book is made from
Forest Stewardship Council® certified paper.

FSC
www.fsc.org

MIX
Paper from
responsible sources
FSC® C018179

Printed and bound in Great Britain by Clays Ltd, Elcograf S.p.A.

Contents

1

Scott

There were two of them. Both had very long silky black
hair cascading all the way down to the small of their backs.
They were pretty Asian dolls in extremely short dresses.
The one on the left wore a fire-engine-red, slinky design
that was revealing enough to display her well-toned,
tapered legs to their best advantage. The one on the right,
if anything, was even more attractive. She was characteris-
tically slim, but her chest was unusually large – presumably
the result of artificial enhancement. Their stiletto heels
made a loud clatter on the concrete as they strutted past.
The crimson bit of temptation spared him a short,
self-possessed glance. Oh, she knew he was checking her
out – what red-blooded American male wouldn't have?

Scott wished Robert was there already. His friend was a
trained plastic surgeon and would know at a glance if those
boobs were real. Except for their breasts the women looked
very much alike. He permitted himself a brief fantasy: what
if they were twins? How sweet would that be?

He wondered what they did for a living. They could be
call girls – very expensive ones – or perhaps strippers.
Without a doubt they were women who were hot for a
living. They just had that particular ... way about them.
An awareness that men got hard around them. He watched
their swaying, confident strut, not bothering to hide his
interest.

The women walked up to a doorway under a bright
yellow sign and rang a doorbell. Scott smiled. His instincts
were right – they just rang the doorbell to Hot Summer's,

perhaps the most well-known strip club in town. It had a justifiable reputation as the place to go to if you wanted to see some really hot girls – assuming you had the money.

There was a sign:

Today's Performers:
AMBER
BECKY
TINA
MICHELE
HEATHER
TIFFANY
PRINCESS

He scratched his nose and slowly nodded to himself. Obviously, these two were 'performers'.

Scott wondered what names they used. None of the names were Asian. He wandered closer but the doors swallowed up the twin dolls.

A tall blonde approached from the direction of the parking garage. She had very long, tanned legs. They were so impressive, Scott nearly forgot to shake his head in mute appreciation of her cleavage. Those luscious tits had been given every possible opportunity to draw interested stares. They were trapped by the slimmest of margins by a flimsy halter top of white polyester. The word 'SEXY' spelled out the obvious, an utterly superfluous designation composed of silver sequins. The blonde spared him a single bored glance as she approached the doorway. He grinned at her, appreciative of the lack of ambiguity in her attitude and attributes. Scott was enjoying his favourite spectator sport.

She halted at the doorway and rang the doorbell.

Scott gulped air, startled by the sound of a car's horn. He flinched and turned to face the road. A bright-red car, tiny, convertible and expensive-looking, pulled up to the curb. Robert sat behind the wheel. This had to be Robert's pride and joy, then.

Scott walked over and examined the car. The thing was practically alive and had a catlike character. It wasn't just idling alongside the curb; it was curled up, engine purring, waiting to leap. Robert pumped the horn on the steering wheel with his fist, producing yet another burst of brassy perfectly pitched sound. He was of average height, smooth shaven, with sparkling brown eyes and chestnut-coloured hair. He wore a red golf shirt and khakis.

'Dude, *this* is the car?' asked Scott. Robert had been talking about it for weeks now, but this was the first time he had seen it with his own eyes.

'Sure is,' said Robert, beaming. He brushed an invisible speck of dust from the walnut dashboard. 'It's an actual 1961 Austin Healy 3000.'

Scott whistled. He ran his hand over the side. 'I admit it, it's a hell of a car. I'm impressed.'

'Everybody likes it. Even Holly likes it, although I think she's a little jealous. She says I want to marry the car.'

'Oh yeah, women. I wanted to ask your professional opinion about these two chicks . . .' He looked around in vain. The two Asian dancers had already been swallowed up in the dark rectangle of the club entrance and Scott's searching gaze snagged on the statuesque blonde. The door to the club was wide open, she just needed to pass through a curtain of burgundy velvet to go inside, but she stayed rooted in place, looking at them. No, not at them, at the car.

Robert fiddled with the stereo. 'Sergeant Pepper' came on and he closed his eyes, leaning back in his seat. Scott waved to the blonde. She seemed completely absorbed by Robert's car, but she looked up eventually and gave him a tight smile.

Maybe he ought to come by the club for a beer or something. Might as well start his vacation early. He definitely deserved a drink. Slaving away in a cubicle at the Bureau of Vital Statistics, processing mind-numbing applications all day, chipped away at the soul of a man. A stiff drink, some skin, a vacation in Jamaica – it was definitely high time for all three. He hopped in the car. The song nearly over, Robert put it in gear and they peeled out into traffic.

'What were you looking at?' asked Robert.

'You didn't see her?' He pointed at the doorway but all he saw was the parting shot of a slender ankle and stiletto heels before the curtain swung back into place, blocking his view. 'Dude, you should have been here earlier, there were these two really hot Asian chicks ...'

'Naw, not me.' Robert laughed. 'I'm happily taken, thank you.'

'Yeah, yeah ...' Scott replied, chuckling. 'I know. So in any case, I'm nearly out of here!'

'Oh yeah, Jamaica!'

'Right. Leaving tomorrow.'

'Send me a postcard, you hear?'

'Too bad you can't come.'

'I'd love to ... But I'm swamped with work. I have a symposium on my oncology research and way too many operations.' He lovingly stroked the dashboard. 'Maybe this spring, after I'm done with my research, I'll take this beautiful girl cross-country.'

'Great idea! Can I come?'

Robert laughed. 'I'm sure Holly would just love to have you along.'

'Oh come on! You know you'd rather be with your buddies, man.'

'Sure, sure.'

Robert made a right. He zoomed into the left lane and drove north. The wind raked through Scott's hair and the sun sparkled. 'Where are we going? Don't you have to go back to work?'

'I do, but I barely ever get a chance to drive my sweet baby. Another five minutes and we'll stop for food, don't worry.'

'Good, I'm starving.'

Finally Robert pulled over. He listened to the engine's purr for a few moments before shutting it off with a happy sigh. He motioned towards the restaurant sign. 'It's been ages since I had good Chinese.'

The restaurant was nearly full and they got a table near the kitchen. The hostess had a slim body, tight as a drum, encased in a sleek black dress.

'You really have a fetish, you know,' said Robert, commenting on his friend's appreciative stare.

Scott felt slightly defensive. 'So? Everyone has a fetish.'

'I don't.'

'What about Danielle?'

Robert chuckled. 'Head Nurse Danielle? I still think she had that uniform shortened. That's the only explanation for those legs. But you do have a point. I can't say I wasn't tempted. She never gave me the time of day, though . . .'

It was Scott's turn to chuckle. 'Maybe she was into girls?'

Robert raised an eyebrow and leant back in his chair to stare at the lacquered red ceiling. 'I really don't need that idea in my head. Not that it's a bad idea, mind you . . . But she's gone and now I'll never nail a hottie nurse.' He morosely drank some water.

'But you'd like to.'

'Not any more,' mumbled Robert.

The waitress brought their lunch. They didn't talk much while they ate. Scott ordered a beer, Robert a lemonade.

'I wish I could stay for dessert,' said Robert. 'But I've got to get back to work. Where can I drop you off?'

'Uhm . . . Take me back where you picked me up,' said Scott. 'Maybe I'll try to hook up with those two chicks I saw earlier,' he added, laughing.

'You're incorrigible,' said Robert with a smile.

The club was a shadowy den of spotlights and candles. He didn't stop to soak in the details. Scott negotiated the doorman in front and the cop sitting behind the curtain with a mixture of impatience and excitement. Hot women and beer! This is the life! he thought.

He scanned the shadowy darkness for the two women he had seen outside, finding one of them immediately. She actually came over to him as he sat down at the bar. She reminded him a little of the hostess at the restaurant. She had that all-natural slim body and wore a tight blue dress.

'Hello,' she purred. 'I'm Tina.'

'I'm Scott.'

'So how're you doing, Scott?'

5

'I'm doing great, Tina. I'm doing just fantastic, actually.' God, this girl was so hot! 'Can I get you a drink?'

'I'd love a drink, Scott!' She giggled prettily and tossed her glorious long black hair back over her shoulder. She gestured to the bartender. 'Mai Tai, Henry.'

He couldn't quite stop grinning. 'You're gorgeous, Tina. Was that your sister I saw with you outside?'

'Yeah, sure. That's my sister,' she got a hold of the Mai Tai and wrapped her crimson lips around the straw. She watched him while she sipped. 'You like my sister?'

'I like you, I like you . . .' Scott laughed. 'But your sister is pretty too. You're both very pretty.' He finished his first beer and motioned to the bartender for another round.

'I'll ask her to join us,' said Tina. She caressed his arm, her hand feathery light. 'You stay here, honey.'

'Oh don't worry, I'm not going anywhere.' Scott grinned. 'You just bring your sister. Tell her I want to buy her a drink.'

'You like Tina and Heather, Scott?' asked a seductive contralto voice.

Scott turned on his chair. The voice belonged to the tall blonde who had observed his departure earlier. She was definitely one hot number, a total package with a great tan, long blonde hair, big tits, curves . . . She had changed already. Her new outfit – work outfit – was a black lace corset, a tiny black miniskirt, a garter belt and black patent-leather sandals with stiletto heels.

'Wow,' he blurted. He sensed that his mouth was agape and he closed it. 'Yeah, sure, I like them.' He drank down some of the beer to cool his head and held out his hand. 'I'm Scott, by the way.'

She took his hand and pressed it softly. 'I know, I heard you introduce yourself to Tina. Hello, Scott.'

'What's your name?'

'I'm Michele. So you've come to party with Heather and Tina, Scott?'

He grinned. 'Sort of, I guess. I'm going on vacation tomorrow and I thought I'd start the party early.'

'Where is your friend?'

'What? You mean Robert?'

6

'Is that his name, Robert?'

'Yeah, the guy I was talking to when you came in. You like him?'

'He's got a nice car.' Michele smiled. 'It's very hot.'

'It's his little baby.' Scott nodded. 'Maybe I'll bring him the next time I come.'

'I'd like that,' said Michele. 'So what do you do, Scott?'

'I work for the Bureau of Vital Statistics. Death and marriage certificates, name changes . . . Stuff like that.'

'That's *very* interesting.'

Scott stifled a wry grin. No doubt a garbage man was also 'very interesting' as long as it got her some tips.

Tina returned. She was accompanied by her so-called sister.

'Scott, hello,' she said. 'My name's Heather. You know Michele?'

'I'm due on stage in a minute.' Michele smiled. 'Show Scott a good time, girls. I think we'll be very good friends.'

Scott withdrew some more cash from the in-house ATM. After all, he didn't need a lot of spending money in Jamaica. It was not an expensive place. Just a few hundred should be enough. He would be gone for only a week, for crying out loud.

'Oooh, thank you, Scott!' Heather giggled, taking her second Mai Tai. She leant against him, resting her scented head on his shoulder. She slid her manicured fingers up and down his arm. 'You're so strong, Scott!'

'Thanks, Heather.'

'I think you're strong too,' purred Tina. 'You like my sister and you like me . . .' She glanced at Heather.

The girls exchanged a peculiar look and giggled mischievously.

'Scott, take us to the champagne room,' whined Heather. 'You'd like the champagne room. We would show you a really good time.'

He laughed nervously. 'Champagne room?'

'We want to give you a lap dance,' cooed Tina. 'First we sit on your knee and then you get to . . .'

'Spank the one who was bad?' he said, grinning.

7

'Yeah, you get to spank the bad girl,' she agreed at once. She tilted her body and slapped her gorgeous tight ass. 'Spank spank spank the pretty tight buns until they're all red and I just have to beg you to stop. And when you stop I'll be so grateful that I'll . . .' She lowered herself over his lap by way of demonstration. Her ass settled over his raging hard-on and clenched like a vice. 'Like this, you know?' She giggled. Heather got up and stood behind him. She draped her long, scented black hair over his head while her sister squirmed all over his erection. They smelled like roses burning.

'I guess . . . Hold on,' he gasped. This champagne room was bound to be expensive. 'How much . . .?'

'Just two hundred!' Tina caressed his cheek. 'It's sooo much fun!'

'You know, I just can't . . .'

'You go and have a good time, Scott,' purred Michele. She had apparently overheard the latest exchange. The tall blonde was wearing something else again. That had to mean that it was time for another one of her sets. How many beers had he had? It was hard to tell how long he had been inside. The place was like a casino, there were no windows to let in any sunlight. Michele's latest outfit was an astonishingly short black dress. Since she was standing, Scott had an unhindered view of a pair of frilly white lace panties.

Michele caught him admiring the view. She gave him a bitchy smile and leant forwards, thrusting her ass out while knowingly looking over her shoulder. She swayed back and forth. 'You like my lace panties, Scott?'

He turned red but replied with an emphatic 'Yeah!'

'You should go upstairs with Tina and Heather,' she said. 'You deserve a treat!'

'I'm sure, but I . . .' He wanted to say, 'but I'm not going to have any spending money in Jamaica if I blow it all here on you girls', but he immediately realised these girls would be ignoring him faster than a speeding bullet if he was stupid enough to admit being close to broke.

'Oh, girls!' Michele frowned, bending a little lower. Her pussy was a shaved mound of gorgeous pink behind the frilly lace. 'We're all so mean, teasing poor Scott like this!'

8

Even her frown was sexy, thought Scott. His gaze wandered over to Tina. My God, she looked delicious.

Michele noticed. 'Let's go to the ladies room, Heather.'

'OK,' replied Heather, giving Michele a questioning look.

The blonde whispered to her. Their hair clashed, the golden blonde generating a shocking contrast against the raven black. Heather nodded and they glided away with seductive grace.

Scott finished his beer while Tina was doing her set. He noticed Heather returning from the ladies room. She negotiated the jungle of tables with professional skill. She stopped to talk to men who talked to her but shook her head frequently, once in a while pointing in the direction of his table.

Scott grinned. Had he made an impression?

Heather returned and sat at his table just as Tina rejoined them. The two girls had a brief rapid-fire exchange in a language he did not recognise. He thought about asking if it was Chinese but then realised if it wasn't they might get offended, and if it was they might think him ignorant.

'What's up?' he asked after they finished.

'We are taking you upstairs to the champagne room,' said Heather. 'We're gonna show you a good time.'

'But I . . .'

'Don't worry, Scott.' Tina smiled. 'Michele is treating you!'

'Really? Why? I mean . . . that's great!'

They pulled him up the stairway, stroking him here and there, caressing his arms. 'You're sooo strong!' purred Tina. 'So handsome!'

Upstairs there were curtained-off little rooms. Heather parted the curtains and pulled him into one. Tina pushed him from behind at the same time and he fell forwards, landing on an unexpectedly plush leather sofa. He sat up and they sat down as well, just as they had promised: on his knees.

'This is when you get some *personal* attention,' cooed Heather. 'You want me with the big titties –' she shook them, obviously gloating '– or flat little Tina with no titties?'

'I have titties and they're not little!' Tina pouted. She stepped on top of the couch, her stiletto heels nearly gouging a hole in the leather, and smoothly knelt down next to Scott. In this position her breasts were at eye level. She pushed them together, tweaking her nipples mere inches from his transfixed gaze. 'You don't think they're little, do you Scott?'

'They're great, Tina,' Scott replied. 'They're fucking great.'

Heather pushed Tina aside and plopped herself in his lap. Her sister – if that is indeed who she was – crossed her arms, pouting. Heather began to manipulate his cock with her ass, through his pants, applying one slow, sensuous stroke of her clenched cheeks at a time.

Tina leant her head on his shoulder while Heather was busily dry-humping his aching hard-on. She rubbed her tits up against his face. 'Tell me again how nice and big my titties are, Scott!'

'They're awesome,' he said. Her nipples were perfect, erect and so close to his lips. He longed to suck on them. They smelled sweet.

'Are you enjoying your lap dance, Scott?' purred Heather. Her ass gripped his cock and released it. Gripped his cock and released it. Slid higher and higher . . . Gripped his cock and released it. 'You like my ass around your big hard cock, don't you Scott?'

'Yeah,' groaned Scott. 'Oh yeah.'

'I can tell how big it is,' crooned Heather. 'Would you like to play with my big titties, Scott?'

'Yeah,' said Scott. He thought of the gorilla downstairs. 'Can I?'

'For a friend of Michele . . .' said Heather, trailing off meaningfully. 'Of course!'

He reached out with trembling hands and cupped the big luscious tits of the Asian girl dry-humping his cock. He had to lean forwards and his face brushed up against one of Tina's perfect nipples.

She pulled away and playfully slapped his face. 'Big strong Scott *likes* the personal attention!'

'Oh, he likes it all right.' The voice was familiar and dripped with contempt. Michele entered the alcove. She made sure the curtain was closed and stood right over the sleazy tableau. She was still wearing the little black dress. 'Song is nearly over, Scott,' she purred. 'Tina, honey, Scott is too busy groping Heather's tits to do anything for himself. Why don't you help him out?'

Tina giggled and nodded. 'Michele must really like you, Scott,' she purred. She leant into the gap between Heather's back and Scott's chest and put a manicured finger on her 'sister's' undulating back. Tina slowly traced her finger down to her ass. Her long black hair cascaded over Scott's head, enveloping him in a scented tent of seduction.

Once again, her nipples were so close . . . He let his head lurch forwards until his face brushed up against one.

Tina giggled and reached below Heather's butt.

Scott felt her questing hand. She searched around until she found his zipper. She tugged on it as her sister squirmed over his erection. Finally, her hand succeeded in its mission.

'Oh my God,' gasped Scott.

'You can remove her hands before she pulls your cock out,' said Michele. 'But I don't think you will. You would have to stop groping Heather's big tits and I think you've grown too attached to part from them.' She caressed Tina's face, neck, shoulders. 'Take out his pecker and play with it until the end of the song, baby.'

Heather slid off his lap. Tina giggled again as her fingers triumphantly latched around his cock. She pulled it out. It was standing at full attention, helpless and rock-hard. The Asian stripper's delicate fingers with their crimson-tipped nails slid up and down, up and down, up and down again, manipulating his erection.

'That must feel sooo good,' crooned Michele. 'It must feel so good to have pretty Tina play with your big stiff cock, Scott!'

Heather pouted. 'He's ignoring me, Michele!'

'You really should do something about that.' The blonde smirked, then squatted down and gave Scott a

11

condescending little smile. 'Would Scott like to put his cock in between Heather's big tits?'

'Yeah,' moaned Scott. His entire being seemed concentrated in his skilfully manipulated member. He reached out and caressed Heather's luscious tits as the girl crawled closer. Tina positioned his cock in between Heather's tits.

Abruptly the song ended and the girls stood.

'What?' gasped Scott. 'What's going on?'

'Would you like Tina and Heather to continue, Scott?' purred Michele.

'Yeah, we wanna continue,' said Heather. 'You liked my big titties around your cock, baby?'

'Yeah, continue!' said Scott. 'Jesus, just keep it coming!'

'The first one was my treat,' said Michele, her voice sweet as honey. 'A lady shouldn't be expected to treat every time . . .'

Scott thrust his hand into his pocket and fished out his wallet. He pulled out the wad of twenties that he had just withdrawn and thrust the money in Tina's outstretched hand.

Tina giggled and the money disappeared. Scott wasn't sure where it went – there didn't seem to be a location for it to disappear to. A heavy, sensual beat started up again.

'There you go, Scott,' said Michele. 'Enjoy yourself.'

Heather trapped his swollen cock in between her tits. She pushed her breasts together, hard. The tip of his member appeared at the top of the tempting mounds until it was a mere two inches from her mouth. 'Oooh,' she crooned and while she stared at his cock she slowly licked her lips. 'Maybe I can make the big white man come on my face!'

'But Scott has to go on vacation,' said Michele. 'He might not want to stay that long.'

Tina put her hand in between his legs and began to fondle his aching balls. Her fingers caressed the base of his helpless, quivering cock. 'This is his vacation, Michele!'

'Oh God,' moaned Scott. 'Oh my God!'

'It would be a shame if Scott came too early, girls,' said Michele in a reproving tone. 'Ease off a little. Why don't you give Scott a kiss?'

Tina and Heather looked at one another and giggled. They positioned themselves on either side of his member and slowly licked it until they both got to the tip. Once there their tongues – and the tip of his cock – merged in a filthy, intertwined kiss.

'I gotta come,' mumbled Scott, staring at the two writhing Asian sluts. 'I gotta come in their mouth, I gotta.'

'But the song is nearly over, Scott!' said Michele, 'The song is nearly over!'

2

Lucille

They were sitting in the salon. It was actually the dining room, thought Lucille sourly, but for now it would have to double as the salon. Rooms ought to have a specific function and stick to them. At least she didn't have to argue with her mother. They were having the tail end of a blissfully agreeable conversation.

'No, of course you can't have a black maid,' agreed Martha, ice-cold with certainty. 'You of all people. And they steal. Everyone knows that.' She lifted her coffee and sniffed it suspiciously. 'A little more milk if you would, honey.'

Lucille poured some more into her mother's cup.

'And some more sugar if you don't mind.'

'Of course ... What do you think of a black driver, though? They look pretty good in a uniform ...'

Her mother sniffed. 'Well, of course a driver is a different breed altogether. They're not in the actual house. They usually have some little cottage on the side. It's not attached to ... it's not a *wing* of the house, naturally. You don't want to socialise with them, they just drive you around. Did you talk to James about getting a driver?'

'I mentioned it in passing,' lied Lucille. Privately she felt that it was a little premature to talk to James about a driver. She had enough trouble convincing him that once they got married they ought to look for a bigger home; the issue of the driver would just have to wait until she had more leverage – until, say, she was expecting his first child.

'Good, good. So what did he say?'

'I'm not sure if he was really paying attention. He works a lot.' Lucille put another sugar cube in her mother's cup before she had a chance to ask for one. She sighed theatrically – à la Scarlett O'Hara missing Brett Butler.

'Oh thank you, honey,' oozed Martha. 'Anyway, why the sudden interest in . . . *staff*? I thought you had a maid come every week.'

'I have so much work with the wedding preparations, I've asked her to come twice a week. I'm just thinking of how much trouble it'll be to keep the new house; I thought live-in help –'

'Domestics,' offered her mother.

'– Domestics, yes, I thought those . . . they would be a good idea. In any case, permanent staff would be impressive. Imagine, mother, I could throw dinner parties every week for executives and bankers and all kinds of people, friends and family. It would advance James's career!'

'You will make a wonderful wife and mother, dear!'

'Thank you, Mom.'

'Some more sugar, dear.'

'Of course. Some more coffee?'

'I don't mind if I do.' Martha laughed, the folds of fat on her cheeks rippling with amusement. 'Make sure the staff you hire know how to make good coffee, dear.'

'I thought about switching to tea.'

'Tea? Really?'

'Yes. It's such a civilised habit.'

'Custom. It's a custom.'

'Anyway, I thought about having tea with some select friends on a daily basis. Wouldn't that be quaint?'

Martha considered the cup of wonderful, toxically sweet concoction in her hand. She seemed unconvinced by the idea of giving it up for tea. She put the cup down, sighing with barely suppressed longing. 'I suppose it would be . . . quaint.'

It was time to move on to important things. 'What about the bridesmaids? Do you have a finalised list?'

'Yes, of course. Holly, Genny, Penny, Wendy, Kirsten, Christen, Jennifer, Jennifer Brown and little Kimmie Lee.'

'And the maid of honour is . . .'

'My *sister*, mother.'

'Pamela, yes, of course. What about Kirsten? Didn't you mention her the other day? She was marrying that English gentleman, that . . . what did you call him again?'

'He's a *peer*,' sighed Lucille. 'It would be nice, yes. But Pamela would have a fit if I didn't ask her. Anyway, if it wasn't Pamela I would have to ask Holly Childress. She's practically engaged to Robert Waverly, you remember.'

Martha catalogued the list by social status. 'Kimmie Lee? Who is that?'

'She is this darling little Asian girl I met at school. I needed to have one more bridesmaid than Wendy had at her wedding and . . .'

'Asian? Are you sure? You aren't thinking of doing anything *ethnic*, are you?'

'God, no.' Lucille laughed. 'Wouldn't dream of it.'

'So why bring her to a . . . to a western wedding, darling? The poor thing will be positively miserable, so out of her *culture* and things.'

'She was in the sorority, mother.'

'Oh, really? You let in . . . I mean, how avant-garde!'

'She's a nice girl. I think she doesn't even speak Chinese. Her father is white; he's the boss of Holly's boyfriend. You know, Robert.'

'Oh, Robert! The doctor! Well, she's still . . . Well, I suppose so. Can't say we're not people with an open mind,' declared Martha with undeniable satisfaction. 'She doesn't have an . . . Does she have a boyfriend?'

'Yes, of course. His name is William Devonshire *the third*.'

'Oh! Well. She's certainly welcome. It'll be so cosmopolitan! I'm so proud of you, honey!'

'Thanks, Mom!'

'What do you have on your plate today?'

'I'm meeting Holly later. She had some good ideas about the wedding cake. She helped Wendy with her cake and I thought she would know exactly who to call.'

'Mom nearly had a fit because of Kimmie,' sighed Lucille and nibbled on her salad. 'You don't know how hard it is to deal with family, Holly. I mean, it's an absolute pain.'

16

'You're doing just fine, Lucy.'

'Thanks!'

They were sitting in the outdoor section of a Mexican restaurant. It was a beautiful day. They were killing time until Trish deigned to make an appearance. She was Lucille's personal shopper and she was in high demand.

Holly glanced at her watch. 'She's running late. I can do my own shopping.'

'You can't do this to me, Holly. I would very much like you to make use of her services. She's a very busy woman; not everyone gets to use her.' She smiled. It was nice to use words like 'make use of her services'. It made her feel like she was in charge. She pursued the motif, gently putting her hand on Holly's arm. 'I insist that you use her as well,' she said, gentle but firm. 'She is a treasure! In any case, she is indispensable for the socially active wife of a prominent doctor.' It was really wonderful that Holly had made such a catch; she could be retained as one of her best friends without Lucille feeling embarrassed when introducing her to James's colleagues.

'I am not even engaged yet, Lucy. Anyway, you could have said "active partner of a young executive". Anyway, I've been told that I have good fashion sense.'

Lucille shrugged. 'Oh honey, maybe so, but you'll have children and then you won't have time to work.'

'I'm a career woman, Lucy, you know that. There'll be plenty of time for kids later.'

'Oh, we all *say* that. Look, here comes Patricia!'

A tall, middle-aged woman in a precisely colour-co-ordinated outfit of orange and light brown appeared on the terrace. She was talking into a cell phone, flipping it shut as she spied Lucille.

She was like a gun firing words. She aimed herself at them and just pressed the trigger. 'I'm swamped! Terribly sorry I ran late, two more clients for tomorrow. You must be Holly Childress, I've heard so much about you, I hope we can be friends.'

'Uh, well, you know . . . Patricia, I . . .' began Holly. 'I'm not sure . . .'

'Let me tell you what I have planned for today!' said

17

Patricia, smiling with her mouth. 'And please, call me Trish!'

Lucille straightened up and tugged the hem of her skirt. She always felt extremely self-conscious in Patricia's presence. The woman had so much style! Now that she had finally introduced a potential client to Patricia perhaps she would be considered a *premier* client. Yes, it was very important that Holly should make use of Patricia's services.

They chatted about Holly's personal taste and profession – she was an accountant, not a lawyer; Lucille had to keep reminding herself of this little snippet of information, otherwise she just kept thinking of her as Doctor Waverly's girlfriend – and Patricia insisted on paying the bill. The busboy, a tall, muscular black youth, cleared the table. He was very tall, at least 6'4", with broad shoulders and a shaved head.

'Are you OK, baby?' asked Holly, giving Lucille a concerned look. 'He is not making you uncomfortable, is he? We can leave right now if you like.'

Lucille blushed. This is why you don't keep friends who have seen you during a moment of weakness, she reflected. That one near-miss would haunt her for the rest of her life, she was sure of it. At least Patricia wouldn't understand the reference.

'I don't know what you mean,' she said and gave Holly a warning look.

The busboy walked by again, carrying a loaded tray of dirty dishes. His hard butt brushed up against her elbow.

She wished she had another margarita. She wished Holly would just shut the hell up. She wished this busboy would stop walking back and forth right in front of her with those muscular arms and perfect buns.

Holly was referring to the events on that night nearly seven years ago.

It started out with a lot of drinking. She was pretty tipsy and her boyfriend was passed out in her dorm room.

No, it all started with him pushing her down on the bed and starting to feel her up. His inexpert groping managed

18

to make her wet and definitely desirous of some kind of resolution, but then it turned out that he was simply too drunk to perform. By the time he finally put it in he was too far gone and eventually just began to snore, his lips erupting rhythmically, nearly visible clouds of cheap vodka and beer.

Asleep, his member was turning flaccid. She pushed him off, frustrated. Lucille wanted to come. She wanted some of Andy's cock right then and there. What if she fucked him in his sleep? Was that even possible? She thought she had read some article about nurses fucking patients while they were in a coma. The idea was strangely appealing.

She wrapped her hand around his cock and tugged at it. He stirred but didn't wake. He did stop snoring, however, which was a positive development.

The dorm rooms didn't have their own bathrooms. There was a bathroom down the hall, shared by all the girls. What she wanted was some lubricant so she could get Andy's cock hard in his sleep, and then ride him. He always got hard faster when she used some sort of a lubricant. Even baby oil would do.

She was still wearing her hottie party-girl outfit – something she wouldn't be caught dead wearing now. On that night she wore hot mules with three inch heels, a black miniskirt and a darling little green top. She looked cute and she knew it. She even wore some red lipstick, although privately she thought it made her look a touch slutty.

There were some people in the common room, all men. They were *black* men and Lucille averted her gaze. Black men were dodgy. They dealt drugs and they could not be trusted. Some of these guys were football players. Maybe all of them were. Cindy's boyfriend, Trent, was a defensive lineman on the football team. He was there on the green couch, huge, powerful, black, beautiful the way a gun is beautiful. He was there with some of his friends. Lucille felt their eyes track her as she hurried to the bathroom. She picked up the first thing she could find, a bottle of suntan lotion in a brown bottle.

She slowed down on her way back to the room. There was no reason for her to hurry – it wasn't like Andy wouldn't be there when she came back exactly the way she'd left him, the combined anthropomorphic personification of a useless cock and the threat of snoring. The football players stopped talking and just watched her as she traversed the common room. She did not see Cindy anywhere – Trent was here alone, then. Everyone else was still at the party. The only people awake in the dorm were these guys and Lucille.

She entered her room. There was Andy with his cock peeking out from his unzipped pants like some half-wilted flower. He was snoring. Lucille poured a dollop of lotion on her hand and smeared it over his member. She stroked his cock, one greasy handful at a time. His snoring stopped – again – but she couldn't tell if he was awake. Soon he did get hard, but not hard enough, not yet. Maybe if she gave him head? She wrapped her crimson lips around his cock, tasting the coconut flavour of the suntan lotion.

It worked. After a minute or so she judged him hard enough to fuck. She pushed her panties down to her ankles and grabbed his cock, pressing it against her drenched pussy lips. Why couldn't he just drink a little less and fuck her? She moaned aloud, frustrated. Without the stimulation of her lips, he was already losing his hard-on. Still, she managed to slide him in and let out a pleased little moan.

'Hey.'

She whirled around, gasping with surprise and apprehension. Trent was standing in the doorway, watching her. 'Can I watch?' he asked, grinning. There were others behind him, all those hot black guys from the football team.

'Wanna fuck?'

'I . . .' gasped Lucille. The idea was preposterous.

The idea was so sleazy.

The idea really turned her on. She blushed and Andy's cock automatically responded to her arousal by slipping deeper into her drenched pussy. She moaned – she couldn't help it – and rose and fell, rose and fell. She could not stop herself from riding Andy's cock despite the presence of the unexpected audience. Trent whistled and the whole gang of them crowded into her room. One of them shut the door.

'Is he passed out?' asked some guy with nearly blue-black skin and incredible biceps.

'Yeah, he is passed out,' answered Lucille, manically riding Andy's cock. The useless lump was getting soft again. 'He's getting soft,' she whimpered. 'God, I'm so ... so fucking wet.'

'So, like I said, wanna fuck?' asked Trent. 'Wanna fuck us?' He pulled his cock out, an incredible ebony monster. *He* was hard.

Lucille blushed. But she didn't stop riding Andy's useless dick. It was all she had. Still, she just had to keep on looking at that majestic black cock and licking her lips.

'I'm guessing that's a big yeah, Trent,' said one of them. 'Fuck the bitch.'

Trent grinned and walked closer, cock in hand. He grabbed her hair and pulled her head down until her mouth was positioned right over the gigantic ebony shaft.

His voice was deep and powerful. 'Suck on it, baby.'

She weakly struggled against his grip but her head was inexorably being forced down towards that gorgeous thing. He was forcing her! The idea nearly made her come. It would have if Andy had a decent erection. She let herself fall forwards a little, like a puppet with the strings cut. Her lips brushed against Trent's cock. Lucille's lips parted slightly and a drop of her saliva fell on his majestic black member.

'Suck on it,' he commanded and she moaned as he pulled on her hair.

'OK,' she sobbed. She tentatively placed her trembling lips on the tip of his cock and let them part a little more. It slid half an inch into her mouth. He tasted salty. She opened her mouth wide and sucked him into her hot wet mouth.

'What a ho,' said one of them, laughing. 'Yeah, suck him off, bitch.'

Lucille gazed up at the ebony god standing above her. He held on to her hair to steady himself while he fucked her mouth. She was nearly drowning in cock. It made her so very wet. She felt Andy and his flaccid dick being pulled out from underneath her. Hard, packed black muscle

21

surrounded her. Big strong hands roved over her back, her hair, her ass, her legs.

A finger found her sopping-wet cunt.

She moaned and bucked against it. Another one slipped inside.

And then, at that exact same moment, Holly Childress waltzed through the door and ... *saved* her. She was screaming at the players, telling them that she was going to call campus police. Trent pulled out and put away his beautiful immense cock. Whoever was fingering her cunt stopped.

She was not going to admit to fucking a black man – to fucking black *men* – with her boyfriend passed out on her own bed. Yes, Holly, they forced me. Yes, Holly, they were trying to rape me, that's why I'm practically naked. Yes, Holly, they made me perform for them. Yes, Holly, he told me he would beat me unless I let him put it in my mouth. At least she didn't catch a glimpse of the guy (guys?) who was fingering her from behind.

Of course Holly didn't keep her mouth shut. Lucille was forced to attend some stupid class for rape victims. Some of those gorgeous muscle-bound guys were kicked off the team and lost their scholarships. They didn't go to jail – after all, there was no physical evidence of rape and Lucille wouldn't testify against them – but thereafter they avoided her like the plague. She only managed to talk to Trent at a party once after that. She was drunk.

She cornered him and told him that she had to do it, that she knew they weren't trying to rape her. She told him that she knew they were not trying to force themselves on her with Andy totally passed out. She told Trent that she knew they were not trying to force her into an interracial gang-bang orgy. She told Trent that she knew they were not trying to plunge their massive black cocks into her, one after another, until all she could do was moan and stumble around, covered in their beautiful come-cream.

She told him a lot of things. She was drunk.

And then Holly showed up *again* and told Trent to leave her alone or she was going to call the police.

One night, she stupidly told Holly she always wondered what would have happened if she hadn't shown up. If they would have had a full-on – what was it called – a gang-bang? What would it have felt like to be used by all *those* men? All those hard, rippling muscles, pressed against her, flinging her around like a rag doll, bending her over, using her like some come-drenched slut in a porno film.

The busboy waved goodbye and Lucille's eyes regained their focus. Still, he did look a lot like Trent.

3

Robert

'Sir, Scott is here to see you.' Amanda's voice was carefully neutral. Scott kept trying to hit on Amanda but his secretary would have none of it. Robert suspected she couldn't stand him.

'Tell him to come in, please.'

'Dude, how's it going,' said Scott by way of greeting. He collapsed on a high-backed chair.

'Going all right,' said Robert. 'Did an operation this morning, got another one tomorrow. How was Jamaica?'

'Awesome! You get my postcard?'

'Not yet. Didn't see much of the beach, did you?'

'Huh?'

'You're as pale as a sheet.'

Scott put a cigarette in his mouth. Robert shook his head. With a rueful grin, Scott slid the cigarette back into the packet.

'I went out at night and slept most of the day. Great nightlife in Jamaica. You'll love the postcard. The girl on the picture is really hot. Anyway, I know you're busy so I'll keep this short. I'm here about James's bachelor party.'

'A bachelor party?'

'It's the very least we can do for the poor guy. You've met his fiancée, Lucille.'

'But we went out for beers the other night, I thought that was the . . .'

Scott chuckled. 'That was just having a couple of beers. I'm talking about a real bachelor party. It would be a blast.'

'Where do you plan to hold it?' He had an ominous feeling that Scott expected him to host the event.

'Don't worry,' Scott grinned, reading Robert like a book. 'I was going to suggest a strip club.'

Robert's lips twitched. With some generosity, it could have been construed as a smile. 'You know I don't like those places.'

'Jesus, Robert, this isn't for you. When your time comes, I'll take you to a bake sale or something.'

'Am I really such a . . .' He trailed off, not quite knowing what term to use.

'Yup, but I still love you, man.' Scott slapped him on the shoulder. 'I thought we could go to that place downtown. You know, Hot Summer's.'

'Isn't that where I dropped you off the last time?'

Scott nodded. He seemed lost in thought for a moment. When he spoke, it was as if he was reading aloud from a script. 'I still haven't had a chance to check it out properly.'

'I really don't think . . .'

'Let me handle it, OK?' Suddenly he remembered something. He passed a thick envelope to Robert. 'More postcards, I didn't get round to mailing them.'

Robert pocketed the envelope.

'Aren't you gonna open it?' Scott licked his lips.

'Later,' said Robert. He was still thinking about the idea of a bachelor party at the strip club. He knew James, the third member of their little triumvirate, was almost as conservative as he was. 'What makes you think James would like that place?' he asked.

'You have to see this place to believe it. I mean, all I've done is look at some of the girls and believe me, man, they are *hot*.' Scott grinned. 'If James was getting ready to enter the priesthood he would have a change of heart after a party at Hot Summer's.'

'That good, huh?' Robert laughed. 'When would this thing be, then?'

'A couple of weeks before the wedding, I suppose.' He consulted Robert's wall calendar. 'How does March second sound?'

'I guess that should be all right,' said Robert without enthusiasm. 'I'll pencil it in. So, you'll make the reservations?'

'Sure. Who are we gonna invite?'

'The groom, obviously, you, me, Dirk, little Scott, John, Dave . . . I'll work on the list. I guess no girls, huh?'

Scott rolled his eyes. 'No, Rob, you can't bring Holly.'

'She's not going to like this,' sighed Robert. 'Why can't I bring her?'

'Dude, have you ever been to Hot Summer's? If you brought her she'd have a fit.'

'Oh, come on . . .'

'Holly isn't gonna let you have any fun, dude.'

'She can be fun.'

'I'm sure she can. But definitely *not* at Hot Summer's. I mean, come on, dude, even if she comes along she'll make us all feel bad about it.'

Robert imagined Holly's reaction to naked women gyrating around a metal pole. Her anticipated reaction was not a pretty sight. The scene in his head included a whole lot of yelling.

'Don't take this the wrong way, dude. I think Holly is hot and kind of smart, but you don't need to put up with her constant . . . badgering.' Scott looked out of the window. 'Anyway, it's not like she has to know.'

'I don't like to lie to her.'

'It's not like you're gonna fuck around on her. You're just going to a strip club for a bachelor party. Hey, I'm going there tomorrow night. You should come along with me and check the place out.'

'I'm working late tomorrow.'

'The cancer thing again?'

Robert began to explain his oncology research and a promising new technique he and his team were developing. 'If it turns out that we're right, the sky is the limit.'

'You've been working on it for years.'

'So? It's a worthwhile project.'

'You weren't so altruistic when you were in medical school.'

'Sometimes we change for the better.' He became

reflective. 'I was doing an all-nighter at the hospital and a woman was brought in, dying. I could make her pretty, give her a facelift, a boob job, a pretty pug nose, but I couldn't save her life.' There was deep emotion in his voice. 'If my research is successful, perhaps I'll make up for that failure.'

Scott leant back in his chair. 'I respect your dedication, man. But I couldn't spend years on end doing gruelling lab work without getting something out of it.'

Robert chuckled. 'There's more to life than money.'

Scott smiled. 'I suppose so. It's nice to think so, anyway. But you're trying to change the topic.'

'What topic?'

'Hot Summer's. Are you gonna come along with me tomorrow?'

'Call me when you get there. If I'm done with work, I might drop by.'

Scott pulled the pack of cigarettes from his pocket, only to put it away again at Robert's disapproving glance. 'Fine, fine. You're such a damn health freak.'

Robert laughed out loud. 'I suppose I am. Listen, Scott, I hate to say this but I have to get back to work.'

Scott stood up. 'No worries. I have to go anyway.' In fact, he seemed strangely eager to leave.

Robert lived with Holly in an uptown condo. It was a good building, new, for 'high-end' professionals. They had not yet discussed marriage or kids, although Robert had a growing belief that the potential for this talk was becoming ever riper with the passage of time. The lobby was always manned by security personnel. There was a laundry and a convenience store, and an underground garage where he stored his baby, the fire-engine-red 1961 Austin Healy 3000 roadster.

Robert extracted the magazines and junk mail from the mailbox. He took the elevator upstairs, unlocked the apartment, entered and hung up his coat. 'Honey?'

There was no answer.

He tossed the magazines (Holly's health magazine and his medical and scientific journals) on the coffee table, got

27

a bottle of mineral water from the fridge and scanned the mail. There were two credit-card offers (he tossed those in the to-shred pile) and a postcard. He looked at the postcard with a disdainful smirk, shaking his head as he beheld the sleazy photograph of a buxom blonde in a thong bikini. He glanced at the stamp but it wasn't anything special – in fact, it was a standard US stamp. The girl was purportedly lying on some Jamaican beach but she seemed lit from the front and the sun was behind her. Even with the US stamp Scott's postcard only got here from Jamaica today, well after he had already returned. 'Having a great time, wish you were here, alone, so you could get some of this!' said the short message. It took a moment for him to make the connection between 'some of this' and the blonde. He glanced at her again.

Robert rolled his eyes. The girl was certainly not his type. Big tits, thin, tanned, your stereotypical beach bunny. Holly didn't look like this girl at all – his girlfriend was short and petite, with dark hair and sparkling dark eyes. She was pretty and he loved her, but she wasn't exuding sex like this postcard bunny. He never could attract women like this one without sensing that they were only after him because he was in medical school. They were an all or nothing deal, either immediately interested in a serious relationship or they couldn't care less about him. He supposed this was the reason why it took so long for him to lose his virginity. He'd never had the chance to play around.

He heard the key turning in the lock and quickly slipped the postcard into his jacket pocket, next to the unopened packet from Scott. The last thing he needed right now was another row with Holly. She was not likely to exhibit either patience or understanding about a picture like this one in his possession. No doubt she would accuse him of thinking about that woman while they were making love. Holly could not tolerate the idea that he might be thinking about another woman during sex. He'd only asked her once to dress up as well. He still paled remembering the episode. It had happened when he was flipping channels one rare bored afternoon. Somehow, he'd navigated on to one of

28

those dating shows. The girl who popped up on screen was a complete bimbo – she wore stiletto heels and a cheerleading uniform, one of those fake ones with an extremely short skirt and a top that was just a glorified bra. It was all extremely revealing. He laughed at the outfit but did not change the channel and he found that he got hard watching her. Like a moron, he mentioned to Holly that he found the get-up arousing.

'You go and fuck her then,' said Holly. 'I guess I'm just not good enough for you. You go and get yourself some stupid bimbo like her, OK?'

'It was just a thought,' he said, lamely. 'I didn't mean to upset you, baby.'

'I want you to love me for who I am,' said Holly, obviously pissed off. 'Not for wearing some whore outfit.'

'Baby, it's just playing . . .' he trailed off when he saw the rage in her eyes.

'Well, it's not my kind of a game, OK? I am not into dressing up like some cheap slut!'

He threw up his hands, defensive, and spent the next two days in Holly's dog house, walking on eggshells. All this was months ago; still, he did not enjoy the recollection. The postcard was not going to be shared with his girlfriend.

Holly walked in, dressed in sensible two-inch heels, a white cashmere sweater and a tasteful knee-length Brooks Brothers skirt. She never wore any makeup. 'Hi honey,' she said. 'Any mail?'

'Only the magazines,' lied Robert. The postcard was burning a hole in his pocket. 'How was work?'

Holly was a top-notch CPA at a major firm. There was even talk of partnership, a nearly unheard-of accomplishment for someone of her age and gender. 'It was fairly routine,' she said. She picked up the fitness magazine and sat down next to Robert. She flipped it open and showed him the picture of an aerobics instructor, glistening with oil or sweat or something. It made the woman look slippery. She was muscular but not overwhelmingly so, and very attractive, wearing a lot of discreet makeup.

'Very nice,' he said guardedly.

'You think?' she answered.

'If you like that type.'

'But we both know that's not your type, don't we?' Holly smiled, watching Robert like a hawk.

'Of course not. I have exceptional taste,' he said, alarmed.

Holly smiled and hugged him fiercely. 'You sure do!'

He relaxed a little. Apparently this was the right reaction.

'Kiss me!' said Holly. 'You won't get to see me tomorrow, after all!'

'Oh yes,' he said. 'Your sorority alumni thing. I'll miss you!'

He closed his eyes and kissed her. Without his meaning it to, the picture of the buxom beach bunny from the postcard invaded his mind and his member stirred. He pulled Holly closer, carefully slipping his hand lower on her back. He was waiting for her to shut him down. She usually did.

For some reason she didn't, not today. He found his hand cupping her tight butt and the postcard faded from his mind as her body responded to his.

Her long thighs wrapped around him like the coils of some serpent. They were oiled somehow and they slid and rubbed against his cock.

Good God he was hard.

She got on all fours, swaying her butt seductively from side to side. 'Fuck my pussy,' she hissed.

Robert gawked at her. Holly never talked dirty. It turned him on. He quickly rose and knelt behind her. In the dim light her legs were so long, so tanned. He positioned his cock and slid into her tight wet cunt.

'That's it baby,' she cooed. 'It didn't take long, did it? Fuck my pussy, Robert. Fuck it, fuck it, fuck it!'

Every time she said 'fuck it' she moved forwards and back, making the command into a self-fulfilling prophecy. 'You like my tight wet cunt, don't you, Robert?'

'Yeah!' he moaned. Holly had never felt this tight and wet at the same time, ever. 'Yeah, I'm gonna fuck your

30

pussy, Holly!' He reached out and grabbed her hair – long, blonde hair, slightly curly – and pulled on it.

She giggled. 'Oh yeah, you like it a little rough, don't you Robert? Fuck the pretty blonde cunnie, Robert!'

He realised something was off but he wasn't sure what it was. Jesus, those legs were incredible. She bump-and-ground against him and he lost his train of thought. He thrust inside her, panting like a buck on heat.

He felt his balls constrict and she looked back over her shoulder – big, luscious tits swaying – just as he spurted an avalanche of come into her quivering wet cunt. She smirked mockingly and he withdrew, gasping.

It wasn't Holly – it was the sleazy bimbo from the postcard.

Robert's eyes snapped open. His member was oozing pre-come. It was still rock-hard. The dream was burning bright in his mind's eye.

Holly was lying right next to him. Her breathing was very spaced, very even. She was in deep sleep. Once in a while Holly slept naked. Tonight was one of those nights. After they had finished she had fallen asleep in his arms without putting on her nightie. He carefully lifted the blanket and looked at his girlfriend's body. Her legs were long too, and her breasts were perky, pretty, a mere handful. His member twitched and he began to caress Holly's butt. It was so tight, so pretty. He leant closer to it and breathed a slight kiss on that perfect derrière.

Holly stirred. The pattern of her breathing quickened.

Robert hesitated and then put his hand in between her legs. He began to pet her exposed pussy. He made his way to her clit and began to tease it with a fingertip. Holly's clit was nice and pink too. He slid down until he was facing the object of his desire and parted his lips.

Holly moaned. She moved a little but not far enough to stop him. He lowered his mouth over her and slowly ground his lips against her clit. He gently nibbled and licked, nibbled and licked.

'Not now . . .' groaned Holly. She sounded dead asleep. 'Not now, honey. Tomorrow, OK?'

'Oh, please . . .' whined Robert.

'What's gotten into you?' Holly yawned. 'Tomorrow, baby. Promise.'

Robert glumly nodded. He was still aroused and there was no way he could go back to sleep. If only she wore pyjamas, maybe then he could get some rest.

He closed his eyes anyway, hoping to get back to his dream.

'Look who's back!' teased the bitchy blonde from the postcard. She was lusciously naked. Now that he knew she was a dream he was not so reticent.

'Yeah,' he said. 'I'm back.'

'Wanna cheat on Holly?' asked the figment of his imagination. Her tits were much bigger than Holly's. 'Wanna stick your cheating hard cock in my beautiful blonde pussy? Watch my slutty red lips wrap around your dick and suck every drop of come out of you?' She came closer, wearing very high heels, and took hold of his hand.

'You should cheat on Holly,' she purred. Her long red nails ran up and down his arm. 'You should shove your dick in my pretty cunt. Or maybe you should slide it into my ass.'

She got on all fours and spread her butt cheeks wide. 'Like this, baby. Wanna get a little freaky, honey?'

He tried to concentrate on Holly. He could not seem to call up her image.

'But baby, you tried!' cooed the blonde. 'You tried and the nasty bitch turned you down. But I'm here for you, honey!' She wriggled enticingly. 'Shove your dick into my cunnie until you come. It'll make you feel so good, Robert. You'll want to do it all the time.'

'Oh fuck,' he whispered. He could not look away from the tawdry vision. 'It's only a fantasy,' he whispered.

'That's right baby,' said the woman. 'It's only a dream. Just slide that cock in my pussy and enjoy.'

He woke up in a cooling puddle of his own come.

Holly was sitting up. She was staring at him and shaking her head. 'Jesus, Robert,' she said and yawned. 'You could have waited a few hours.'

* * *

32

The next day's operation went off without a hitch. When he finished he found himself with extra time. This was a rare treat. He logged on to the private site of the oncology research team. He shared the server space with an exclusive team of other scientists. Robert opened another window to cut and paste interesting suggestions for his own specific research assignment into a text file. Some of the observations from the other researchers were definitely worthwhile. He pulled up the database that contained his experimental data and checked some of the results, thinking about how they fitted in with his theory. Soon he was completely focused on his work. He even turned off his phone.

He was looking for a special cell.

A cell that fought cancer with exceptional ferocity. There were some clues that such a thing could exist. His job was to find it.

If he found it and they could synthesise it . . . He drank some cold water to clear his head. He did not have time for fantasies.

When his mouse finger cramped up he turned off the computer. It was pitch dark outside. As he was logging off, his eyes strayed over to the clock on the bottom right of the screen: 9:04 p.m.

He was tired but not sleepy; he was excited about the research. Sometimes one could feel it, the approach of an imminent breakthrough. He turned on his phone as he was walking towards the metro (there was no point in driving two stops to the hospital).

His phone beeped. He had three voicemail messages. They were all from Scott, asking in his peculiar goofy way where the hell he was.

Now he remembered. Hot Summer's, that was the place Scott wanted to check out tonight. Amused, he chuckled to himself. He didn't have to call Scott with an excuse. He could just go home and have a quiet evening at home, alone until Holly got home.

He was directly under a bright yellow sign – in fact, he nearly walked past it – before its significance penetrated his mind.

HOT SUMMER'S, the sign proclaimed in bright, blazing letters. A huge, muscle-bound guy stood in front of the

33

place, walkie-talkie in hand. He wore a black tuxedo. His bald head reflected the yellow sign overhead. Robert could hear music filtering through the double doors. A sign adorned the wall next to the door. The letters were thick black on a yellow background. 'Tonight's performers are:' and then a long list of obviously made-up names. There was a Heather, a Candy, a Heather 2 . . . he didn't read any further. He got the gist of it.

Scott was in there. Should he go in and say hello? He glanced at the doorman who glanced back impassively. Holly definitely wouldn't like this. Vacillating, he put his hands in his coat pockets, rocking back on his heels. His hand brushed up against a cool, smooth surface, a paper rectangle. He reached in and pulled it out. The postcard with the picture of the buxom blonde seemed to mock him. She had big tits, tanned skin, blonde hair. You couldn't tell what colour her eyes were; she was wearing sunglasses, an article with a larger surface area than her bikini.

Robert shoved the postcard back in his pocket. He felt the envelope of postcards Scott had given him. He pulled it out and tore it open. The top postcard depicted the same blonde model. She was posing in a flimsy bikini, her skin glistening with oil. The others were all similar. All the postcards were of the same model.

He was an adult, wasn't he? He could have a drink with his friend if he so desired, even if it was in a place where naked women danced!

He furtively checked the street – it would not be proper to be seen entering this den of iniquity – and walked towards the door. The doorman barely glanced at him, just spoke into the walkie-talkie. 'One,' he said and stood aside.

Robert walked through the doors and found himself in a dark foyer, the small room heavily overlaid with a sweet, fruity scent and cigarette smoke. It was close to pitch dark and before him was a deep-burgundy velvet curtain that presumably led into the interior.

A uniformed cop sat on a stool guarding the curtain. 'ID,' he said. Robert nearly chuckled but then decided to play along – he showed his licence to the cop who glanced at it and then handed it back in the same motion.

Robert walked through the curtain.

It was a dark, spicy realm on the other side, filled with flickering candles and violet-blue lights. It was full of cigarette smoke and Robert nearly turned around right then and there. As an oncologist, he despised cigarettes. On his right was a jukebox, and in front of the jukebox . . . Robert swallowed hard, and realised he was staring. She was a blonde Barbie doll with long tanned legs. She wore something that no nurse in a real hospital would ever put on, unless she meant to seduce the rest of the staff. Her breasts were huge; they nearly burst from the confinement of the tight white polyester. Her nails and lips were a bright scarlet and she wore a lot of blue eye makeup. She wore absurdly high white stiletto heels. She was a carbon copy of the woman on the postcard.

'Sir? Can't stop here,' he heard. 'Must sit at a table.'

He tore his eyes from the vision before him and forced them to refocus on a gorilla-like man in a black suit. 'A friend of mine is already in here,' he mumbled. He looked around. The room itself was a long rectangle. On the centre-left was a huge mirror, fronted by a stage with two metal poles. The stage was surrounded by tables. On the stage . . .

On the stage was a naked girl with red hair, swaying seductively to the beat of the music. She ground herself against the mirror, pushing her nipples against the cold glass. She moaned softly and swayed seductively to the music. The only things she wore were red go-go boots and a garter belt. It was stuffed with banknotes.

From the corner of his eye he saw that the girl had finished at the jukebox and was now walking – no, walking was not the right word, she was strutting provocatively – deeper into the shadowy depths of the club. Robert stumbled after her. The girl's uniform was so short and tight that he could see the perfect tan of her ass, a perfect, hypnotically undulating contrast against the white of that flimsy uniform.

'Dude!'

The girl stopped to chat with a fat man in a brown suit who was sitting at a table in the company of another stripper. She had fluffy platinum-white blonde hair, mammoth-sized breasts and vacuous blue eyes. The nurse bent over the table to make conversation, and Robert found himself envying the fat man's view of her cleavage.

'Dude!'

Finally, the familiar voice penetrated the crimson haze clogging Robert's perception and he lifted his gaze to search for the caller. A scant two tables away he spied Scott. When his friend saw that he finally had Robert's attention, he raised his glass from the table, saluted and grinned.

Robert hastily seated himself. He had not remembered having an erection like this for ages. Unless he counted his wet dream from last night. 'Nice place,' he managed.

'You were staring at Michele like she was the second coming.' Scott smirked. 'Not that I blame you, she is definitely a looker. You should talk to her, you're her type.'

'You know their names?'

'Well, yeah ... the blonde in the nurse's uniform is Michele, her friend with the big tits is Becky, the redhead on stage is Princess – or Tiffany, I'm not sure. The two Asian ones are Tina and Heather. I think Amber is Asian too – or so I've been told – but she only talks to Congressmen.'

'Really? They talk to the customers?'

'Yeah, they come to the tables before and after their sets and chat with the guests, milk them for tips.'

'You're kidding.'

'No, not at all. Watch.'

A tall brunette with beautiful legs sauntered by. She smiled at Scott and then at Robert. Her eyes were green and her lips exceptionally full.

'I'm Scott,' he said and brandished a five-dollar bill.

'I'm Princess,' she replied, smiling. She turned her leg to give Scott access to the garter. It was a slow, calculated movement, playful-lazy yet full of sensual energy.

He slid the money under the garter. 'You're gorgeous, Princess.'

'Thank you, Scott,' she said, and levelled her smile at Robert.

'Would you like a drink?' said Scott. 'My friend would like to buy you one if you would come by later.'

'Sure, I'd love to,' she purred. She swayed closer until her perfectly proportioned, long legs were a scant few inches from Robert. She waited.

Scott leant close enough to whisper in his ear. 'Give her something! A couple of bucks? You're embarrassing me.'

'Oh, I'm sorry,' Robert stammered and fished out his wallet. He looked inside and saw that he only had twenties. He looked to Scott for advice but his friend was immersed in admiring the latest dancer on stage, the large-breasted bleached blonde whose name he had already forgotten. Confused, he took the twenty out and held it out to the stripper. She smiled broadly and lifted her garter. He wanted to ask how she was going to make change but realised that was no longer possible. He put the money under the garter. His fingertip brushed up against her warm, perfect skin, sliding against it as he put the bill in place. She let go of the garter and it snapped into place, trapping his twenty against her flesh.

'Thank you so much, Robert,' she trilled, oozing appreciation. 'I will come by later for that drink, OK?'

'OK,' he said breathlessly.

'Ooh, big spender.' Scott smirked after she had left. 'Better watch out, once she tells the others we'll have company.'

'She will tell the others?'

'Maybe.' Scott shrugged. 'Or maybe she'll try to keep you all to herself.'

'I had no idea it was like this,' said Robert. His eyes were glued to the stage. He vaguely heard Scott order him a beer. Becky was slowly, seductively strutting around the metal pole. She pushed her breasts together and used the tip of her tongue to explore her upper lip.

'Gotta love good ol' Becky,' said Scott. 'She gives a hell of a lap dance, too.'

'What? I hate to sound like a fool, but what exactly is a lap dance?'

Scott pointed at the stairs opposite the stage. 'You see those stairs?'

'Sure.'

'The girls make most of their money by giving lap dances upstairs in the champagne room. That's a room with these ... I guess they are booths, with curtains. They've got leather couches in there and the girls make you sit and then they hop on your lap and *squirm* to the music. I hear Michele can turn a man into a puddle of jello in under a minute.'

There was something in the way he said 'squirm' that made Robert break out in a sweat. 'They sit in your lap? Is it expensive?'

'Yeah, but it's really not a lot for what you get. It's only a hundred bucks.'

'A hundred dollars?! That's extortion!'

'You don't have to do it. It's a helluva time, though. You really ought to try it before you say it's all bad.'

In the meantime, Becky's set was building to an erotic conclusion. She got on all fours and began to crawl around on stage, sliding her giant tits against the glistening floor. She made eye contact with Robert and licked her lips. As she slowly rose from the floor, she began to tweak her nipples with her long, hot-pink fingernails.

'You've got to give her a tip for that, dude.' Scott laughed. 'That was above and beyond!'

Robert was vaguely wondering how there was enough blood in his body to make his face blush when all of it seemed concentrated in his member. 'Oh, come on,' he said weakly. 'I can't ... what would Holly think?'

'Holly'll never know!'

Robert found himself standing. There was a business-man who just tipped the stripper a dollar and then it was his turn and the owner of those huge tits was watching him with those vacuous big blue eyes.

His eyes roved over her body.

She seemed to know the direction of his gaze and used her hands to stroke her flesh exactly at the same spot.

Robert fumbled with his wallet as he realised he still didn't have change. Swallowing hard, he fished out another twenty. He noticed his fingers were trembling. Becky's blue eyes glittered as they took in the size of the unexpected offering. She stood slowly and walked closer, draping her long bleached-blonde hair over Robert's head. Suddenly, he found himself in a seductive tent of the stripper's making. The scent of her hair and the proximity of those huge tits made him dizzy. The dancer pushed her breasts forwards until Robert found his lips firmly pressed against the heaving flesh. Her skin was warm and her breasts exuded an exotic, spicy scent. His head was reeling.

When she let him go he just stood there, numb, staring at the lewd display before him. She was naked except for her high heels and her garter belt. Her pussy was shaved and pink. She giggled and stroked herself; it was so fake, it was such a blatant effort at sexual manipulation, it took his breath away. And it made his dick hard.

He managed to stumble to his chair and collapse in a worn-out heap. He picked up his beer and drained it in a few tortured gulps.

'She put her tits in my face!' he gasped. 'I can't believe she did that!'

'Just wait until she comes by later.' Scott grinned. 'You've been marked as a big spender now.'

Sure enough, his appreciation of Becky's charms was interrupted by a soft touch on his shoulder. The seductive vision of Michele loomed over him, those devastating curves on full display in her slutty parody of a nurse's uniform.

'Hello, I'm Michele,' she purred.

'I'm Scott and this is my friend Robert,' said Scott.

'Nice to meet you, Robert . . . and Scott,' said Michele, pointedly looking at the empty chair at their table.

'Ask her to have a drink, dude,' said Scott encouragingly.

'Would you like to have a drink with us?' said Robert, lamely.

'I'd love to.' She smiled and sat down on the empty chair, crossing her gorgeous legs. She put her hand on Robert's arm. 'I've never seen you here before, Robert.'

She kept her hand on his arm. Her nails were long, crimson, lacquered. 'You have nice biceps, Robert,' she said and moved her hand up his arm, then down. The gesture was like a red-hot stroke on his cock. He knew he could not stand up, not now; he would never live it down. Scott would mock him for that erection for the rest of his life.

Now that she was sitting next to him, he could not help himself from trying to get a good look at her body. She was gorgeous; her hair was long, a cascading avalanche of golden curls. She had the skin of a woman who went to the tanning salon on a regular basis, and large, definitely fake tits. Still, whoever did them knew his stuff. She wore white stiletto heels.

Michele giggled and petted Robert on the head. He felt the long fingernails on his scalp. 'I'm thirsty!' She pouted.

A waitress in a tight red top and matching hotpants seemed to materialise out of thin air. 'What can I bring you?'

'I'll have a glass of champagne,' said Michele.

'I guess I'll have a coke,' said Robert.

Scott chuckled. 'Are you kidding? There is no point . . . It costs ten bucks for a drink whether it's a scotch and soda or a coke.'

Michele nodded. 'You guys should do some shots!'

The waitress smiled at Scott. 'Two tequilas, then?'

Michele yawned theatrically. 'I'm *so* tired!' She put her heels in Robert's lap. The white stilettos poked into his belly. Those sleazy shoes settled right over his painful hard-on.

'Do you want to do shots?' asked Scott.

'Uh . . .' began Robert, not sure how to say 'No, I do not want to do shots'. He had work tomorrow, the oncology department expected a research brief, and . . . He shook his head and opened his mouth to make his case.

Michele squirmed in her seat. She stretched out her long tanned legs and the pointy tip of her shoes pressed directly on the stiff flesh of Robert's straining cock.

He gasped.

'Don't be such a spoilsport, sweetie,' cooed Michele. 'Have a good time, live a little!' She giggled.

'Sure, let's do some shots,' mumbled Robert, red-faced. He was desperate to hide his discomfort. 'Let's all do shots, I guess.'

40

The waitress delivered the shots nearly instantaneously. Robert stared at the drink like a mouse before the baleful stare of a serpent. He never could handle his alcohol.

'All right!' said Scott, grinning. 'Now we're talking! I knew I should have brought you in here before.'

'Yes, Scott, you should have brought him in a lot sooner,' agreed Michele. 'I *like* him!' She slid her hand down until her fingers enveloped his hand. She guided his fingers until they were securely fastened around the shot glass. 'On three!' she commanded.

She counted down from three and when they arrived at 'one' they all drained their glasses. Robert's eyes filled with tears – the tequila went down smoothly, however. A warm sensation coursed through his veins. Not so bad, he thought.

The stripper leant in close. Her skin was heavily scented with a sweet, cloying perfume. Her lips brushed up against his earlobe as she communicated her offer via a delicate whisper: 'Would you like to come upstairs with me, sweet Robert?'

'What – what's upstairs?' he croaked. Paradoxically, his throat felt parched but he was drooling. It was difficult to think with her nibbling on his ear. Her sweet feminine scent was pervasive.

Michele's breasts pushed against his arm as she slithered even closer. He didn't think that would have been possible without her actually sitting in his lap. Her voice had the consistency of crystallised honey. 'Would you like me to sit in your lap and do a little dance, Robbie?'

'I really can't,' he whimpered. The idea of Michele squirming over his erection . . . He did not want to think about it. He couldn't stop thinking about it.

'Of course you can.' She giggled and continued to stroke his hand, slowly sliding those long fingernails over his skin. Her huge blue eyes bore into his own like a serpent sizing up prey. 'Just come upstairs with me, Robbie, it'll be so much fun!'

Robert hadn't been this aroused since . . . maybe *ever*. He couldn't seem to tear his eyes from the tempting offering. Feeling weak, he tore his eyes from Michele and addressed his friend. 'Scott, Holly is going to kill me!'

41

'Don't be stupid, dude, just don't tell her!'

'It'll be our little secret, Robert!' promised Michele, tightening her grip. She stood and pulled Robert after her. He had no choice but to stand – the only alternative was to make her look foolish, which he could not make himself do. She led him to the stairwell where another one of the apelike security men stood.

As they approached he began to look expectant. He glanced at Robert. His eyes were flat, dark, unreadable. When he spoke the words lacked emotion. 'No touching at all. Keep your hands on your side at all times. Pay in advance. Tipping is optional.'

Robert opened his mouth to protest. How could they possibly think he would grope some woman who was not his girlfriend?

'Thank you, Robbie, for taking me upstairs!' purred Michele and she pressed herself against him, only separating after a mind-boggling two seconds. He could not remember his planned protest at all. Something about not wanting to touch a stripper, no matter how hot she was.

Dazed, Robert looked at the security man. 'That'll be a hundred dollars,' said the man.

Robert pulled out his wallet. He always had a hundred-dollar bill in his wallet, for emergencies – he pulled it out now and passed it over. The security man slid the bill into a thick brown leather wallet. Robert glumly registered the details of the transaction. Vaguely, he realised that the next day would be full of regrets.

'Ever had a lap dance before, Robert?' asked Michele.

'Never been to a stripcl– to a gentlemen's club before,' he responded.

'I'll make sure you'll never forget, then.' She squeezed his hand in reassurance, not letting go.

She led him up the narrow, dark staircase.

Robert had nowhere to look but at the inviting, swaying bottom of the temptress in front of him. He could see underneath the sleazy nurse's uniform, directly at her perfect tight ass and the glittering silver thong she wore. She knew what he was looking at – she looked back at him and giggled as she caught him staring. 'Like my ass,

Robert?' she asked playfully. 'Your friend liked my ass too.'

'No, no. I mean – yeah,' he sputtered, blushing. 'It's really – nice.'

'Just nice?' Michele pouted and stopped on the staircase, gripping the handrails on both sides. He nearly bumped into her.

She rotated her ass very slowly, a seductive circle that made him break out in a sudden sweat. 'Don't you love my ass, Robbie?' she asked.

He could feel the heat of the tequila in his blood as his trapped gaze followed the swaying motions of the stripper above him. 'It's beautiful,' he admitted, the drink making him reckless.

'I'll have to teach you to love it.' Michele pouted again. She reclaimed his hand in hers. She pulled him up the last two stairs until they stood in a shadowy, well-appointed room. There were curtained alcoves in a circle, with little rooms discreetly hidden from the eyes of anyone entering the main chamber by curtains of plush red velvet. Music was pumped in via hidden speakers. They were exuding a heavy, rhythmical beat. There was a small bar with a shallow depression containing ice. It was almost full of champagne bottles.

'We should open a bottle,' said Michele. 'Once Becky popped one and the champagne soaked her top,' she said sulkily. 'I had to take everything off her and it got *very* sticky.'

'I'm not sure . . . I'm a bit out of cash.'

Michele nodded thoughtfully and parted one of the velvet curtains. A plush black leather couch occupied the alcove. There were speakers on the side walls. A painting adorned the centre wall, a cheesy erotic rendering of two Roman-era women kissing each other.

She caressed him. 'There's a cash machine downstairs. Becky kind of liked being sticky . . . but I'm nice, I don't have to be sticky,' she said with a mischievous smile.

He said nothing and Michele shrugged. 'Such a good boy you are, Robbie.' She giggled. 'Let's see what I can do about that. Sit down.'

'OK,' he said, nervous. He sat down. The couch was like a giant leather beast; it seemed to swallow him up. Robert was genuinely curious about what was going to happen next.

Michele smiled and looked him over.

He could not help but think that he was being measured. There was a sense of calculation behind those cold blue eyes. 'So what do you do for a living, Robert?' she asked, unbuttoning two more buttons on her already revealing uniform.

'I'm an oncologist,' he answered, wondering why he was telling the truth.

'What's that?' She pouted and put her thumb in her mouth, sucking on it like a baby. He found it impossible to look away.

'I'm a doctor specialising in cancer research,' he explained, feeling absurdly pleased about the opportunity to show off.

'A doctor.' Michele giggled. 'I always wanted one of those. You are such an important man, researching and all . . . You like nurses, Doctor?'

'Uhm . . . Yeah.'

'It's your lucky night, Doctor! You deserve a treat.' She finished unbuttoning her uniform, but did not take off the top. Somehow, the shadowy glimpses of her naked breasts were a lot more arousing in their semi-covered state than if she had uncovered them completely. 'Oooh, I get to be the doctor's nurse tonight,' cooed Michele. 'Doctor . . .'

'Waverly,' he supplied.

'Dr Waverly, does your wife know about you and that little slut nurse, that Michele?' she asked, mock-serious. She put her hands beneath the uniform and pushed her breasts inwards and up, until they were exposed to his gaze. 'Does your wife know that you get hard looking at slut nurse Michele? Does she know that you play with yourself all the time, thinking about slut nurse Michele's big, beautiful tits and tight ass?'

'I'm not married. I don't have a wife,' he stammered, captivated by the teasing display.

'Good boy.' She giggled and sat down on his lap, facing him. Her thighs were firm, warm vices. She petted his face.

44

'I'm so glad you are not married, Dr Waverly,' she purred. 'If you were, your wife would be curious as to why you spend so much of your valuable time with that slut Michele.'

'But I don't . . .'

'You *know* you'll be back, Dr Waverly.'

Robert gasped as the stripper rose and turned her back to him. She lowered her gorgeous ass over the rigid tent of his erection. Her butt slid over the outlined shape of his painfully hard cock and she began to move up and down to the beat of the music, milking his trapped member with consummate skill. 'You like to do the night shift with nurse Michele, don't you, Doctor?'

'Oh my God,' moaned Robert. 'That feels . . .'

'Amazing, doesn't it, Dr Waverly?' cooed Michele triumphantly. 'You want to feel me up, don't you, Doctor?'

'No, never,' whimpered Robert.

'You want to touch pretty slut nurse Michele, don't you, Dr Waverly?' She grabbed his hands and put them over her luscious naked tits, sliding his hands underneath the shiny polyester of her uniform.

'I – I guess,' whimpered Robert, feeling his fingers tweak the nipples of his irresistible seductress.

'Doctor Waverly!' Michele giggled in mock outrage. 'I can't believe you would try to press yourself on an innocent young woman in your own department!'

'God, you're amazing,' croaked Robert.

She rode his erection, up and down, keeping his hands over her naked tits, her manicured fingers keeping his hands trapped against the hot flesh.

The song was coming to an end. Her movements became quicker, more calculated. She ground her ass into his member, milking his trapped cock.

'What is it you want again?' She smirked.

'I want to touch pretty slut Michele,' answered Robert, frantic with need. The methodical manipulation of his member brought him to the edge of an unbelievable orgasm.

The music ended and she stood up.

'Jesus, please don't stop,' he gasped.

'Would you like me to continue?' she asked sweetly.

'Yes!' he groaned.

'You have to pay in advance,' said Michele. 'Let me take you to the cash machine.'

He opened his mouth to say 'no' but she pressed herself against him. Her breasts pushed against his sweater and her legs wrapped around him like a boa constrictor. His intention to walk away died on his lips.

'You were great, Robbie,' she whispered, eyelashes fluttering. 'I really like you, Dr Waverly.' She giggled. 'Slut nurse Michele gets wet thinking about Doctor Waverly.' She motioned for him to go ahead. 'This way you can look up slut nurse Michele's dress, Doctor,' she explained. 'Every time you turn around to tell me that you don't want to come back upstairs, you'll have to look at me and when you do that –' she smirked '– you'll change your mind, won't you?'

It was as if she had read his mind; he did indeed turn his head to tell her that he had changed his mind, that he was no longer interested in going back up on those narrow stairs into the sordid lair of temptation, but when he did so, he encountered those long, tanned legs, those stiletto heels, that swaying, seductive flesh on brazen display, accentuated by the sleazy white folds of slut nurse Michele's uniform.

She giggled and softly prodded him with her heels. 'Go on, Robbie. Faster you pay, faster we can be back upstairs.'

He stumbled out of the stairwell and stood to the side as she emerged behind him. She said something to the tuxedoed ape who had taken his first hundred. He didn't say a word, just nodded in acknowledgment.

She took his hand and pulled him after her. Her bottom was swaying to the slow, sensuous music that blared from the speakers.

'Dude, how was it?' Robert heard, vaguely. He turned red with embarrassment.

'Hold on,' mumbled Robert, avoiding Scott's eyes. 'I'll be right back.'

46

He meekly walked after Michele. There was a small cash machine blinking with yellow and green lights.

He numbly took out his wallet and put his ATM card in the slot. The machine swallowed it with admirable speed and he punched in his password: H-O-L-L-Y-1.

A nearly physical wave of shame washed over him as he punched in the name of his girlfriend. This was wrong!

'We should have something else to drink, Robbie,' said Michele, leaning into him. Her hands kept sliding against his arm, against his torso, incidental strokes that made him want more.

'I really can't stay,' said Robert, abruptly. 'I have to go.'

'Robbie, I want to go back up,' whined Michele petulantly.

Shame fought lust and shame won, albeit barely. He pressed one of the two hundreds that came out of the machine into Michele's hand and rushed out, refusing to listen to her crooning calls after him. From the corner of his eye he saw Scott rise and say something but then he was at the curtain, past the cop and the doorman, outside in the cold, fresh air. Almost at once his cell phone began to ring – it was Scott – and Robert turned it off.

He walked a block north just to get away from the club before turning right to get to the metro. He was shaking inside. How could he do this? If it wasn't for Holly he would be pissing away his hard-earned money being dry-humped by some sleazy gold-digging stripper!

He swore he would make it up to Holly. She could never know, of course, what he had done, but he would swear never to do it again – which he never would, of course.

Inside the club, the machine finally printed out Robert's receipt. Long manicured fingers reached out and held the piece of paper up to the light so their owner could study the contents, before folding it up and sliding it beneath the lace of a garter belt.

4

Robert

'Darling!' Robert smiled, exuberant. He gave her a crushing hug and kissed her.

Holly disentangled herself from the unexpectedly vehement embrace and gave him a measured, sidelong glance. 'You look very happy to see me.'

'Why wouldn't I be?'

'I don't know ... How was your evening all by your lonesome?'

'Had a drink with Scott,' said Robert carefully. 'I got home fairly early though.'

'Sounds nice.'

'Yes, it was.'

'Scott is a bit of a party animal, isn't he?'

'Oh, yes, sometimes, I suppose.'

'So where did you go?'

'Sorry?'

'Where did you go for that drink?'

Robert walked to the window and peered out into the darkness. 'Is it snowing outside?' he asked nervously.

'Robert, are you deaf? I asked you a question!'

'Scott wants to do a bachelor party for James.' Robert gulped. 'He wanted me to see the place where he wants us to go –'

Holly cut him off. 'A bachelor party? Where?'

'It's a place called Hot Summer's, it's – ah, well ...'

Holly's voice was unnaturally level. 'Did you go to a strip club, Robert Waverly?'

'Yes, I suppose so. There were girls there, yes!' he battled back gamely, knowing full well it was futile. 'Scott asked

me to check out the place before we finalised arrangements
. . .'

Her voice was honed and sharpened, a swooping ma-
chete. 'So. Did you have a good time, Robert?'

'It was OK,' he mumbled.

'So you enjoyed yourself, did you?'

He raised both hands, as if warding off the evil eye. 'It
was really cheesy, honest!'

'I can't believe you've done this to me!' Holly stood and
stormed into the bedroom. The door nearly slammed into
Robert's face as he hurried after her. His hand was moving
to turn the knob as an audible click permeated his
distressed consciousness: his girlfriend had locked him out.

'Holly, please!' he pleaded. He could hear elaborate
sounds issuing from the bedroom.

'Why don't you go back to your little strippers, I bet you
would like that!' came the muffled, angry recrimination.
'Go on, I won't be here by the time you get back!'

Robert felt incredibly guilty – Holly's suggestion made
him recall (again) the sordid events in the champagne room,
Michele and Becky and Tiffany and . . . and his member
grew hard. The insistent vision of the nurse-uniformed
stripper standing over him had turned into a seductive
goad. His fevered imagination kept replaying the scene in
the stairwell, over and over. In his mind, Michele's uniform
kept getting flimsier and flimsier, until she was practically
naked, becoming a bitchy, mocking essence of addictive
femininity. Her voice kept percolating through his mind:
*This way you can look up slut nurse Michele's dress, Dr
Waverly. Every time you turn around to tell me that you don't
want to come back upstairs, you'll have to look at me and
when you do that . . . You'll change your mind, won't you?*

He shook his head to clear it of the persisting visions.
'Please, Holly! I love you!' he begged. He politely knocked
on the door. 'I love you so much! It was a mistake! I – I
didn't know it was a strip club . . .'

'You are stupid, then! Do I want to date a – a cheater,
or an idiot? I don't think I want either!' screamed Holly,
her voice practically drilling into his head through the
thick door panel. 'How could you!'

Her yelling grew jumbled until the sounds finally turned into incoherent weeping.

He sighed and sat with his back against the door, dejected.

'After all I've done for you,' sobbed Holly, finally talking after a minute's worth of sobbing. 'How could you? And I thought we had something special together! What a fool I've been! To think that I considered – *marrying* you!'

Robert wiped his forehead with his hand. He was sweating. 'I'm so sorry, honey. I'm so sorry. Let me make it up to you, please!'

'I'm not sure I can believe in your commitment any more, Robert,' said Holly. The bedroom door finally opened and she walked out. Her eyes were red with tears. She was dragging a bright-yellow suitcase.

'What are you doing?' asked Robert, flabbergasted.

'What does it look like? I'm going to Mom's, Robert. I can't believe I'm forced to go back to my mother's!'

'Jesus, darling . . .'

'And don't you dare take the Lord's name in vain, Dr Waverly!'

'Sorry, sorry . . . I mean, please don't go. I love you!'

'Funny way to show it – maybe next time you will buy me a bouquet of hookers? Were the whores pretty, by the way?'

'What whores?'

'Those stripper whores with their fake tits, Robert!'

'No! They were ugly, you know I don't like that type!'

'Now you are lying! I seem to remember that TV show and that retarded bimbo in those high heels that you were drooling over!'

'No, they were ugly,' muttered Robert, quickly moving to embrace her. He wanted to use the warm sensation of her body against his to chase away the memory of Michele's luscious tits in his grasping hands. 'You are a hundred times more beautiful than those stupid – girls,' he added in what he hoped was a calming tone.

She shrugged off his arms, audibly sniffed and folded up a pair of sensible white cotton panties. 'I guess I'm going to let you think up a way to make it up to me, Robert, but you're not getting any sex for the next couple of weeks. And I don't want to see Scott for the foreseeable future, is that clear?'

Robert didn't say anything for a long moment. When he spoke, it was in a very quiet tone of voice. 'What about the bachelor party?'

Her eyes practically popped. 'You are worried about that stupid bachelor party when our entire relationship is at stake? Let me make myself absolutely clear, Robert Waverly: you are not going back to that place, ever! If I find out that you've gone within a mile of that – whorehouse – I'm breaking up with you for good. Do you understand, Robert?'

'Yes,' he said, miserably.

She picked up a gilded photograph taken last year at a charity function organised by Holly's sorority. She shoved it in his hand. 'While I'm gone you can look at this picture to see what you are missing.'

He looked at the picture in mortified silence. Holly looked good in it. She wore a conservative, fairly low-cut black dress and two-inch black heels. She even wore some lipstick. For Holly, that was as sexy an outfit as you were going to get. For a moment Robert considered how Holly would look in slut nurse Michele's uniform and he felt his member rise to the occasion.

Holly kept on folding white, grey and khaki outfits and placing them into the suitcase. She stopped for a moment and gave her boyfriend a baleful stare. 'I guess you can bring them here. I'm sure I don't have to tell you to behave?'

'The bachelor party? To the apartment? Are you sure you are OK with it?'

She rolled her eyes. 'I'm not some ogre, Robert. They can come here, talk football, drink and make a mess. I know what men do.'

'I guess that'll be OK,' he said tentatively.

She looked at him for a moment longer and snapped the suitcase shut. 'That's that, then. I'm leaving. When I come back, let's say three weeks, you'll have a lot of work repairing the damage you've done to our relationship.'

'I'm sorry. Darling, I will make it up to you.'

'Oh, you will, you can bet on it,' said Holly and she pointedly stared at the packed suitcase. 'I guess it would be too much to ask you to put this in the car?' she asked sardonically.

'I'm sorry,' he said again, and picked up the bag. He followed Holly to the parking garage where he placed the bag in the trunk of her car.

He waved her goodbye but she pointedly ignored him. He watched her disappearing tail-light and returned to the apartment with a heavy heart.

He met Scott for a drink and told him what had happened. His reaction was not at all what he had expected.

'Dude, that's fantastic!'

'What are you talking about? It's an absolute disaster!'

'I don't see the problem. She is giving you carte blanche for the next three weeks. We can have the bachelor party at Hot Summer's, she'll never know.'

'Scott, I'm never going to that place again. Ever.'

'Oh come on, I mean . . .'

'I will not say it again, Scott. Don't even try. I'm not going back to that place.'

'We could hire some . . .'

'Absolutely not. I'm not even sure what exactly you were going to say but I can guess. Like I said, no way.'

Scott remained silent for a moment. When he finally spoke it was like bidding at a poker table. 'What about at your place? I suppose we could save a ton of money. Hot Summer's is an expensive place for one of those things.'

'I guess.' Robert was pleased Scott was not making a big deal out of his refusal to have the party at the strip club. He felt some measure of compromise was not unreasonable.

'Don't worry about it at all. I know this is a bit on short notice, but I was thinking of doing it next week.'

'Next week? I thought the wedding was months away!'

'Just got a call from James last night; Lucille's mom is trying to get a date at the cathedral, and if she does get it they'll be having the wedding in, like, three weeks . . .'

'Good Lord. I need to tell Holly, she might have a conflicting obligation.'

Scott grabbed Robert by the shoulders and softly shook him.

'What are you doing?'

'I am shaking you down, looking for your balls. Oh, I know! They are in Holly's pocket, I remember now! Dude, Holly is a bridesmaid, you think Lucille of all people will let her forget?'

Robert forced himself to laugh. 'Very funny. Yeah, I guess she would know.'

'Anyway, how about next Thursday night?'

'I will have to ask all the guys,' said Robert. 'I'm not sure if it's doable on such short notice. Let's keep it fairly civilised, though. I'll pay for the drinks and we can use the apartment, but no strippers, Scott.'

'Oh, come on . . .'

'I mean it, Scott. If Holly finds out . . .'

'OK, OK! Enough already! I'll handle the – arrangements.'

Robert glumly nodded. 'If it's a go, I will hit the liquor store on Wednesday, pick up some chips and things.'

Scott nodded and left.

When Robert woke up the next morning he felt miserable. The apartment felt empty without Holly. The bed was too large – he had found himself tossing and turning all night. He put Holly's picture on the bedstand, on her side, finding himself scooting closer and closer to what was usually her place in bed. Robert ended up sleeping on her side. When he woke up his eyes immediately strayed over to her picture.

He glanced at her made-up, 'sexy' look and took the rare opportunity of his solitude to ogle his girlfriend's picture without the dangers this sort of behaviour normally engendered. His hand strayed over his morning hard-on and freed his cock without a second thought. Jerking off to his own girlfriend hardly seemed objectionable – he figured she would be pleased on some deeply buried subconscious level if she ever learned by some divine miracle what he was doing. His eyes roved over the meagre amount of exposed flesh of Holly's legs on the picture and over her modest cleavage. His hand continued to bring himself to ever-higher levels of arousal. Robert closed his eyes as he neared orgasm – and a nearly living vision shoved aside the feeble echoes of Holly.

Her portrait slipped from his weakened fingers as his lips parted, forcing his voice into a high-pitched, mindless repetition of Michele's mockery. 'This way you can look up slut nurse Michele's dress, Doctor Waverly. Every time you turn around to tell me that you don't want to come back upstairs, you'll have to look at me and when you do that . . . You'll change your mind, won't you? This way you can look up slut nurse Michele's dress, Doctor Waverly, this way you can . . .'

He repeated the manipulative stripper's words over and over, thinking of the luscious mounds of her breasts in his hands, the feeling of her tight, gorgeous ass around his mindless, trapped erection, the view of her long, tanned legs from below . . . He whimpered pathetically as great gobs of come spurted from his tortured member. The forgotten portrait was exactly in the wrong spot – the mocking results of his orgasm spilt all over his girlfriend's picture, covering her entire tastefully clad figure with oozing white come.

He was immediately overcome with guilt. He took the picture into the kitchen and scrubbed it carefully. He was horrified to discover that a drop of water had mixed with his come and the mixture somehow seeped beneath the frame, smearing the top edge.

He put the picture back on the nightstand and sat back down on the bed, thinking. It was obvious that he could not go on like this – he must get Michele out of his system for good. After he ate breakfast he reviewed his email and read one of the many medical journals that he periodically contributed to. He had a lot of work to do – he was close to a breakthrough, he was sure of it, and he could not afford distractions.

Robert could not immerse himself in oncology, however. He was still bothered by the events of the last few days, and soon enough he found himself back in the bedroom. He picked up Holly's picture again and concentrated on the memory of his girlfriend's body, trying to feel arousal. It was just no good. Robert numbly unzipped his fly and began to stroke his member, concentrating on the picture. As he worked himself into a state of frazzled lust, he found that his lips were mouthing what seemed to have become a sort of mantra, once again: 'This way you can look up slut nurse Michele's dress, Doctor Waverly, this way you can . . .'

When he realised what he was doing, he stopped. Robert reluctantly zipped up his pants. He felt that he had to find something to counteract the memory of Michele's seductive charms – it was unfortunate that it would not be Holly, but anything was better than his present predicament. He walked into the foyer and searched through his coat pockets until he had found the postcard Scott sent from Jamaica, along with the envelope full of unmailed ones.

His eyes roved over the luscious tits of the blonde on the pictures (they were all of the same woman) and his cock hardened with approval. He resumed masturbating. Soon he was on the edge of a shattering orgasm. After his cock spent itself, he put the postcards in the envelope. He was about to return it into his coat pocket when he hesitated. It was still at least a good week before Holly's promised date of return – he would need to distract his mind from the insistent tug of Michele's luscious, tempting offer. He opened the top drawer of his nightstand and put the envelope inside.

He returned to the postcards twice that day. It allowed him to concentrate on his work. After each climax he was be able to focus on research for at least an hour or so – until the memories of Michele's manipulative caresses resurfaced once again, like poison gas bubbling up from a pool of quicksand. As always, his urges had driven him into the bedroom where his trembling hands quickly put the postcards to use. As the day dragged on he found himself less and less able to keep his mind off the filthy memory of the stripper's alluring charms. He stared at the picture of the beach bunny from Jamaica and realised that he had been comparing her breasts to Michele's and Becky's.

If he hadn't known any better, this model could be Michele.

'Damn,' he cursed aloud. He would have to work doubly hard the next day to make up for all this wasted time with his dick in his hand. It was as if he was some hard-up teenager again. Robert shook his head, disgusted at himself. He decisively marched into the foyer and put on his coat. He found himself outside, walking along the avenue in the direction of the metro station. The local branch of his bank was just around that corner, he realised. He fished out his wallet, shamefaced. For the first time in years, he had no cash on him at all. The wallet was completely empty. It even lacked the customary hundred he always carried for emergencies. Once he thought about what he could do about that, he became a little happier. His pace quickened as he rounded the corner, pleased that at least he could return his wallet to something resembling its normal state.

He inserted his ATM card into the machine. Robert forced a smile as he punched in his PIN. Obviously, he would need a hundred dollars to replace the squandered emergency fund. And he would need a little ready cash for incidental expenses. He really ought to spend a little money on Holly as well. After all, she did say he would need to make up for the damage he had caused to their relationship. Yes, he would definitely have to buy her something nice. Not all stores took credit cards. He really ought to take out some extra cash just in case he found something that she might like, in a store that didn't take credit cards. It was all so simple, really.

Robert put the thick wad of twenties in his wallet and began to walk down the street. He was cheered by having accomplished at least this much. Tomorrow he would start work early and finish late. He would not spend another sweaty day jacking off to some stupid postcards.

His walk took him in an unexpected direction; he found himself near his office on a familiar stretch of avenue. He gave an amused chuckle, surprised that he was so near Hot Summer's. The club was just a hundred feet away, on the *other* side of the avenue, next to one of those little shops that sold magazines, newspapers, soda and cigarettes.

Really, he ought to buy a paper. How long had it been since he had actually read the newspaper? He couldn't remember the last time! He really should pay more attention to the news. He crossed the avenue, keeping a close eye on the shop. It was really very close to Hot Summer's. Why, from here you could actually read the sign with today's performers:

HEATHER

TINA

AMBER

BECKY

DEBBIE

TIFFANY

JOANNA

MISSY

PRINCESS

He read the sign twice, from top to bottom. So Michele was not working tonight. Good! The apelike security man stood impassively in front of the door.

Robert cleared his throat.

The security man ignored him.

'Excuse me,' said Robert, nervously.

'Yes, sir?' responded the man, finally.

'So Michele is not working today, right?' asked Robert. It was a good idea to double check, he told himself. After all, he did not want to run into her by accident.

'No, she is working on Wednesdays, Fridays and Sundays.' The man reached into his pocket and took out a bright-yellow business card. 'This has the website of the club. There is a schedule posted there every week.'

Robert took the card; he didn't really have a choice, he figured. Only a fool would insult a muscle-bound ape like this by refusing to take it. 'Hotsummersnightclubdotcom?' he read.

'Yessir.'

'Thank you.'

'Coming in, sir?'

'Oh no, no way,' laughed Robert after a brief pause. After all, Holly was out of town. Michele was not working. Surely, just to have a single drink would not harm anyone. Holly would never know. He could just go and watch the girls for a few minutes, have a single drink and not even tip them. His cock stiffened and strained against his pants as his eyes roved over the list, assigning tantalising images to each name: Becky with her mammoth tits, Princess with her long, slender legs . . .

As he stood there, paralysed with indecision, the walkie-talkie in the doorman's hand crackled into life. After a brief and unintelligible exchange of words the door swung open. A man exited the club, swaying slightly. He was in his early forties at most, balding, in a pinstriped suit. In each hand he was holding one half of a credit card. Right after he cleared the door he stumbled and steadied himself against the wall. 'Shit,' he groaned.

'Can't stay here, sir,' said the doorman, looming over him. 'Gotta get out of here.'

'Jesus, dude, I just blew every dime I had in there,' said the man. 'Give me a minute to clear my head, OK?'

The doorman got right in the other man's face. He put his hand on the man's shoulder. The doorman did not yell, but somehow it wasn't necessary. There was disdain in his voice. 'Do you want me to call the cops?'

Robert noted that the 'sir' seemed to have disappeared from the doorman's vocabulary.

The man shook off the doorman's hand and scurried off. When he was a good thirty feet away, he halted and threw the cut-up credit card down on the pavement. His eyes were red and Robert realised that the man had been crying. 'You goddamned bastards,' he sobbed. 'You bloodsucking bastards.'

The man's frustrated, painful muttering faded away into the night as he walked away. Robert figured he didn't have the cash for a cab.

'Sorry about that, sir,' said the doorman. 'He couldn't pay his bill. Don't worry about that loser; we're a high-profile place, sir, this sort of thing hardly ever happens.'

'Yeah ...' said Robert. 'I really should go.'

A gorgeous redhead in translucent platform sandals and a tight silver dress approached the entrance, giving Robert a slow, languorous smile. The girl greeted the doorman with obvious familiarity and Robert realised she must be a stripper. They both looked after her as she disappeared behind the doors.

'That's Tiffany,' said the doorman. 'Coming in, sir?'

Robert had lost his erection during the ugly interlude with the ejected man in the suit, but the new arrival re-keyed his lust. Still, he could not forget the ugly little scene earlier. 'Maybe some other time,' he said. 'I'm just here to get a paper,' he added. He motioned towards the shop.

The doorman nodded. He resumed his impassive stare.

Once he was out of the shadow of the club entrance he began to breathe a little easier. He could not believe how close he had been to entering the place again despite Holly's warning. Jesus! He must be really hard up to find those trashy girls attractive. He liked classy, educated women with conservative values, like Holly.

Robert walked into the news shop and grabbed the paper. His eyes strayed over the rack of magazines. Holly's workout magazines were here. He picked one off the rack and leafed through it until he came upon the picture of the toned, sweaty aerobics instructor. He chuckled at the silliness of the picture and casually replaced the issue on the rack. These things were ridiculous!

Speaking of ridiculous, an entire line of glossy magazines at the top of the rack was hidden behind a dark plastic strip. Why, just to get one down for a good look required effort! Still, wearing an amused smile, he moved closer and took down a few of them. He furtively took his haul to the cash register. The magazines were all wrapped in plastic. Tantalising bits of the cover models reinforced his hard-on. He put the newspaper on top of the sordid pile of porn.

'Just these,' he said, his eyes scanning the rest of the shop. By divine grace, the place was empty.

The cashier, an old black man, rang up the paper and the magazines. '46.50,' he said. Robert impatiently peeled off three twenties.

He left the news shop smug with newfound confidence. He smiled at the doorman in front of Hot Summer's, holding the paper bag like some kind of a talisman. He wouldn't be tempted by this place any more.

When he got home he rushed into the bedroom with the paper bag as soon as he crossed the threshold. He unzipped his pants and took his cock out, tearing the plastic wrap off each magazine, frantic with his pervasive need. He quickly zoomed in on one of the magazines with a promising cover. It depicted a blonde model with huge tits. She wore stiletto heels and a schoolgirl uniform. She was sucking on a lollipop. He began to stroke his cock as his eyes devoured the seductive content of each glossy page.

When he came to in the morning, his eyes immediately focused on a pair of enormous fake tits. His face was resting on the glossy pages of a centrefold; apparently he had fallen asleep on pornography. He pushed it away with disgust but his eyes lingered. It was the picture of the girl with the big tits in the schoolgirl uniform. His member stirred again. The magazines were strewn all about the bedroom, beckoning him, albeit with less force than during the night before. He had looked through all of them and they were no longer a seductive novelty, just a known resource to counter the insistent urge to return to Hot Summer's, to return to Michele's squirming, luscious body.

No – today he would dedicate himself to work, to research. He dressed and made himself a sandwich, putting it in his briefcase. He checked his pockets – did he have everything? He walked through the apartment just to make sure.

When he entered the bedroom his eyes strayed over to the mound of glossy pornography strewn all over his bed. He stacked them (keeping the one with the schoolgirl on top) and put them in his nightstand. He hesitated before closing the drawer.

I should just keep one on me, to stave off temptation, he thought. He opened the nightstand and removed the top magazine, putting it in his briefcase. He slammed the bedroom door shut and resolutely walked out. He avoided Hot Summer's on the way to work on purpose, deriving satisfaction from this exhibition of willpower.

Robert managed to get a great deal of work done before lunch. He only realised the extent of his hunger when his secretary asked him if he wanted her to bring him something for lunch.

'I brought a sandwich,' he told her. 'I'll eat it here.'

'All right then,' she said. 'Are you going to be OK here all by yourself for the rest of the afternoon? I asked for this afternoon off last week, if you remember.'

He didn't remember but neither did he mind. 'Sure, sure. Have fun,' he said.

'It's a dentist's appointment,' said Amanda.

'Uhm – sorry, I forgot,' he laughed. 'Hope it won't be too – painful.'

She left and he took the sandwich out. It looked pretty pathetic. The bread had got soggy. Robert had no desire to bite into it. He just wasn't hungry for a crappy sandwich like this: cheese, a single slice of ham, butter – not even a slice of tomato to liven things up. Maybe he should have taken Amanda up on her offer to bring him something to eat.

Maybe he should go out for lunch. He had plenty of cash on him and there were all those little places along the avenue, right by Hot Summer's. Robert wondered if Michele was working today – it would not do to go down the avenue and happen to walk right into the jaws of temptation.

Hesitantly he pulled out the business card the doorman had given him. He read the website's address out loud, chuckling with amusement, but typed it in regardless. He would never check this website to visit the place, of course. He was only looking it up so he could avoid it during those times when it was most dangerous to his peace of mind, his relationship and his wallet.

As the site started to load, he remembered the doorman's words: Michele was working Wednesdays, Fridays and Sundays. He moved to close the browser window just as the site finished loading. A collage of practically naked flesh unfurled on his screen. There was a link to a gallery, a link to dancer schedules, a link to waitress schedules, even a link for 'special services'. What on earth could those be? Certainly he would just be exhibiting the healthy curiosity of an amused spectator if he checked out the offerings. He felt oddly disappointed when clicking on the link only produced a mere two lines of text: 'Dancers may be hired to perform at designated events, such as bachelor parties', and 'click here to schedule'.

Holly would kill him! She would definitely leave him, he thought. A line of pictures began to crawl across the top of the screen, still shots of the girls. Robert's lips parted slightly and his member rose until a little tent formed in his pants. There was Tiffany, bending low and displaying her ass to its best advantage in a skimpy leopard print bikini . . . Becky, tweaking her nipples with those slutty manicured nails . . . Finally, he saw Michele. She was wearing the nurse's uniform. The picture was taken in the stairwell and the camera was looking up the flimsy covering of her outfit. Her stiletto heels helped to show off her long tanned legs to their full advantage.

Holly would kill him. He couldn't hire these – what did Holly call them? Stripper whores with their fake tits? Yes, that was it. He clicked on Becky's picture and waited impatiently as the full-size picture loaded. Her tits definitely could be fake. In fact, they *were* fake. He was a qualified plastic surgeon, after all! Although he had chosen to dedicate his life to cancer research, he was still more than qualified to tell. It was definitely a professional job. What about Michele's tits? He clicked on her picture as well. Yes, those could also be fakes. Just like the ones on the postcards. He pulled one out and compared it to the image on screen. Yes, those breasts and Michele's were . . . He looked at the model's face. With the sunglasses and a perm, she *could* be Michele. His eyes strayed to his office door. Amanda was out until tomorrow and he was all alone . . .

He unzipped his pants. They slid down to his ankles as he began to pleasure himself while soaking in the spectacle of the pictures on the monitor. He switched to his left hand as he clicked on picture after picture.

How much would it cost to hire a stripper, anyway? He clicked on the 'click here to schedule' link. A picture of a blonde (Heather 2) in a sleazy cheerleading uniform and six-inch mules came up. Underneath the picture was a politely worded command: 'Enter name here please.'

He typed in his name (one letter at a time, he could only use one hand) and punched ENTER.

A picture of Becky sucking on an obscenely shaped lollipop loaded on screen. Text flashed below the picture: 'Thank you *Robert*. Please enter the date and address for your event.'

He chuckled – he just wanted to know how much it would cost to hire one of these girls; it was academic curiosity, nothing more, nothing less. He was slightly annoyed that the programmer was putting him through these hoops before he just clicked on CANCEL anyway, but he really wanted to know what they were charging. He put in next Thursday for the date and the address of his apartment for location.

A picture of Tiffany in the black leather get-up of a professional dominatrix filled the monitor. The picture was captioned: 'Good puppy! Such a good boy! You're almost there! Now enter your credit-card information!'

His breathing grew shallow as he stared at the picture. As he hesitated, the picture shifted to the left, to be replaced with a photo of Michele. She was wearing a tawdry pink dress, torn in strategic spots to reveal tanta-lising glimpses of her gorgeous body. The caption now read, 'Go on piggy, you know you want to!'

His left hand subconsciously continued the incessant stroking of his erection while his right hand pulled out his wallet. He typed in his credit-card number and expiration date one character at a time. His other hand continued to manipulate his painfully hard member. He simply could not bring himself to stop. Every time he thought about clicking the site off, another picture would load and he simply had to see them all.

He practically flattened the enter key, hooked on the offerings reeling him in through the monitor.

Becky and Michele were standing in a shower. They were lathering one another up with soap; their nipples were invisible in the steam, under the creamy bubbles. Thumbnails of a dozen girls came up underneath the text: 'Select the dancer(s) you wish to perform at your event.'

He clicked on the thumbnail images of Michele and Becky, his eyes slavishly absorbing every filthy detail.

'You've been such a good boy, *Robert*,' flashed the screen. 'Now just click on *Confirm* and *Michele* and *Becky* will come by to show you a good time on *Thursday*.' A figure flashed next to the word CONFIRM.

'Jesus Christ,' mumbled Robert. 'That's insane! Twelve hundred dollars?'

More pictures loaded as he vacillated. They showed Michele and Becky rubbing up against one another in various sleazy outfits. The cajoling would not stop. Text flashed. 'The girls you have selected, *Michele* and *Becky*, enjoy playing with one another,' the screen informed him. 'They like to rub their tits together and play dress-up for you.'

Robert stared dumbly at the screen; like an automaton, his hand kept stroking his cock. There was simply no way around it.

'They love giving lap dances together to the fortunate man whose friend hires them for a bachelor party,' urged the screen, showing a picture of the two practically smothering some lucky guy on a chair.

Robert's pathetic stroking took him to the edge of a mind-blowing orgasm. Just as his efforts were about to bear fruit, every single one of the pictures filling his screen abruptly faded; only one line of text remained: 'Click CONFIRM, *Robert* and you will get to see more pretty pictures – and *Michele* and *Becky*, in person, live on *Thursday*.'

His left hand in constant motion, Robert lurched forwards in his chair, his drooling face a few inches from the monitor. This close to the screen, his vision blurred until all he could see were the mocking, blinking words in the centre of the monitor. With a pathetic whimper, he pressed down on the mouse, the audible click travelling

64

through his arm and straight into his spasming, happy member. The screen blinked and filled with a stream of explicit pictures featuring Michele and Becky, one after another, fuelling his arousal and the addictive waves of pleasure.

'You've been a good boy! You've been a good boy!' scrolled text over and over on the bottom of the screen. 'You've been a good boy!'

'I've been a good boy,' gasped Robert and felt his balls contract, spurting his come all over himself. 'I've been a good boy!'

He stayed slumped over the keyboard, mumbling the words.

'Next Thursday?' asked Scott, incredulous.

'Yes,' said Robert. He felt completely exhausted. 'Next Thursday, 7 p.m. sharp.'

'Everyone is OK with this?'

'Yeah, I've called everyone.'

'You know they'll expect girls.' Scott looked at Robert meaningfully.

After a moment's pause Robert looked away. 'I took care of it.'

'*You* took care of it?' asked Scott suspiciously.

'Yes. I have – two girls coming,' sighed Robert. 'I don't want to talk about it, OK? It's frigging expensive!'

'Dude, I'm so proud of you!' Scott slapped him on the back. He shook his head and gave an appreciative chuckle. 'You surprise me all the time, man. See? All you needed was a little time away from Holly to find your balls.'

'Scott, please don't talk about Holly like that. I wish she *was* back.'

'She'll be back soon enough, dude. You'll be humping her in no time flat. You can tell her what a good boy you've been!'

Robert flinched.

He did not really have a choice – after Amanda's return to the office the next day, he was forced to rush home at lunch. He leafed through a couple of the magazines but they weren't helping. He turned on his laptop, typing in the address of the Hot Summer's website. In less than a day he managed to look through all the pictures. He masturbated to all the girls in the gallery, but the pictures of Michele, Becky and Tiffany were particularly effective in helping him get off. The constant masturbation was taking a toll on his work – he barely got any of the research done that he had promised the non-profit committee that co-ordinated the entire cancer-research effort.

He promised Holly and himself that he would never go to Hot Summer's again. Of course it didn't help that the club was so close to his office and the lab. He walked past the place several times every day, furtively glancing at the names on the bright-yellow sign, although by then he knew the schedule by heart.

His cell phone beeped. He received a text message: 'I guess you don't miss me much. Holly.'

Overcome with guilt, he wrote back, 'I love you. I miss you very much. I bought you a present.' He rushed to make his lie true. There was a jewellery store on the other side of the street. He counted the cash in his wallet, excepting the customary hundred he kept for emergencies.

'I'd like something for my girlfriend,' he told the sales girl. She was a ditzy blonde with big tits – at least he would have considered them big a week ago, until his exposure to the enhanced versions at Hot Summer's and in the glossy magazines stuffed into his nightstand. Still, he found them attractive and soon enough he realised that he was drawing out his description of what he wanted, just so he could get a better look of her cleavage. 'Just something to make her feel special,' he added at the end and leant lower over the counter.

'Sure thing,' she said with a white-toothed smile. 'Let me show you a few of the more popular pieces.'

She pulled out a couple of earrings, a medallion and a few bracelets. Some of them had small diamonds.

He picked up the medallion and glanced at the price tag – it was 240 dollars. 'We also have a large selection of chains to go along with the medallion,' she added.

He held up the medallion against the sunlight coming in from outside. He had a clear view of the club from here.

He nearly dropped the medallion when he recognised Michele's blonde hair and characteristic strutting walk. She disappeared inside the entrance. 'Yeah, that'll be OK,' he said in a hurry. 'I'll take it.'

'Would you like a chain as well, sir?' she asked.

'Yeah, sure, why not,' he said, distracted. Even from this far off, Michele looked incredible. She wore white platform heels and a short white miniskirt, topped off by a white fur coat – probably a fake, but you could never tell. She looked like a high-priced toy (which she was, now that the thought occurred to him).

The sales girl showed him a few chains and he just nodded at the one she sounded most enthusiastic about. The total for medallion and chain came to 426.99; he opened his mouth to protest but then reconsidered. If anything, Holly deserved a much more expensive gift than this little trinket. After all, he had just spent 1200 dollars on two strippers! He watched the girl put the chain and the medallion in a velvet box and came to a decision as she gift-wrapped the box.

He resolutely kept his eyes away from the girl's cleavage. Pocketing the box, he marched directly across the street to the club entrance. The doorman glanced at him. 'Is the manager in?' he asked. He wasn't sure if this was the same guy who had witnessed his hesitation the other day – they all looked the same to him.

'Yessir,' said the doorman.

'I have to talk to him.' He steeled himself against a run-around.

The ape's response was unexpectedly mild. 'Just go on in and wait for him by the curtain.'

There was a characteristic scent to the club, a mix of sweet body rub, cigarette smoke and lust, a sensual, spicy odour that wormed its way underneath his resolve and gave him an instant erection. A slow, seductive beat permeated the place like bacteria in diseased meat. He knew Michele was inside, but he was temporarily sated; the last few days' masturbation provided an odd sort of defence against his lust.

The cop nodded to him and told him to wait. Soon enough, a greasy-looking guy in a double-breasted black

suit arrived. He looked Robert over and nodded.
'Hiyyadoin',' he blurted. 'I'm Dennis, I'm the manager on
duty. What can I do for you, sir?'

'Well . . . I was on your website the other day,' he began
with some difficulty, 'and I wanted to see how much it
would be to hire some of the – dancers to work –
to perform at a bachelor party.'

'Sure, yes?' said the manager. He spoke too quickly.
'The girls are great at it. They're really professional, a great
time, is there a problem?'

'Well . . . The only way I could see the price was by
clicking all the way to the end, and then I accidentally hit
confirm and it charged my card, but then I . . . the wedding
has been postponed . . .' he trailed off, realising he sounded
completely hapless.

'Oh, I see.' The manager did not sound upset. 'Well, you
see, I can't issue a refund. The bachelor party gigs go
straight to the dancers. It's a perk for the girls who work
at Hot Summer's – most other clubs take a big cut, but
here they get it all . . .'

'Really?' said Robert, feeling a sudden flash of panic.

'Yes. There is a screen with pictures of the dancers; you
click on the one you want at the party and she gets the
money. The credit-card company processes it for them
directly, not for us. Who did you click on?'

'Uh . . . I think her name was Becky,' said Robert.

The manager nodded.

'And Michele.'

'They are our most popular duo,' said the manager.
'Please stay here, I'll bring Michele. Becky is off today.'

'Uh – OK.'

'You hired two of them?' said the cop. 'I'm not surprised
you want a refund.'

'Why?' asked Robert, surprised and not a little appre-
hensive.

The cop shrugged. He was about to say something when
the manager returned with Michele following close behind.
'Robbie!'

His resolve suddenly crumbled into glowing red shards
of lust. He could not take his eyes off the tempting vision

68

before him. Michele was wearing the platform white heels he had spied from the jewellery shop, but she had taken off her fur coat to display a white lace teddy that only served as a token shield to hide her full luscious tits. She pressed herself against Robert, the mounds and curves of her firm young body pushing against him, carving up his will into small manageable bits.

'I'm so glad you came back, Robbie!' she cooed. 'I was so glad when I saw that you asked for me and Becky to do your friend's bachelor party! I wanted to call you and let you know how *appreciative* I was. But you *never* gave me your number, Dr Waverly!' She pouted and stomped her foot, a definite threat to the feet of bystanders with those heels. Her chest jiggled.

'No need,' he managed, vainly trying to keep his eyes on her face and not her body. The manager was gone – how he managed to disappear during the heartbeat that Robert was distracted, he did not know.

She seemed to recognise the conflict raging within him and put her hand on his, pulling him into the club through the curtain. 'We can talk upstairs, the club is almost empty,' she said.

'No, I can't,' he groaned, feeling her long fingers pull him into the semi-darkness beyond. He stumbled after her. The shadowy gloom of the club was like a vacuum pulling him in. He scanned the space. She was not exaggerating; the club was practically empty.

The stairwell was unguarded. He said something about it and she nodded. 'It's still early, Robbie. You don't mind if I call you Robbie, do you, Dr Waverly?' She giggled. 'You didn't mind the last time!'

'Well, sure, of course not,' he answered somehow. Her grip was like a vice around his wrist. She pulled him into the bottom of the stairwell and his cock responded to the oh-so-well-remembered site of her merciless teasing. He seemed to hear her mocking voice echoing off the walls: '*Every time you turn around to tell me that you don't want to come back upstairs, you'll have to look at me and when you do that . . .*'

'I really can't, I don't have time,' he said in a near panic. 'I can't go up there!'

'Oh, poor Doctor Waverly.' Michele giggled. 'Are you afraid of little ol' Michele? Would you like me to put on my nurse's uniform, Dr Waverly? Would little Robbie like to play with slut nurse Michele?'

Her words were like manipulative caresses over his now fully attentive member. He felt compelled to obey his mindless erection; it was pointing straight at the gorgeous swaying bottom of the manipulative dancer. He followed his new compass up the stairs to the champagne room.

'Are you looking up my skirt, Dr Waverly?' she teased.

'It's hard not to,' he said finally. 'You have a really beautiful – bottom.'

'You're so cute, Dr Waverly. Just call them tits and ass, all the girls do. So you like my tight hot ass, Dr Waverly?'

'It's really sexy,' he said, dry-mouthed. She seemed to play to his arousal, purposefully moving her legs in such a way as to exaggerate the swaying, hypnotic motion. He wanted to look away but it would have required – looking away.

'Here we are,' she purred, having arrived in the champagne room. As with the last time, the place was empty. The champagne bottles were still there, however. 'Let's sit down, Robbie.'

'Where?'

'Silly man.' She giggled and led him to an alcove. Michele parted the velvet curtains. She pushed him down on the sofa until his head bumped against the back. 'I said sit down, Dr Waverly.' She sat down next to him and rested her head on his shoulder. The scent of her body rub was a sweet cloud in the air. Her cleavage was wide open and from his vantage point he could see the pink of her nipples.

'Did you enjoy feeling up my tits last time, Doctor Waverly?' she said in a smirking, bitchy tone. 'I just *know* little Robbie wants to feel them up again.'

'Yes, I mean, no!' he said, aghast. 'I mean ... Michele, I'm sorry, I was throwing a bachelor party and I accidentally clicked on confirm and the wedding is – well, I'm sorry, I just wanted to, you know, cancel the appointment ...'

'But it would be so much fun, Dr Waverly. I mean – you went through all that trouble giving your name and address and credit card information, and you clicked on confirm – it was all a big accident, wasn't it, Dr Waverly?'

He nodded miserably, thinking of a plausible lie. Maybe he could claim that he was just checking how much it would cost and when he clicked confirm he was actually trying to click the window off. Maybe he could claim it was a computer malfunction.

She smirked knowingly, lifting her skirt with both hands. Her motion was deliberately slow. She took off her panties, watching Robert's trapped gaze with amused condescension. The tawdry offering of her shaved sex silenced Robert's planned explanation. Her mound was pink, a contrast to her crimson nails.

She mocked his silence. 'Ooh, the doctor likes slut nurse Michele's nice pink pussy, doesn't he? Have you been a good boy? You've been playing with your weewee thinking about pretty Michele's ass, tits and pussy?'

He was frozen, thinking she must be a mind-reader. 'Why would you say that?' he said weakly.

'You can't even look away, Dr Waverly. You've been coming around the club every day for the last two weeks, drooling like a puppy.'

He opened his mouth to protest but she silenced him yet again by taking off her flimsy lace teddy. Her tits sprung free right in front of his face. He felt saliva collect in his mouth; now he was drooling more than ever.

'Why don't you just give in, Dr Waverly. Don't you want to feel up my titties again? I know you want to.' She giggled cruelly. 'Go on, put your hands on my big, firm titties and feel them up, you can whack off tonight thinking about them.'

'I have a girlfriend,' he said, desperate. He lowered his trembling, more than willing hands. His cock was oozing precome and straining against his pants.

'Does she know you spent twelve hundred dollars on two strippers?' She smirked. 'Does she know her boyfriend is a drooling tent-popper?' She put her hand on top of his

71

pants and touched Robert's tortured member through the fabric. She stroked the outline of his erection with those long, manicured fingernails. 'Robbie,' she said, her voice turning into a manipulative, demanding whine. 'Robbie, I decided that Becky and I are going to do your little party. And then, Robbie, we are going to have a nice little talk, just you and I, about what I can do about your little problem.'

'What problem?' he gasped. Her fingers seemed to know just what to do to keep his arousal at fever pitch without granting relief.

'I think Dr Waverly's erection is telling me "I need you!"' purred Michele. Her fingers sought out his zipper and she pulled on it until his member sprang free. She collected his rock-hard cock in her hand, examining it with a critical eye. 'Robbie! Dr Waverly!' she cried out, her voice dripping with condescension. 'I think your cock needs more of my pretty pink pussy!'

'I have a girlfriend,' he said, desperate. He was sounding weak even to his own ears. 'I love her.'

'Lucky me.' Michele smirked, cruelly caressing his erect member with a manicured forefinger. 'I'm sooo glad your dick loves *me* instead.'

'No,' he moaned as she began the methodical stroking of his cock, using both hands. She manipulated him slowly, rubbing up against him every once in a while in between series of strokes. 'Your little girlfriend that you love so much, I bet she doesn't dress like pretty Michele or Becky?'

'No,' he gasped, watching her degrade him. 'She is pretty conservative.'

'You want to fuck my pretty tight pussy, Robbie.' She giggled. 'You've been coming by, tent-in-the-pants, every single night, wanting to come up here and give slut nurse Michele more nice hundred-dollar bills, so she would sit on your lap and rub up against your cock.'

'No,' he whimpered. 'I have to go,' he gasped. He tried to squirm away but her hands were latched around his member.

'Of course,' she said, laughing. 'But we will talk again, won't we, Dr Waverly?' She cruelly let go of his cock. The sudden cessation of her manipulations was nearly painful – it was such a loss of pleasure that it almost made him cry.

'Go, then. We will see you at your house, Doctor Waverly, at your friend's little party.'

He stumbled down the stairs, dazed, zipping up his pants just as he got to the bottom. A huge black man stood there in a tuxedo. 'That'll be a hundred dollars,' he said impassively.

'But I ...' said Robert, about to launch into an explanation. He quickly reconsidered his intention; the man's face became a rigid mask. This gorilla probably didn't know about the arrangement. Michele or the manager must have forgotten to tell him. 'Let me go back up, she'll come down and ...'

The man shook his head meaningfully and put out his hand.

Robert pulled out his wallet and handed him the five twenties, the ones that he had put away for emergencies. 'Fine, fine,' he muttered, angry and frustrated. He stormed through the club, barely acknowledging the cop's goodbye. The doorman nodded to him as well. 'Nice day we are having, sir,' he said conversationally.

Once outside, still dazed, he slowed down enough to nod back. The doors of the news shop glowed with yellow light; he marched inside, making a beeline for the rack with the porno magazines. He went through them in detail, stacking them in his arm, collecting all of the ones with the sluttiest-looking girls on the cover. A couple of them were fetish magazines.

There were people in line, an old couple and a little kid with a skateboard. He shouldered past them, ignoring the old woman's protest. He needed to get home as soon as possible. 'Here,' he snapped at the old man manning the register, spilling the huge pile of porn magazines all over the counter.

He paid for his purchase with his credit card – he was out of cash, again. 'Dammit,' cursed Robert. He did not worry about the credit card, of course; even with the 1200 he'd blown on Becky and Michele, he had a very high credit limit.

He took the brown paper bag (it was pretty heavy) and crammed it into his briefcase.

As soon as he got home he rifled through the pile, laying the magazines out on the bed. He looked through them until he found some women who looked similar to Michele; large breasts, tanned, long legs, blonde hair, nice luscious lips, long painted fingernails. He stroked himself to an altogether unsatisfactory orgasm and fell asleep.

The next day was Saturday; normally Robert went to the lab to work on research, but this weekend he was determined to get a fresh start, to clear his head, to clean his life. The last few weeks had been hectic and he had been fielding calls from other members of the oncology research team. They were demanding the results of his tests. Even his boss at the hospital – important, after all, as the boss of the department that paid him his salary – well, even he was unhappy with his performance. Over the last week he had come in late twice and left early twice. He had to get creative to get out of that mess.

He had taken a good five minutes off from his busy schedule of masturbating to the magazines to talk to Dr Rainer, his boss. 'I'm sorry, Wayne,' he told him. 'It's been very busy at home. Holly and I had a little fight, you know how it is . . .' he trailed off, hoping Holly's name would ward off his boss's irritation. He had caught Wayne checking Holly out at several department events, although the older man had never had the nerve to try anything. He just blushed and stammered every time they came in close proximity.

Sure enough, Wayne's tone changed immediately; if anything, it became happy. 'Really? That's too bad, Robert. I'm sorry to hear that.'

'I'm sure it'll pass,' said Robert quickly, not liking it. He felt anger, although he wasn't sure who he was mad at. Anyway, Holly was his girlfriend, not some piece of meat!

'Let me know if I can be of help, OK?'

'Sure thing, Wayne,' said Robert, nearly rolling his eyes. At least the fool should learn how to disguise his stupid little infatuation from him.

In any case, that had been yesterday. He had a lot of work to catch up on, but he decided to take the day off and really face his demons. It was obvious that he had to do something about the constant masturbation, about the pornography piling up in his apartment, about the imminent bachelor party that was rapidly spinning out of control: about Michele.

He slammed his fist into the wall, angry at himself. How could he let himself become this – *billygoat*? Like some horny teenager ... Tight-lipped, he gathered all the magazines and threw them in the trash, feeling somewhat purified by the gesture.

He walked to the kitchen and looked at the calendar. He had circled Thursday with a pink highlighter in a moment of weakness; the mark had been mocking him every single day for the last week. Would you look at that, he thought. He hadn't yet crossed off today. He picked up the highlighter and crossed off yet another day. Robert looked at the new mark with nothing less than surprise, his eyes inexorably travelling down even though he tried to resist. He weakly leant against the door of the refrigerator and circled Thursday with the highlighter again, sobbing with helpless, pent-up lust. Michele's words were echoing through his head, her bitchy, condescending seduction a living drill boring into his will. The pink of the highlighter reminded him of another pink: the condescending offering of Michele's beautiful shaved pussy.

Maybe he shouldn't have thrown away all of the magazines. He went to the trash can and pulled out a couple of the ones on top. These were not the best ones. He wanted the one with the sleazy blonde that reminded him of Michele, the one that had the girl with the pretty shaved pink pussy and the high heels. He dipped his arms into the trash can and feverishly rummaged through the garbage-stained contents until he found the right magazine, with the pictures of the slutty-looking, big-titted blonde and her nearly identical playmate. His eyes soaked in the images and he stumbled into the bedroom, mouthing Michele words. These were words she would say, he was sure of it. 'Ooh, the doctor likes slut nurse Michele's nice

75

pink pussy, doesn't he? Have you been a good boy and played with yourself thinking about pretty Michele's ass, tits and pussy?' He stroked himself until he came, finishing with the words from the computer screen, moaning them like some mantra: 'I've been a good boy, I've been a good boy . . .'

He fell asleep in his own filth. Robert's face rested on the obscene photograph of a blonde, her legs wide open, seductively stroking her shaved slit. The picture was partially crumpled and stained around the edges, just the way he had reclaimed it from the garbage.

5

Robert

Thursday finally arrived. Robert did not go to work, even though he had an operation scheduled; he took a sick day. Rainer had to pull in Doctor Henderson to cover for him.

'I'm sorry, Wayne,' he coughed into the receiver. 'I'm really under the weather. I hope I can make it in tomorrow. Uhm – Holly mentioned you over the phone, by the way.'

After a moment's pause: 'Really?'

'Yes, she said – she said that we should really have dinner with Wayne sometime.'

'That's very nice of her,' said Wayne, obviously stunned. 'I'd love to come.'

I bet you would, you perverted old bastard, thought Robert. Still, it's not like he had a choice. Holly was coming back soon and he had to come to terms with his newfound appetites. He needed to go out and buy chips and some alcohol for the party, get dressed, sweep the place. He had to hide all the porn magazines.

At the grocery store he bought some snacks and a huge tray of sushi.

All that remained was alcohol. In the liquor store he found a large display unit of champagne. He noticed that it was the same variety they had in the champagne room of Hot Summer's, but here it was merely a little over twenty dollars for a bottle.

'It's on sale by the case,' said the salesman. Robert picked up a bottle and looked at it. 'Just two hundred.'

77

'Really?' he asked, dry-mouthed. He could recreate the Hot Summer's champagne room in his own house, however inexpertly; just having the champagne there would be almost like being there.

'I'll take two cases,' he found himself saying. The memory of the champagne room made him think of his first time at the club, the taste of the shot he had had with Michele, what was it . . . ? 'And some good tequila too.'

'Sure thing. Some ice?'

He nodded impatiently and handed over his credit card. Despite his efforts to make good time, it was mid-afternoon by the time he had finished shopping. He only had a few hours left. He put one case of champagne in the bedroom, in a cooler full of ice that he also purchased at the liquor store, and somehow managed to fit the rest of the bottles into the refrigerator. There was not enough room unless he moved some stuff. What *could* he move? There was some of Holly's health-food stuff – some kind of a mix involving organically grown vegetables, sealed in plastic containers. Strictly speaking they ought to last for a single night out of the fridge, Robert was certain of it. Well, pretty sure anyway. He wasn't a food chemist. He put the boxes on top of the fridge and put the champagne in their place. He wasn't sure if you were supposed to chill tequila, but could it really hurt? Hesitating, he put it in the fridge but then took the bottle out again. So which was it? Chilled or room temperature?

Maybe he should look it up on the net!

After all, it was his responsibility to be a gracious host. To serve chilled tequila was maybe like serving red wine with ice – he just didn't know; he didn't want to look like a fool.

He turned on his computer. As soon as he was online, he typed in the address for Hot Summer's. He told himself he didn't know why. His eyes sought out the luscious, tempting body of Michele, his member forming the now familiar pop-up tent in his pants.

He made to unzip his pants when his gaze fell upon the bottle of tequila on his desk. 'Oh shoot,' he mumbled. He needed to relax, to unwind, to stop thinking about sex. He

78

twisted the bottle open and took a deep swig straight from the neck. If only Scott could see me now, he thought.

The tequila went down smoothly. He took another long swig and turned off the computer. He would be gracious host no matter what – chilled tequila was not going to make a difference one way or another. After all, hadn't he hired two hot strippers as entertainment?

He checked his watch – it was a Rolex, a gift from his father. 'Three more hours,' he mumbled. He swallowed the tequila in his mouth. It sure was getting warm. Robert put out a few bowls and filled them with chips and settled down to wait. He picked up a book – *Crime and Punishment* – and tried to read, but his eyes kept straying over to the wall clock.

Two more hours until 8 p.m., he thought, frustrated. James and the rest of the guys were coming at 7 p.m., of course.

At 6.45 p.m. sharp his doorbell rang. He rushed to open it. Scott stood there, wearing a big grin. 'Dude!'

'Hi, Scott,' said Robert. 'Glad to see you.'

Scott sniffed the air. 'Did you get an early start with the party?' He grinned. 'What have you been drinking?'

'I tested the tequila,' admitted Robert. 'Want some?'

'Sure, let's do shots. When are they coming, again?'

'At eight,' sighed Robert.

'I thought you said seven,' said Scott, frowning.

'I mean, seven.'

'Wow, man, you are a bit out of it. Drink up, it'll calm you down.'

'You're right,' said Robert, and poured the drinks. They moved into the living room.

'Dude, where is the salt? And the lime?'

Robert stared at the shot glass in his hand. 'We need that?'

'Uhm – yeah?' Scott rummaged through the fridge. He pulled out the big tray of sushi. 'What is *this*?'

'Sushi. Put it on the coffee table.'

'Raw fish? But Be–. But I hate this stuff. And no lime?!'

'Sorry,' he said.

Scott chuckled and shook his head. He put the sushi on the coffee table and they drank anyway, slamming their glasses back. They spent the next few minutes with inane banter until the doorbell rang again.

The boys were on time.

There were only seven of them. Besides James and Robert, the only other attendees were Scott, little Scott (or as he liked to call himself, Skot), Dirk, John and Dave. They'd been friends for ages.

'I've got champagne and tequila,' said Robert. 'And there is scotch in the cabinet. Got some beer too . . .'

'Excellent.' Scott grinned, toasting Robert with another shot. They tossed it down and Robert popped a bottle of champagne, pouring a drink for James. They toasted the groom.

'I'm very happy for you,' said Robert. He tried to think of something tactful. 'It's great. Lucille is a nice girl.'

Lucille was nice, sort of – at least she was definitely *decorative* if you liked the typical sorority-sister type. James had just been appointed as chief information officer for a Fortune 500 company and Lucille had latched on to him like some kind of a predator. She had been planning the wedding ever since they'd met.

'You know, Robert . . . Well – can you spare a minute?' asked James. He looked uncomfortable.

'Sure, what's up?'

James pulled him into the living room and through the open balcony door, until they were standing in the open air. 'This is not the right time, but – you're not going to like this,' he began. 'Your girlfriend has been staying with Lucille.'

'What?' gasped Robert. 'She said she was going to her mother's!'

'Well, she didn't. Lucille is . . . You know how Lucille is. She wanted me to ask you if you were going to reconcile *soon*. Apparently Holly is very upset about you not calling her and what not . . .'

'I've been very busy,' said Robert defensively. 'It's been hectic at the hospital, and I've been busy with research.'

'Yeah, I heard about your research. I think it's great that you are doing it for free.'

'Thanks, I appreciate that.'

'You had that offer to go to that plastic surgery clinic a year ago, didn't you? They were offering you a small fortune!'

'Oncology was always a passion for me. I know it's an odd combination, being a surgeon and a research oncologist, but I managed thus far.'

'I am just proud to know you, Robert. I think it's great what you are doing. I hope all will clear up with Holly. She is a – nice girl too.' James sipped his champagne.

'Thanks!'

James laughed. He pulled out a small video camcorder. 'Holly had the gall to ask me to take pictures. I guess she wanted to make sure there weren't any girls.'

'You wouldn't spy on me for her, would you?' asked Robert, suddenly uncomfortable.

'No, no way. Scott told me there might be some strippers,' he said, suddenly grinning. 'I've never been to a bachelor party with strippers, so I brought two blank tapes. I'll film some scenes of us drinking and stuff and show that tape to Holly; is that OK?'

'That's a good idea.' He checked the wall clock again. It was already 8.15 and there was still no sign of Michele and Becky. 'You'd better do some recording now; the girls are already late.'

James nodded and turned on the camera, focusing in on a bowl of crisps. Skot and Dirk cornered him and pulled him away in the direction of the kitchen.

Robert sat down on the couch, facing the foyer and the wall clock. The second hand was ticking away with agonising slowness.

Scott came by and brought him another shot of tequila and another glass of champagne. Irritated, he drained them both, one after the other. Scott brought him another round.

He opened his mouth to say something to Scott when the doorbell rang.

Robert sprung from his seat, stumbling a little. The tequila and the champagne were making him light-headed. The sound of the doorbell was enough to stir his member. He rushed to the door and opened it within a heartbeat of the bell's chime.

Becky and Michele stood in the doorway. His eyes roved over them, drinking in the delicious view. Both of them wore the sleaziest form of Catholic schoolgirl uniforms: tiny little miniskirts and stiletto heels (pointy white on Becky and black on Michele). Becky's mammoth tits in particular were close to the point of ripping the straining fabric of a fuzzy white top. Their midriffs were exposed.

Both girls carried kit-bags.

'So eager to see us, Doctor Waverly!' Michele smirked. 'It's so nice to be wanted. You know, Becky, I haven't seen Doctor Waverly at the club lately.'

'It's true, Michele. Anyway, aren't you gonna invite us in?' purred Becky.

Michele smiled sweetly and said, 'You can stare at her tits better inside, Doctor.'

Robert blushed and glanced over his shoulder to see whether anyone had witnessed this humiliating exchange. James was the only one within hearing range of the doorway. He was facing it and holding a glass of champagne. The groom was blushing furiously yet his eyes were locked on the newcomers. It was apparent his mind hadn't registered a word of the conversation.

'Come on in,' said Robert just a second too late, as they had already waltzed into his apartment without actually waiting for permission. He followed them closely, breathing in the cloying scent of their body rub, perfume and hair spray. The scent awakened the memory of his lap dance and he felt saliva collect in his mouth as they sauntered into the centre of the living room. By now all remnants of conversation had ceased. The men were all looking at the two dancers. 'Oh – my – God,' said John, his mouth open. 'I was not really expecting this, not at Robert's place . . .'

Michele handed Robert a CD. 'Put this on,' she commanded.

Becky was staring at the platter of sushi wearing an expression of utter revulsion but then she forced herself to look away and smile.

Robert went to the stereo, put in the CD and pressed play. The slow, sensuous beat of something vaguely Middle Eastern came on.

Michele glided into the centre of the living room. She raised her voice until it overrode the music. 'Now, Robbie was a good boy and he invited us to do a little show for you.' She put her hand on his neck and scratched him behind one ear. 'You've been a good boy, Robbie.' She smirked. 'The thing is, Becky has been a bad girl, right, Becky?'

Becky nodded with a strange mix of apprehension and eagerness. 'I've been a baaaad girl, Michele.'

'As hall monitor I've been given the job of making sure that Becky learns her lesson. Becky has been teasing the boys.'

'I've been a little slut, Michele,' sobbed Becky. She put her hands on her tits and pushed them together, massaging them with her hands. Her long, pink fingernails slipped beneath the lonely, bright-gold button, and snapped it off. The flimsy white top peeled right down, exposing her enormous breasts.

'Oh my God,' said James, echoing John's words. He was sitting on the couch, just a few feet from the incredible artificial wonders.

Michele heard; she turned her head to face him. 'Just because she is a wet-pussy slut doesn't mean she doesn't have to obey school rules. Becky needs to learn there is a system here at Slut High. If you could just do whatever you wanted, Becky, what would you do to James here?'

The bleached-blonde stripper strutted over to James. Even with the absurdly high white stilettos on her feet, it was obvious she was exaggerating the swaying motion of her ass. She thrust her chest straight ahead; as she loomed over James, she let her hands fall to her sides, letting her tits fall against his face. His eyes glazed over as she rubbed the huge mounds against his head. She rhythmically smothered James's flushed face.

The rest of the guys were staring, mouths agape.

Robert wanted to take out his cock and jerk off but obviously couldn't, not now; he picked up James's video camera and began to film Becky's sleazy seduction of his friend, for later use in private.

'Becky is such a slut.' Michele giggled. 'Don't you boys think Becky is a total bimbo whore?'

'Yeah, she sure is,' agreed Robert fervently.

'I think Becky likes the groom,' said Michele, bitchy condescension oozing from every word. 'Becky wants his loyal, engaged, hard-working cock to slide in and out of her drenched slut pussy.'

'No,' protested James, but his voice was muffled by Becky's big tits. 'I can't, Lucy ... I won't cheat on Lucy.'

'We're just playing, James ...' cooed Michele. 'After all, slut Becky's pussy is not free. Becky's pretty pink pussy is very expensive.'

Becky got off James.

The groom took a shuddering gulp of air as the mounds of flesh left his face. His skin was ruddy red. 'Oh my God,' he gasped.

Michele picked up the tequila bottle and pressed it in his hand.

'Go on, have some more,' she urged him. 'Go on!'

Absently, he nodded and raised the bottle to his lips. He drank but his eyes remained locked on Becky. She began to strip, each motion a seductive, subtle series of movements until she was completely naked, except for those white stiletto heels. She got down on all fours, parting her ass cheeks with her hands. Her pussy was glistening.

'Your pussy is so wet, Becky,' observed Michele. 'I bet somebody here would give a lot of money to slide their straining hard cock into your pink fuckhole.'

'Wow,' said James, laughing nervously.

Scott resurfaced from the kitchen; he was carrying two champagne bottles, freshly popped. 'James and Robert, those are the loaded guys at this party.' He grinned. 'It's your last night as a free man, James, so drink up!'

Michele turned away from the others. 'Robert is such a good boy,' she cooed. 'I hope James will be a good boy too. Let's all drink to Robert being a good boy!' She pressed a full bottle into his hand.

James laughed; he drank again. By now his face had turned very red and his eyes kept straying over to Becky's wantonly exposed glistening cunt.

'You see, James, Becky likes to play with her lollipop to give the teachers a stiffy. Once they get a stiffy they do whatever she tells them.' Michele took an elongated, cone-shaped lollipop out of her kit-bag. 'Are you like one of bimbo Becky's pussy-whipped teachers, James?'

James laughed and sucked down some more champagne. His eyes remained locked on Becky's pink slit.

Michele began to tease the big-titted bleached blonde's glistening pussy with the long lollipop. She teased her pussy lips and circled the fleshy knob of her clit with the shiny red tip. 'Bimbo Becky likes it when her pussy gets sticky with yummy candy.' She laughed. 'She makes her tent-popper teachers lick her clean.'

'Yeah, fuck my cunt with the lollipop, Michele,' moaned Becky, trying to manoeuvre her pussy lips around the obscene striped candy cane. 'Fuck my pussy with the lolly!'

'Would you like to fuck Michele's naughty cunnie with the lollipop, James?' cooed Michele. 'Would you like to fuck her expensive pink cunt until she just drips yummy sweet candy?'

'Oh, I could never,' whispered James. His voice was barely audible.

'I think James might change his mind if we just gave him a chance. It looks like he might have a taste for that expensive pink pussy,' smirked Michele. 'Why don't we leave them alone for a few minutes, OK?'

She picked up the camera from where James had left it and herded the rest of them into the master bedroom. She closed the door and turned the lock.

Michele picked up Holly's picture from the nightstand. 'Is this your girlfriend, Robert?' she asked in an amused tone.

'Yeah, that's her,' said Dirk. 'She's got him on a short leash.'

'Little Robbie likes to be put on a leash?' asked Michele, obviously interested. 'You like to be put on a leash and taken on walkies?'

The men laughed.

'Oh, come on,' said Robert. 'That's ridiculous!' He sat down on the edge of the bed.

'Is that why there is a come stain on it?' asked Michele,

laughing. 'Once she had you on a leash she made you jerk off to her picture?'

'No,' he replied, laughing but embarrassed. 'She is very conservative.'

Scott picked the picture up from where Michele had put it. He examined it and chuckled. 'It really does look like a come stain, dude.'

'Oh, lay off it, I don't know what it is.'

Michele yawned and laid down on the bed – on Holly's side. She stretched, arching her feet and resting her slender black heels on Robert's lap. The stiletto heels pushed against his stomach.

Robert stared at the feet in those slut shoes. They were exquisite and small, and she kept moving them with infinite subtlety. He imagined bits of his will flaking away with every humiliating little movement.

Scott cleared his throat. 'Why don't we go get a drink in the kitchen?' he asked the others. 'Robert is busy here.'

'Yeah,' purred Michele. 'Why don't you do that?' she added in a bitchy, contemptuous tone.

After a moment's pause, his friends filed out of the room. Robert finally opened his mouth to tell her off – nobody was going to talk to his friends in that tone!

She giggled and pressed harder with those whore heels, pushing against his cock, making the manipulation of his member obvious and undeniable. She kicked off one shoe and put a perfect foot over his erection. Her toenails were painted a lurid pink; they squeezed and went up and down, up and down.

Robert groaned.

'Becky's pussy is very expensive,' said Michele conversationally, manipulating his cock with her pedicured, arched foot. 'I hope your friend can afford to keep Becky's pussy happy. Can little spooger Doctor Waverly afford to keep slut nurse Michele's pussy happy?'

'Michele . . .' groaned Robert. 'I – why are you doing this?'

'All you have to do is just tell me to stop, Robbie,' said Michele, laughing. 'Just tell me to stop and I'll stop milking you dry, little Doctor Waverly.'

'I have to tell you to stop it,' he mumbled weakly. 'I just have to,' he told her, trying to convince himself of the truth of it.

'Oh, shut up, Doctor Waverly. Can't you see your cock doesn't want me to stop? You have to tell me to stop, but you didn't ... Little spooger Robbie just doesn't want pretty Michele to stop jerking his cock off with her pretty feet. Spooger Robbie's hard prick is telling him what to do now, I can tell. Why don't you just relax, do what your weewee tells you and unzip your pants. I can tell you want to, Doctor Waverly!'

A faint sob escaped Robert's lips – there was no way around it. He unzipped his pants. His frantic hands even pushed them down to his ankles until his aching cock was fully exposed in its shameful erect glory.

Michele smirked with gloating triumph; she slid her other shoe off and placed her feet around his member, her pink toes forming a tunnel of irresistible sensual stimulation.

Robert's eyes were trapped on Michele's perfect feet, so pretty, so perfect, so absolutely in control of his member.

'I want you to watch very carefully, Doctor Spooger,' she said, giggling. 'Make a home movie, even.' She put the camcorder that James had brought into Robert's hand. 'Take a picture of slut nurse Michele's pretty feet jerking off your worthless erection, Doctor Waverly. When you cry over your bank statement you'll need something to remind you of what you're getting for all –' she applied pressure with her toes and pulled on his cock, up and down, accentuating each word '– your – hard – earned – money!'

His head reeled with lust and tequila; he picked up the camera and zoomed in on the pathetic sight of Michele's toes manipulating his helpless manhood. His cock was like a hard, flesh-covered toy at the mercy of the stripper's pretty toes.

'You enjoy being milked, don't you, Doctor Waverly?' Michele giggled and prodded his cock with a playful little kick before resuming the stroking.

Robert gasped; he was so close he could feel his balls

beginning to contract. He leant into each filthy caress, assisting his own absolute degradation.

'I think you've had enough, spooger.' Michele laughed. She removed her toes from his cock and sat up on the bed.

He whimpered and tried to squirm after her, to rub his cock against her retreating foot. 'Please don't stop!' begged Robert, nearly crying with frustration. 'Why did you stop?'

'But Robert,' said Michele, her long, fake eyelashes filtering the calculating blue of her eyes. 'It's not *your* bachelor party, you know. You hired bimbo Becky and slut nurse Michele to show your friend James a good time, not you.'

'But Becky must have . . .' he said frantically.

'Oh *no*, Doctor Spooger. Bimbo Becky's pink pussy requires a lot of pretty presents before it becomes – available – even for a good boy like your friend James. Now it's time for me to help Bimbo Becky show the groom a good time.'

'Put my shoes back on my feet, Doctor.' She prodded his hand with an arched foot and he put her shoes back on, one at a time.

She rose and strutted to the door, then opened it. She slid her manicured nails over her breasts, her flat stomach, her long tanned legs, all seductive, manipulative little touches. She glanced back at Robert. 'If only you asked us over for a private party, just the three of us.' She giggled. 'Oh well . . . Maybe some other time.' She shut the door.

Robert tried to run after her, but he stumbled and fell over; his pants were still around his ankles. His lust-addled, drunk mind realised that he was essentially naked and he reluctantly pulled up his pants. He heard vague moaning from the living room and his curiosity got the better of his nearly unbearable need to touch himself. He picked up the camera and moved into the living room.

James was with Becky. It only vaguely registered in Robert's mind that the rest of their friends seemed to have left. Becky was on all fours, her mammoth tits looking positively gigantic as they lusciously drooped forwards. Her breasts were so large that her big pink nipples actually touched Holly's carpet. The stripper's entire ass and shaved pink pussy were glistening with moisture. There was no sign of the lollipop. Robert zoomed in on Becky's pussy, roved over her entire body, then moved on to Michele's slutty heels, her long, tanned legs, her nearly exposed cunt.

'Keep the camera on Becky and James, Doctor Spooger,' ordered Michele, scratching him behind the ear again. He obediently followed her instructions; her touch was like fire on his skin.

James was licking his lips. His face was red and his expression entirely dazed. His zipper was open but he didn't seem to notice.

Michele unzipped the other kit-bag and took out something that resembled a huge, shiny black dildo, affixed to the inside of a pair of black rubber panties. She also withdrew something that looked like a small TV remote. 'Now, James, I can tell that you've been a good boy, much like your friend Robbie,' she began. 'I know you really, really want to put your eager prick in bimbo Becky's wet pussy, but we both know you didn't earn that privilege yet. Isn't that right?'

'Bu– but . . .' said James, stammering. He was obviously drunk. He lifted the champagne bottle and drank straight from the neck. The foamy gold liquid ran down the corner of his lips and stained the expensive cashmere of his sweater – yet his eyes remained slavishly locked on the oddly glistening ass of his seductress.

'He has been a very good boy, Michele.' Becky giggled. 'I am all clean now!'

'Bimbo Becky, you've been a naughty whore again!' sighed Michele. 'I'm going to have to teach you to stop making engaged men lick your sticky cunt clean! You go and cover yourself!'

She slid the panties over Becky's six-inch white heels, pushing the monstrous dildo up in between her legs until it pressed against her pussy lips. It was a huge rubber cock, shiny black and at least thirteen inches long, with a cornucopia of knobs and protrusions along its entire length.

'This big-titted bimbo needs her pussy fucked,' said Michele. 'But without making tribute to her expensive pink pussy, all she'll let you do is lick her cunt clean – or she might let you fuck her with this remote-controlled vibrator.'

Becky put her hands over her ass and spread them wide, leaning forwards and exposing her yawning slit.

'If only some generous, generous man wanted to fuck Becky's pussy enough to make her happy,' purred Michele, 'she might let him slide his rich, hard cock right into her cunt. Like this, she would let him think about what he might be doing . . .' Michele extended a stiletto-heeled foot and used the point of her shoe to push the giant rubber cock into Becky's yawning hole.

The bleached-blonde stripper moaned and spread her legs even wider. She turned her head to watch Michele's ministrations. Her hair swung around like a pale yellow corona. 'Fuck my cunnie, Michele,' she begged. 'Fuck my wet pussy, pweeease!'

Michele finished pushing the vibrator in with her shoe. 'Nice and snug, bitch?' she asked. 'Fills up your pussy, doesn't it? Better than the lollipop?'

'Yeah, Michele,' moaned Becky. She licked her lips. 'Please turn it on, I wanna come!'

'Becky is addicted to this thing.' Michele laughed. She put the remote in James's hand. 'Push this button, James. Fuck her pussy, you know you want to fuck her slutty wet pussy.'

'But . . .'

'Dammit, James, fuck her pussy,' snapped Robert, nearly bursting with the overwhelming urge to fuck, or at the very least see someone, anyone, get some action. 'Push the button, make her squirm!'

'You are such a good boy, Doctor Waverly,' cooed Michele and she petted his head. 'So nice and helpful!'

Becky turned her head until her eyes locked on James's. 'Jimmy,' she said, pouting, 'please fuck my cunnie! Pweeease . . .' she begged petulantly, sounding like some manipulative little girl.

Something snapped in James. It was as if a barrier of some kind just shattered. He pushed the button. The faintest buzzing emanated from the direction of the buried vibrator inside Becky.

An inarticulate moan escaped the stripper's lips; she lurched back and forth. Whatever was happening inside her was giving her delirious, spasming waves of pleasure. 'Fuck me harder,' screamed Becky, turning over on to her back. She grabbed the giant mounds of her tits and tweaked her nipples with her long fingernails.

James was standing with his mouth wide open. 'OK,' he said lamely, groping at his crotch. 'I have to,' he gasped. 'I have to fuck her.'

'Oh no, not like that.' Michele laughed, slapping his fumbling hands as they strove to free his cock. 'You get to fuck her like this, with the vibrator. Maybe if you bring her some pretty presents, maybe then she'll let you put that eager little prick into her pussy ... But first you have to *earn* her pussy, Jimmy.'

James pushed another button. Michele showed him a dial.

'Turn it up halfway,' she commanded.

He obeyed.

Becky let out a helpless, keening wail, and began to squirm in a sweat-drenched, shuddering heap, bumping into the coffee table and the couch.

'Now turn it off.' Michele said, laughing.

James pushed the button.

The big-titted stripper began to cry as soon as the faint buzzing sound stopped. 'Come on, Michele,' she sobbed. 'Fuck me some more, please!'

'She'll do anything.' Michele smirked. 'Watch this.'

She picked a piece of sushi off the plate on the coffee table and prodded the other woman's lips with the morsel. 'Eat some of this raw fish, Becky!'

'Yuck!' she gasped and squirmed away from the offering.

Michele took the remote from James and turned on the vibrator. She turned the dial two thirds of the way to the right. Becky immediately began to thrash and moan on the floor.

Michele leant over her, putting the sushi right in front of her lips. 'The more you eat, the higher I'll put the setting,' she said.

Becky sobbed and opened her lips. Her first tentative disgusted bite became a series of frantic, insatiable gulps as she gobbled down the contents of the tray one piece at a time, her disgust overwhelmed by the pleasures emanating from the vibrating instrument in between her legs.

'Bimbo Becky makes a good pet.' Michele giggled. She turned to James. 'Would Jimmy like to play with my pet?'

6

Holly

'Darling, it's your place too,' said Lucille reprovingly. She held up the porcelain cup to the morning light filtering in through the window. 'This china is just darling, I really like the pattern. I positively adore the pattern. I'll have to make a note of it for the registry.'

'He hasn't called, not once!' sobbed Holly. 'You think – maybe he found someone else?' She sipped her tea, not really enjoying it. It contained milk. Lucille insisted on observing English custom, or at least English custom as she understood it. Specifically, for Lucille, English custom meant tiny, expensive porcelain cups and milk in her tea. Holly found Lucille's come-hell-or-high-water quest to become a member of high society a bit unnerving; during her sophomore year in college, Lucille was anything but high class. Her typical night usually included a beer-dazed frat party and a well-hung guy in bed. Considering the near-rape Lucille experienced during her freshman year, Holly considered her tastes rather peculiar.

Lucille rolled her eyes while she deigned to answer Holly's question. 'I really don't think he found anyone else. Just go home and confront him, darling.'

Holly furtively tried to catch Lucille's eye. 'You aren't tired of me, are you, Lucille?'

'Of course not. Of course not. After all, you're my very best friend! Why don't I call you a cab? I'm sure he has just been busy with his work at the hospital, those surgeries or operations and all . . . It's really just so nice that you'll be marrying a doctor, darling. I mean, I am marrying a computer person. I used to think it was a touch vulgar, didn't you? Of course he is now a CIO – the Chief Information Officer of a Fortune 500 company – really a top-notch executive. I was so foolish thinking he was just some geek; we'll be so happy together. You, on the other hand, you must be so pleased, you are marrying a *doctor* . . .'

'Lucille, what're you talking about? You keep talking about Robert as if we already set a date! He hasn't even asked me yet!'

'He will, he will! You're upset for no reason, darling. Let me call you that cab, and call me as soon as you have that little talk with him.'

'I told him I wouldn't be coming back for another week or so.'

'Why did you tell him such a silly thing? He'll be thrilled to have you back! Just look at you, so pretty and so miserable, he'll just pop the question right away when he sees you. He has been probably pining away after you all this time.' Lucille looked over at the French doors that connected the dining room with the family room, her attention clearly on something else altogether.

'Well . . . It's my place too. My bed is there and all my clothes,' mumbled Holly. 'I really have every right to go back there.'

Lucille put her hand over Holly's and squeezed encouragingly. 'That's right honey, you go and talk to him right away. He'll be so happy to see you!'

'Oh my God,' whispered James. He shook Robert again. 'Robert, what have I done?'

'My head,' groaned Robert. 'Don't talk so loud, please!'

'How much of what I remember –' mumbled James. 'How much of what I remember is real?' His eyes were bloodshot and they had a far-off quality to them, as if they were watching something inside his head. He wore his undershirt, shirt and boxers – but the shirt's buttons were all missing. His fingers kept sliding up to find them. Their absence was somehow the icing on the cake of this nightmare.

'I'll make some coffee before we have this conversation,' said Robert slowly. 'Just don't worry about it, James. Whatever it is that you remember, Lucille is not here and she'll *never ever know*.'

The look of absolute terror on James's face subsided somewhat. 'Well – that's true. Let's have some coffee and I'll try to calm down.' He licked his lips and his eyes bulged with the shock of recall. His skin turned the colour of fire. 'Uh – do you have a spare toothbrush? And mouthwash?'

'Yes, in the cabinet behind the bathroom mirror.'

James practically ran into the bathroom. His voice filtered out to the kitchen. 'Ugh ... Have you seen my pants?'

'I think they're on the living-room floor by the balcony,' yelled Robert, raising his voice to overpower the sound of rushing water from the bathroom.

Robert looked through the cupboard for coffee. He couldn't find any; he didn't really touch the stuff except for a single cup in the morning, but even that he usually picked up at a little breakfast place next to the hospital, along with a double toasted poppy-seed bagel with egg, cheddar cheese, bacon and tomatoes. Just thinking about it made his mouth water.

'James, I'll give you a pair of sunglasses and we will go out for a breakfast bagel and some orange juice.'

'Coffee,' groaned James.

'Right. Let's get out of here, at least for a few hours, all right?'

'Whatever,' said James.

James showered. When he emerged from the bathroom in his boxer shorts and socks, hair dripping, he looked a smidgeon better. He spied the crumpled heap that consisted of his cashmere sweater and linen pants and put them back on. The sweater sported a gigantic multicoloured stain. Some of it was champagne. Some of it was not. 'Oh God,' he moaned, staring at the ruined fabric. 'This was a present from Lucille!'

'We will drop by the mall. Lucille shops at three stores, nothing else is good enough for her,' said Robert. 'We will find where she got it and just buy a new one.' Those endless discussions with Holly concerning Lucille's mind-numbing snobbery and spending habits were good for something, apparently. He handed James a pair of sunglasses.

James looked at him through the brown filter with new-found respect. 'I had no idea you were this resourceful, Robert.'

'I just want you to be happy, James. I know what it's like to live with a – uh – *strong* woman.'

'Yeah,' said James with some uncertainty. 'She is really looking forward to the wedding.'

'Holly told me about that. Let's talk about it on the way, though, I'm starving.'

They left. Robert pulled the door shut behind them.

Holly went to work. She was in a foul mood. The floater for the day, Betty – what a slutty name – was chatting with one of the copy-centre boys. The girl was wearing a sundress that was way too revealing, way too short, way too young.

Holly hadn't heard from Robert in ages. She could see it in her mind's eye – he'd met someone, some little skank wearing a sundress (the vision bore more than a passing resemblance to Betty) and she was going to be the one who got dumped.

She surprised herself. 'Betty, after you're done with your conversation, please come by my office.'

She saw the expression of casual flirtation swept away under a tide of apprehension. It felt perversely satisfying.

'I can come right now, ma'am.'

The girl came in behind her and just stood there while she took her seat behind her desk. 'You may sit,' she said.

Betty sat down. From behind the desk she caught a glimpse of white in between the floater's legs.

'Betty, my dear,' she began, 'I realise this is an HR issue, but I thought I would help you before they took formal action.'

'I'm sorry?'

The little tart looked scared. Good!

'Your attire. It's not professional.'

96

'I'm sorry, ma'am, I didn't mean to . . .'

'It really can't continue like this.'

'I promise . . . I mean, I won't wear this dress again, ma'am. I didn't think it . . . I mean, it was a gift from my boyfriend.'

Holly nearly snarled. Boyfriend indeed! 'You ought to take a sick day and come back in something appropriate for this office. Before you're asked to leave, that is.'

Betty's departure did not improve her mood. She made up her mind to go home and confront Robert.

Holly parked in her spot next to Robert's car. She at least knew he loved that stupid thing. She checked her appearance in the mirror of the elevator. Holly had actually borrowed some of Lucille's makeup, applying it before she left the office (although it made her feel mildly revolted to use someone else's stuff) and she thought she looked damned good.

She took a deep breath in front of the door and rang the doorbell.

There was no response.

She rang the doorbell again before fishing out the keys and opening the door. Her eyes drank in a vista of utter devastation.

'Oh my God!' she gasped aloud, appalled. The apartment was destroyed! Empty champagne bottles littered the carpet – her carpet! – and there was an empty bottle of – tequila? They were drinking tequila and champagne? Potato chips, discarded sushi wrappers, garbage, for God's sake, *garbage*, there was garbage everywhere!

She sat down on the couch, shuddering as the cold wetness registered in her consciousness. She stood and touched the Italian fabric. She leant low and sniffed it – yes, champagne. And something else – something sweet – perfume, perhaps?

Holly furrowed her eyebrows. Is that how it was? They had their bachelor party and they had female guests?!

Shaking with rage, she walked through the whole apartment. Those stupid champagne bottles were everywhere – not even good champagne, just low-end mediocre, bordering on cheap. The kitchen was a mess. She opened the fridge.

With the exception of two bottles of that pitiful excuse for champagne, it was practically empty. Something was off about that and she picked up one of those bottles, staring at it while she tried to recall what was amiss.

'Where is my food, Robert?' she finally hissed at the empty space in front of her, imagining her boyfriend. In her mind's eye he was already cowed and wearing a properly terrified expression. Her eyes roved through the kitchen, finally coming to rest on the forgotten containers on top of the refrigerator. 'No,' she said with utter frustration. 'You didn't, Robert! How could you?'

She tossed her expensive and now ruined food into the garbage and took the bag out. Depressed and angry, she returned to the apartment and went into the bedroom.

She was so stunned she simply had to speak out loud. 'What the hell?' she screamed. 'Is this some kind of a joke?'

The bed – her bed! – was a crumpled mess of sheets. The air reeked with that disgusting cheap perfume. A kit-bag that she did not remember lay on her side of the bed, the zipper halfway open. She grabbed it and rummaged through it.

Holly pulled out a collection of beads on a rubber-coated wire. They were heavy and slightly oval-shaped. They looked like twisted prayer beads. Next she pulled out a long, supple and textured yet hard object, bright blue in colour. It took her a moment to recognise it for what it was and she dropped it with a disgusted shudder. It was a fake penis, a dildo! It wasn't the only one either. She tossed the implements back in the kit-bag and moved into the living room, where there was more light. Holly looked around in shame, but the apartment remained deserted and she resumed her examination of the filthy things. The dildo quivered slightly in her hand, a shiny abomination under the blazing light of the chandelier. She poured the rest of the kit-bag's contents on the living-room floor, nearly nauseous as device after device – all obviously battery-powered – hit the carpet.

She went back in the bedroom, collected the sheets and marched over to the washing machine, violently stuffing the stained fabric into its gaping maw. The coffee table was filthy – it was covered in a stale puddle of champagne and in the centre of that puddle was . . .

Mortified, she picked up her camcorder, the same one that she had given to James to record the party with. Surely he hadn't been stupid enough to actually tape anything that would upset her or Lucille? Then again, he was a man . . .

She knew how to operate this camcorder. It had been a Christmas present from her father two years ago. She hit rewind, pacing back and forth. How could Robert do this to her? He'd told her that she was the love of his life! How could she trust him again after this?

After the rewind was complete she hooked it up to the TV and pressed play. The screen flickered to life, showing a bowl of chips. The apartment was clean. She saw Dirk and Dave in the kitchen. The men were talking in quiet tones. There were no women in sight. Holly sat down, sprayed some window cleaner on the filthy coffee table and scrubbed it gleaming and glistening clean with some paper towels.

Still nothing incriminating on screen. Holly pressed STOP and then FORWARD, hoping to find something juicy that she could simply show her boyfriend as proof of his debauchery – hell, after this, maybe ex-boyfriend – when he dared to waltz back into this – *frathouse* – that he had dared turn their shared home into.

The picture flickered and resolved to show the long tanned legs of a woman. Holly gasped in anger and shock. It only got worse; the cameraman swung over to a naked woman on all fours. For a moment Holly thought they must have recorded the chips and stuff in the beginning over a porno movie, but then she recognised an addled, obviously drunk James on the couch – the couch with the stain, the one she had sat on earlier. Mortified, she turned up the volume. A female voice was giving instructions: 'Keep the camera on Becky and James, Doctor Spooger.'

The camera wobbled but kept the sordid duo of the big-breasted blonde and James in clear focus. James looked disgusting. His face was red and he was drooling. He was staring at the cheap bleached-blonde whore as if he found her attractive. His zipper was open!

The female voice continued in the background: 'Now, James, I can tell that you've been a good boy, much like your friend Robbie. I know you really, really want to put your eager prick in bimbo Becky's wet pussy, but we both know you didn't earn that privilege yet. Isn't that right?'

Holly paled – did that whore just call her man a good boy? 'Bu– But . . .' said James, such a pathetic bastard, he was obviously drunk. Still, he kept on drinking, swilling champagne like some kind of pig. He dribbled booze on the sweater that Lucille had bought for him for Valentine's Day, and he didn't even stop to try to fix it while there was still time. He just kept ogling the obviously fake tits of that bitch on the carpet, and kept staring at her ass. It was probably oiled or something, it was so shiny.

'He has been a very good boy, Michele,' said the one on the floor. She giggled like some stupid bimbo. 'I am all clean now!'

'Bimbo Becky, you've been a naughty little slut again!' said the first one – now that she knew her name, Holly decided to call her Bitch Michele. She hated her condescending, bitchy tone, and the way she spoke about Robert as if she owned him. What did spooger mean anyway? 'I'm going to have to teach you to stop making engaged men lick your sticky cunt clean! You go and cover yourself!'

Holly gasped so loud it qualified as a scream. She put her hand over her mouth, her eyes wide open, as they absorbed the sordid events unfolding on screen. Bitch Michele slid some foul panties with a big fat black dildo over the other bimbo's whore shoes until the giant phallus was nearly inside her. Holly glanced at the pile of filthy sexual aids on the floor – sure enough, there was that same monstrous fake penis, shiny black and at least thirteen inches long, covered in disgusting, odd-looking protrusions. It was attached to the centre of that pair of shiny black panties, made of some kind of rubbery material.

'This big-titted bimbo needs her pussy fucked,' said bitch Michele. 'But without making tribute to her expensive pink pussy, all she'll let you do is lick her cunt clean . . . or she might let you fuck her with this remote-controlled vibrator.'

The camera zoomed in on the bimbo's pussy. The whore put her hands over her ass and spread them wide, leaning forwards, and exposing herself. It was so fake, Holly wanted to scream. Those bitches were manipulating them!

'If only some generous, good man wanted to fuck Becky's pussy enough to make her happy,' purred Michele, obviously in charge. 'She might let him slide his rich, hard cock right into her cunt. Like this, she would let him think about what he might be doing . . .' The bimbo in charge actually used her whore shoes to push the disgusting, fat, huge, hard dildo all the way into the blonde hooker with the big tits.

The other one really liked it. She kept on screaming for more. 'Fuck my cunnie, Michele,' she begged. 'Fuck my wet pussy!'

'Nice and snug, bitch?' asked the first one. 'Fills up your pussy, doesn't it?'

'Yeah, Michele. Please turn it on, I wanna come!'

'Becky is addicted to this thing.' Michele laughed. She put a remote in James's hand. He took it, looking like it was Christmas in July. 'Push this button, James. Fuck her pussy, you know you want to fuck her slutty wet pussy.'

Holly could not believe her eyes. Or ears. Where was her boyfriend? Where was Robert?

'But . . .' mumbled James, looking embarrassed for a refreshing change.

'Dammit, James, fuck her pussy,' said Robert, sounding like he was more than willing to do it himself. 'Push the button, make her squirm.'

'You are such a good boy, Doctor Waverly,' cooed that fucking whore Michele. 'So nice and helpful!'

'Jimmy,' said the one on all fours, 'please fuck my cunnie! Pweeease . . .'

The picture became very slightly fuzzy – whatever James did created some interference.

The blonde whore with the big tits began to scream and gyrate, looking like she was really enjoying herself. 'Fuck me harder,' she screamed and turned over. She played with her tits and James was eating it up, that cheating asshole.

There was more interference on screen as that tall tanned blonde trained James to fuck the big-titted wonder using the remote control. The bleached blonde was putting on a real show, squirming and looking for all the world like she was actually having an orgasm.

Deathly pale and shaking, Holly rewound the scene and pressed PLAY again, focusing on the stupid lines the naked bimbo was feeding those two drunken idiots. They were lapping it up; she wanted those insipid phrases burned into her memory so that she could quote the whore in the break-up speech.

She uttered the lines of the sluts on screen, one after another, in a hyper-exaggerated, overly feminine mockery of each. 'Ooh, fuck my cunnie, Michele, fuck my wet pussy! You've been a good boy, Doctor Waverly! Oooh, fuck my cunnie, pweeease!'

Sobbing with shame, she rewound the scene again. Suddenly, the whole situation just became too much for her. It was unbearable, what they'd done to her. She had always been a good girlfriend. She was going to be a great wife, a good mother. She was going to be a loyal and supportive life partner to Robert.

Holly began to cry. She stumbled into the kitchen, weeping hysterically. 'Why? Why?' she gasped, tasting the salt of the tears that were streaming down her face. 'Why did you do this to me, Robert?' She opened the fridge and bitterly grabbed one of the champagne bottles, then opened it with violent, jerky movements. She looked through the cabinets but all the champagne flutes seemed to have been used – and a large number of them were covered with pitifully cheap, hot-pink lipstick.

'You asshole!' screamed Holly and drank straight from the bottle. She marched back into the living room just in time to see another close-up of Becky's pussy. James really got into the act of fucking the whore with that disgusting sex toy and its remote control.

'Oh, I'll make you pay,' hissed Holly and drank some more. The stupid fake moans coming from the TV made her shake with rage. Gritting her teeth together, she guzzled down the cheap champagne in great shuddering gulps.

'Is this what you want? Some cheap, sleazy whore with obviously fake tits?' she cried, addressing the television. 'Some stupid bimbo whore who will play with a goddamned vibrator?' Holly picked up the odd-looking panties. That big fake cock was obscene; it was covered in bumps in unusual places and there was some weird four-pronged thing at the base of it. She rewound the scene again. There was Becky – Bimbo Becky, she reminded herself, what an appropriate name – impaling herself on this stupid toy and faking an orgasm for these stupid men.

She stared at the thing in her hand. Her head was spinning – she was not used to drink. She had an idea. She could pretend she didn't know what had happened – and then when they went to bed and they were about to make love, she would undress and he would see her wearing this foul toy and she would give her speech and make him feel like the tiny-dicked cheating asshole that he was. And then she would march out of here and she would make sure, oh yes, she would make goddamned sure that every woman on Earth learned about this whoring. No woman of class would approach this prick, ever again.

She rewound the scene again and squirmed out of her white silk underwear. 'Oooh, fuck my cunnie, pweeease!' She mocked the scene as she pulled the panties up. It was difficult; the enormous phallus rubbed up against the inside of her thighs as it sidled towards her private parts. She drank again, then put aside the empty bottle. The big fake cock was now rubbing up against her pussy lips. It slipped a little and rested just barely within her, a light but obscene presence.

She raised the bottle and tried to drink, remembering only then that it was empty. She rose. It was hard to move around with the panties not being all the way on – all the way *in* – and she was forced to move in stunted little steps. The tip of the gigantic artificial cock, positioned the way it was, kept rubbing up against her as she stumbled into the kitchen. Holly let out a startled little gasp and managed to come to a stop at the refrigerator, where she got the second bottle. 'That prick,' she sobbed aloud. 'How could he do this to me? I've always been so loyal!' She opened the bottle and drank deeply. Now that she had stopped, the panties were supremely uncomfortable. The panties slid down a little and the dildo slipped from her pussy. Holly put her hand on the foul toy and re-centred it. Now the tip of the artificial member was once again pushing up against her pussy lips. She let out a surprised little squeak when she felt the tip slip a fraction of an inch inside of her once again.

She went back into the living room. Becky was getting fucked by this very same device on screen. She felt the big, fat, hard artificial dick in between her legs and she slowly pulled the panties higher. The big, rubberised penis slid into her pussy one inch at a time. She was surprised to find that she was wet.

'Oooh, fuck my cunnie, pweeeease,' she sobbed and pulled the panties up all the way. The huge penis filled her completely. Those odd prongs slid right over her clit and caused a pleasant, tingling sensation. Holly's eyes bulged out – she had never felt this full of – full of – cock; yes, she thought, cock. She drank some more of the crappy sparkling wine. 'Fuck my cunnie, Michele,' she mumbled Becky's line. She began to pace back and forth in front of the TV, nursing the bottle. Obviously she was too upset to stay seated. Just pace back and forth, stop here, rub those legs together when turning, pace up and down, rub those legs together, rub them together, like that ... 'Fuck my cunnie, Michele, fuck my cunnie, pweeeease,' Holly whimpered. The pace of her turns increased until she was practically whirling back and forth, revolving around the gigantic prick in her pussy. After a few minutes of this she let out a frustrated moan and collapsed in a sweaty heap. She began to rub her thighs together. Her hand pushed down on the prongs that encircled her clit. She began to massage them through the rubbery material of the obscene panties.

The doorbell rang.

Holly let out a frustrated, pathetic moan. She kept on rubbing herself. Maybe if she just touched her clit directly, without those prongs in the way, she could relieve all this tension, all this humiliation. She tried to put her hand directly over her clit but the material of the panties was too tight. She couldn't slide her fingers past a certain point.

The doorbell rang again.

Holly crawled to the couch. She draped her legs over the side but the edge was too wide to grind herself against. The sound of her sobbing interrupted only by the occasional helpless moan, she ran into the spare bedroom, stopping every few feet to rub her legs together.

Holly essentially used the spare bedroom as an extra closet, for the storage of clothes. Once in a while they used it as a guest room; sometimes Robert's mom slept there. It was furnished lightly, with a small but valuable 19th-century four-poster bed, matching dresser, another dresser (Holly had a sizeable wardrobe) and an easy chair. It was this easy chair that brought Holly here now. The edge looked just narrow enough to work. Her right leg dangled over the side and her left leg rested on the cushion. Sitting like this, she felt the every gram of quiescent mass inside her drenched pussy. Those oddly shaped prongs pressed against her clit. She began to push, rub and turn against the edge of the easy chair, push and rub and turn, push and rub and turn . . .

She heard the door slam shut! Somebody opened the door, came in and shut the door!

Holly nearly screamed in panic but somehow managed to master the unexpected challenge of remaining silent. Wanting to howl with frustration and trembling with apprehension, she scrambled off the couch and dived into a pair of sweatpants from one of the dressers. There was simply no way to undertake the drawn-out hassle of taking off the pleasure-panties, not now. When the visitor left, then there would be plenty of time.

Who could it be? Maybe it was James! Holly knew it couldn't be Robert – why would Robert ring his own doorbell? If it was James she fully intended to make him sweat blood before she marched off. She could already envision Lucille's expression as she watched the sick porno on that videotape. She listened for sounds by the intruder. After a few seconds, her effort was rewarded: she heard the characteristic sound of high heels on the parquet floor. A woman – a woman in high heels! – entering the apartment – her apartment!

Holly's alarm was swept away by a tidal wave of fury. This had better be your long-lost sister, Robert, she thought, silently mouthing the words.

She stalked out of the spare bedroom and came face to face with a tall, very pretty woman. Holly despised her on sight. She was tanned, with big, all too obviously fake tits. Her eyes were an empty blue, accentuated by way too much blue eye-shadow. She wore bright-red lipstick and entirely too much foundation. The woman towered over her in very high black stiletto heels. She was gathering the toys that Holly had strewn over the carpet and replacing them in the kit-bag. There was something very familiar about her. Surely this bitch couldn't be the woman from the video?

'Can I help you?' asked Holly, her voice vibrating with menace. 'You are trespassing.'

'I was here the other night and I left some stuff,' said the woman, calm as ice. 'I'll leave in a minute.'

Holly's breath stuck in her throat – this confident cunt was – what was the name, this woman *was* Michele, the bitch who dared call Robert a – a spooger! This fucking bitch had the nerve – the unbelievable gall – to come back here and gloat over her conquest!

'How dare you come here!' she shrieked, shaking. 'How dare you come here after all you've done!'

Michele smirked. 'I don't know what you think you know but don't worry your pretty little head about it. I have everything, almost.'

'Get out!'

'Have you seen a pair of panties with a vibrator? It's . . .'

'Certainly not!' screamed Holly. 'Do you want me to call the police?'

Michele frowned. 'That's really expensive, I don't want

106

to leave without it. I know I can find it in a second . . .'
She rummaged through her purse – pink sequins, how
tacky, thought Holly – and produced a metallic rectangle
with buttons and a central dial, a remote control.

Holly glanced at it with barely disguised impatience. She
recognised the thing, of course, but that was irrelevant at
the moment. 'I believe I asked you to leave,' she said with
icy formality. 'I never want to see you in this building
again or I shall have to call the police. This is a building
for upstanding professionals, not some . . . bimbo slut like
yourself.'

'Look, just relax. It was a bachelor party, that's all. I'll
find it when I hear the buzzing.' She pushed a button on
the little remote and tilted her head, listening in one
direction then another. 'I can't hear it yet,' said Michele,
looking disappointed. 'Can you hear anything?'

Holly weakly leant against the wall. It was all she could
do not to moan like a bitch on heat. The enormous cock
in her cunt was pulsating, squirming, filling her up. Part of
the thing – no, a couple of parts – were actually rotating!
The prongs that surrounded the fleshy knob of her clit
were vibrating and rotating at the same time.

'It doesn't have a long range,' said Michele. 'If it was in
the other room it might not work at all.'

'Go in the other roo– rooo– room then,' stammered
Holly. 'Just go.' She stood on tip-toe; the prongs on her
clit pressed a little harder that way. 'T– take your time.'

Michele gave her an odd look and went into the master
bedroom. Holly collapsed on the sofa, squirming with
wave upon wave upon wave of intense, mind-numbing
pleasure. She came, then came again. Suddenly the big fake
dick inside her cunt grew motionless. Now that she had
had some measure of satisfaction, Holly managed to
gather her wits enough to sit up as the stripper returned to
the living room.

'I can't find it,' said Michele. She looked glum.

'Too bad,' whispered Holly.

'I'm sorry, what did you say? I couldn't hear you.'

'Did you look everywhere?'

'I thought I did. This is a nice apartment, but it's not

huge. Maybe I would hear the buzzing if I turned it up all the way.'

'You mean a few minutes ago, it wasn't at full?'

'Uhm – no? Why should that matter to you?'

'Well . . . Uh . . . Nothing. I just thought if you wanted to hear the buzzing you would have turned it up all the way, that's all.'

Michele shrugged and took out the remote control again. She turned away from Holly and slowly walked back into the master bedroom, turning the dial all the way to the right as she did so.

Holly stood stock still. She froze with shock as the sensations in her pussy and around her clit overwhelmed her nervous system. She saw Michele disappear into the master bedroom and finally found enough strength in her muscles to flee the living room, squirming her way back to the easy chair. She somehow had the presence of mind to lock the door behind her and collapsed over that convenient narrow edge, a heap of quivering orgasmic pleasure. She was gasping for air. The filthy thing inside her pussy and over her clit was pleasure incarnate, a mind-blowing non-stop ride that made her want to moan until the day she died.

And then it stopped.

'Can I look in here? I thought I heard some sound coming from here,' Holly heard from the other side of the door. The handle turned. 'But it's locked! We were never in here. I don't understand why it would come from this room . . .'

Holly got up and wiped the sweat off her face with a T-shirt from the dresser. 'One moment,' she said, feeling oddly detached. She moved like a machine. She opened the door and admitted the woman. 'Go ahead and search, then.'

Holly looked around. 'These are all your things? They look like your style.'

'What exactly do you mean by that?' asked Holly, irritated. Instead of trying to listen for the buzzing the woman was making small talk. She didn't even have the remote in her hand!

'I just mean they are conservative – very classy.'

'I don't need your approval, you know,' said Holly. She had no interest in making conversation with this whore. 'I saw that videotape,' she said, hoping to see some measure of guilt. 'I heard you call Robert all those names.'

'Did you like it?' Michele giggled. 'I really enjoy putting on a good show.'

Holly gasped. 'Get out! Get out now!'

'Hey, I was just kidding . . .'

'You are some kind of bimbo whore and I want you to stay away from Robert, do you understand?'

'Why're you calling me names, I don't . . .'

'Shut up! Get out or I'm calling the cops! Out! Now!' She marched to the door, her resolute walk turning into a parody of a tight-legged, sensual strut as she rotated her hips around the big prick in her pussy. She opened the door and stood there, silent, waiting for the stripper to leave.

Michele pulled out the remote. 'I didn't try it in the foyer yet,' she said slowly. She pushed the button and turned the dial halfway to the right. 'I can hear something but I can't figure out where it's coming from. I'm sure if I could come by later . . .'

Holly's intention to continue telling Michele off drowned in the waves of filthy pleasure coursing through her quivering clit. She just wanted to moan and rub up against things. She sobbed with the injustice of it all.

'Here.' Michele took a card out of her wallet. 'Call me when you find it, I'll send someone to pick it up. Don't worry, it won't be me.'

'Get out – please,' gasped Holly. She needed a long cold shower; she needed something to clear her head.

Michele rolled her eyes and put the card into Holly's violently trembling hand. 'Please call anytime, OK?'

'OK,' said Holly impatiently. She quickly shut the door and collapsed, sliding down into a shuddering heap. She stroked the wonderful panties with a worshipful hand, over and over, feeling the vibrating, twisting, rotating pleasure in and around every inch of her orgasming, ecstatic pussy.

The sudden cessation of pleasure was a rude and unwelcome development. Frustrated, she rose. After a moment's hesitation, she opened the door. After all, that filthy slut could still be lurking about in the hallway. It was her duty to check. Her eyes scanned the deserted hallway. She even walked to the elevator bay, arching her foot, walking in tiny little steps. She discovered that strutting that way maximised the pressure on her clit. Michele had already left – and obviously the panties were out of range of the remote – or Michele had finally remembered to turn it off.

She tossed the crumpled business card in the trash.

Holly

Obviously she needed to tell Robert off and punish him severely for this terrible lack of judgment. He needed to show proper humility and beg for her forgiveness – without admitting his guilt he could never be trusted again. She looked at the clock, depressed. It was already 6 p.m. and Robert still hadn't shown. Where could he be?

Still, there was no point in moping about. She finished cleaning up the apartment and sat down on the couch. Holly picked up the remote and turned on the broadcast of some concert. She stared at the jumbled images for a few seconds but her mind was not really registering them.

She needed to tell Robert off. How should she go about this? Maybe – maybe the most effective method for this was by quoting the blonde bimbos he hired to fuck James.

She pushed the PLAY button on the camcorder again.

Obviously, it was time to go over her lines again so that she could demonstrate his moral turpitude by presenting him with a mocking parody of his whores' sleazy behaviour. Oddly enough, however, she felt compelled to watch only the one scene that she had chanced upon when she first viewed the tape. She did not want to feel any angrier at Robert than she already was.

There, she was at the beginning of the scene. The glistening pink of bimbo Becky's cunt filled the TV screen. Holly dutifully repeated every word issuing from Becky's lips, eager for her cue to put on the pleasure panties. After the second viewing she decided to keep it on; after all, Robert could be home any moment and she needed to show him just how busted he was. She fell asleep on the living-room couch, with the quiescent, gigantic prick inside her pussy. She wore a contented smile on her lips as the scene played over and over and over, burning into her subconscious.

Holly woke up sweating. She did not remember exactly what her dream had been but it had something to do with the remote control and she wanted some, now. Right now.

She stumbled around in a sleepy daze, looking for the remote until she found it. She pushed the ON button and jumped as the television came to life. Holly gaped at the jumble of loud colourful babble and shuddered with irritation. This was the TV remote! Unless . . . She aimed the device at her panties and pushed each of the buttons. She didn't feel anything.

She sobbed softly as the facts of the situation slowly resolved themselves in her conscious mind. This was so unfair! That whore Michele had the remote and Holly had told her never to come back again.

She pulled off the panties and tried to play with herself using only her hand – for her, a woefully underdeveloped skill – but after the mind-altering experience with the activated vibrator, her mere fingers felt boring and utterly inadequate to the task.

She got up and began to walk around. She experimented until she found the right posture to maximise the rubbing and the pressure of the prongs on her clit. It required her to stand with her shoulders erect – arms back and chest forward – keeping her butt sticking straight back out and her feet arched, almost as if she were wearing heels. This way every time she took a small, dainty step, the prongs pushed and rubbed up against her needy, demanding clit. She moved all over the apartment, cleaning, putting things away, dusting, sweeping and vacuuming. By midnight she was howling with frustration. The apartment was beyond spotless; she had moved on to reorganising the contents of the drawers, folding clothes as she paced back and forth, back and forth, turning swiftly with her chest and ass thrust out, her feet delicately arched, rubbing her thighs against one another, wishing for more, wishing for vibrations, for the rotation of those prongs, for that sensation.

Maybe she wasn't moving fast enough. Could it be that simple? But she was exhausted. Maybe she could just move her legs while lying down, she reasoned. She squirmed, the way she had seen Becky do, but it didn't really work. When she didn't put her weight on her feet the dead vibrator in her pussy didn't seem to do its magic at the same level of intensity as when she was moving around.

Also, she was tired of arching her feet. She rummaged through her closet until she found a pair of two-and-a-half-inch heels. She hated them; she had only worn them twice. Both of the occasions were despised job interviews.

She tried to run in the heels but they made a fearful clatter on the hardwood floor. It was past midnight already; she had better do this somewhere else. Yet the brief gallop had been enough to reveal that the efficacy of the obscene toy in her cunt was indeed enhanced by an increase in speed. She laid down two blankets over the carpet and ran on those, but the heels kept catching on the soft fabric and she fell on her face. Holly sobbed with frustration.

She put on a sweatshirt and left the apartment, continuing to jog inside the elevator, squirming, gyrating her ass to maximise the stimulation on her clit. She ran through the lobby where one of the cleaning crew, an old, black man with salt-and-pepper hair and a long, silver goatee, stared at her with obvious surprise. His stunned gaze took in the sweatshirt and the sweatpants and came to rest on the high heels.

She sniffed with irritation. 'Stop staring at the residents,' she said testily. She paced back and forth while delivering a few manic words. 'I don't believe you're paid to ogle me. I will report you to your supervisor. What is your name?'

'I'm Kevin, ma'am. Sorry, ma'am . . .'

'You just keep on – washing the floors, do you understand me?' She raised her arms to ward off his words as he opened his lips to speak. 'I don't have time for this, I don't speak your – *dialect*, OK?'

He nodded and cast down his eyes, concentrating on his work. He pulled the mop over the red marble, leaving a shiny streak.

She half strutted, half ran out of the lobby, her ass gyrating just – like – that. God, yes. Once she hit the concrete of the sidewalk the jarring shock of each step – as long as she maintained her posture with her tits and ass sticking out and kept her feet arched with the help of those silly, hateful shoes – travelled up her legs and transferred a tiny, pleasure-filled little prod via one of the prongs resting upon her starving, needy clit. Her pussy was soaking wet; the big rubbery prick kept sliding in and out of her for about half an inch if she squirmed just the right way. She clattered down the street. She ran back and forth in front of the apartment building, moaning softly.

She ran faster and faster, her clattering high heels delaying audible signals of the drumbeats of pleasure that kept on falling on her clit. She was going to come, she was going to come . . . She put on a desperate spurt of speed but just before she hit that magical threshold she was forced to stop. She collapsed on a bench, wheezing. Her vision was full of glittering little sparkles. She could have cried.

'Why are you doing this to me?' she whined pitifully. 'Why?' She buried her head in her hands. She sobbed. It was so unfair!

'Miss, you OK?'

She looked up. It was her neighbour, Gordon Parks, a happily married, workaholic assistant District Attorney. Why was everybody giving her grief tonight? 'I'm fine,' she snapped. Stooped over on the bench, she could barely feel the prong on her clit and the big rubbery cock in her cunt was not positioned correctly. It was a decidedly unpleasant, maybe even painful sensation. She straightened up, pushing her tits forwards. As her spine assumed the slightly exaggerated upright posture, the echo of pleasure returned. She stood up with a long, drawn-out motion that emphasised the movement of her ass, still breathing hard. 'I'm just doing a little running tonight,' she said.

'Running? In those shoes?'

'I'm breaking them in,' said Holly angrily. 'It helps. Take care, Gordon. Give my best to Irene.' She stalked off.

Her feet were killing her. She grudgingly admitted that perhaps Gordon was right. Each step was excruciatingly painful and she was utterly exhausted. Even if her feet felt good enough to run with (a preposterous idea in these shoes), she did not have the conditioning to continue. Below a certain rate of speed the bulging device in her cunt was not as pleasurable.

Holly ran back home. She stormed past the janitor. His staring was really starting to piss her off. His perverted, beady little eyes focused on her heels as if wearing heels was all that unusual. It looked like he had just finished mopping the floor. The marble was glistening wet. It was hard enough to walk fast in these shoes – much less run – and she was relieved when she made it to the elevator without slipping. Next to the elevator bay stood a row of potted plants.

The janitor's obvious interest really made her angry. She marched over to the pots. 'You missed a spot,' she snarled, and twisted, rotating around the cock in her pussy. Her elbow 'accidentally' knocked over one of the plants and the pot shattered. Ceramics and soil spilled all over the freshly mopped floor.

His face was inscrutable.

'Oh, so sorry,' she sniffed and entered the elevator. She saw him sigh and walk towards the mess as the doors closed. When she got back in the apartment she took the high heels off and threw them in the closet. Walking on tip-toe, she strutted into the living room. Maybe there was a way to activate the vibrator without the remote ... She whimpered with the pain of parting as she wriggled out of the panties. She felt so empty, so unfulfilled without the sensation of the gigantic rubber cock in her pussy.

She examined the panties and the vibrator in detail. There were no switches or buttons on it, just those wonderful protrusions, prongs and little balls dotting the glistening black material. Maybe if she took the batteries out and put them back in it would come on?

115

She didn't see a place for batteries. Maybe the thing could be unscrewed? She gave it a careful counter-clockwise turn and the vibrator indeed separated from the base. She found gold leads that looked familiar. She sat back up, feet arched and shoulders pushed back, dismayed. Those were the same kind of gold leads that were on the back of her cell phone. The device required a custom charger, not simple batteries!

Holly was utterly exhausted. Sleep eluded her, however. To allow for easier access, she replaced the sweatpants with the shortest skirt in her wardrobe – a mid-thigh plaid piece that she got from Lucille last Christmas. There were buttons running from top to bottom on the left side. Holly thought the buttons on the side made the skirt a touch too revealing – slutty, in fact – and up until now she had refused to wear it. Still, now the thing came in handy. She put the panties back on and buttoned the skirt over it. Squirming in place she turned on the video. Maybe Becky – who was supposedly addicted to this filthy toy – knew how to turn it on; maybe her actions on screen would give Holly a clue to the secret.

She watched it over and over, repeating Becky's lines, until she settled on the one that most closely represented her immediate, overwhelming need: 'Fuck my cunnie, please, fuck my cunnie,' she whimpered over and over. 'I need it!' she sobbed.

She strutted out to the kitchen and pulled out the garbage can. Her arms went elbow-deep into the filth of the bachelor party until her frantic fingers finally found what she was looking for. She nearly cried with relief when she recognised the business card.

Pacing back and forth, she dialled. By divine grace, the number picked up after the fourth ring.

'Hi!' said a seductive, bitchy purr. 'This is Michele.'

'Michele, this is Holly, I am sorry about how I've acted, listen, I've been thinking . . .' blurted Holly in a single breath.

'I am not available right now; just leave your name, baby, and I'll get back to you as soon as you deserve it. *If* you deserve it.' After a fake-sounding giggle a tone sounded.

Frustrated, not knowing what to say, Holly hung up. She paced. Maybe Michele set her phone to silent mode! Yeah – that's what she must have done. She dialled again. She listened to the stripper's bitchy purr over and over, hoping that she was going to pick up.

She dragged the easy chair from the spare room and called again and again, riding the edge, listening to Michele's words. She tried to distract herself from her plight by going through the video again for some clue on how to activate the vibrator without the remote. Under no circumstances did she want to miss Michele answering the phone, so she put the television on mute. In absolute silence, she kept watching the big black dick – the one inside her – disappear into Becky's pink slit. She kept on replaying that segment, hoping for clues.

'You're an eager little boy,' she heard Michele's voice. For a moment Holly gaped at the TV before she realised that the voice was coming from the receiver. 'Who is this?'

'Hi, I'm Holly,' she stammered. Her voice sounded lame to her own ears.

'Holly . . .?'

'Yes. Robert Waverly's girlfriend? We've . . . We met this afternoon.'

'Yes, I remember.' Michele's voice turned decidedly unfriendly. 'What do you . . . Did you find the panties?'

'You know, I think I could find them. I'm sure I could find them. It would be no problem if I could just use that remote. I thought I heard some buzzing just a few minutes ago. Yes, I think I definitely heard something. Anyway I thought if I just had it I could look for them and you wouldn't even need to come by, I would bring them to you as soon as I found them.'

After a moment's pause: 'I see. Yes. You told me never to set foot in your place again, remember?'

'Yeah – you know, I may have gotten a little carried away. I mean, I'm a little jealous, you know, Robert is just such a catch, I just don't like to see him with pretty women . . .'

'He's an oncologist,' said Michele.

'Yes. He's also a plastic surgeon but he hates that work, it doesn't let him do his research. He's only doing it

117

sometimes so he can make his med-school payments,' blabbered Holly. 'So you can understand why I would be concerned about him in the company of two . . .'

'Bimbo whores, I believe that's what you called us,' said Michele. 'Bimbo whores.'

'Well . . . I was angry, I already said I was sorry,' said Holly, panicked that Michele was going to hang up. Her inner thighs were getting raw as she rode the easy chair. She paused the video at the spot where Becky began to squirm and tried to duplicate the movement.

'No, you didn't say you were sorry until now,' said Michele, sounding a touch mollified. 'That's better.'

Holly felt absurdly relieved that she had managed the apology. She kept on rubbing her stuffed cunt against the edge of the love seat. 'I am terribly sorry for having upset you, Michele,' she said, stuffing her fist in her mouth to stifle the keening moan of a tiny little orgasm. There was something inherently erotic in the humiliating apology. 'Please let me find the panties for you, Michele. I'll come and get the remote from you. Where do you live?'

'I think I'll come by instead . . . Don't you go anywhere, baby.'

'I won't,' Holly promised, gasping. The phone slipped from her fingers and she fell forwards on the carpet. Pressing play on the camcorder, she arched her feet, feeling the obscene toy slide deeper into her cunt.

It took forever for the doorbell to ring. She sprung up from the edge of the love seat and ran to the door, opening it with trembling hands.

'Remember me?' said Michele. She wore a white fur coat and a tiny pink miniskirt. Her feet were clad in open-toed stiletto sandals, pink with white stripes. Both her toenails and fingernails were painted a lurid tawdry pink, the same colour as her miniskirt. She was carrying a kit-bag.

Holly nodded, fidgeting. 'Aren't you going to invite me in?' asked Michele after a moment's pause.

'Ah – sure, come in,' said Holly. She moved to the side to allow the stripper easier access into the apartment. 'I hope we can find it,' she said. She felt her lips trembling.

Why wasn't Michele taking the remote out of her purse? Why?

Michele put a manicured finger on her lips. Thoughtfully, she murmured, 'Maybe we can find it without turning it on!'

'I looked everywhere,' Holly protested. 'I cleaned up very thoroughly.'

'Yes, I can see that.' Michele smirked. 'You must have been running all over the place, cleaning it up. Exercise is very important.'

'God, yes,' gasped Holly. She sat down on the couch and crossed her legs, then uncrossed them, then crossed them again, then uncrossed them. 'Aren't you going to look for it?' she asked.

'You really think I should?' asked Michele. 'Why, I'm not even sure if I brought the remote!' She giggled. 'So tell me, Holly, how did you find out about me and Becky?' Without asking for permission, she lit a cigarette.

'Robert hates it when people smoke in here,' said Holly.

'Really? I didn't notice. He seemed to enjoy whatever I did.'

'You're not a very nice person, are you?' asked Holly, getting angry. 'How can you talk about him like that? You don't even know him! You're just . . .'

Holly's voice cut off – Michele was holding the remote, dangling it in between two long, delicate fingers.

'I dropped it the other day and it had to be repaired,' she said, smiling sweetly. 'It would be such a shame if I dropped it again.'

'Yes,' said Holly, watching the remote. Her eyes filled with tears. 'Please be careful.'

'Very good idea to call me here, to have me look for the big fat cock Robert and James used to fuck Becky with,' purred Michele. 'Let's see just what they've done, OK?' She delicately pushed the central button on the remote.

Holly gasped – she crossed and uncrossed her legs and squirmed to the edge of the couch.

'I can't hear any buzzing!' said Michele with hyper-exaggerated innocence. 'Let's turn it up some!' She turned the dial and pressed a few more of the buttons, watching Holly's squirming, gasping body with infinite satisfaction.

'I – I think I can hear something,' gasped Holly. Her eyes were dazed and she was shaking all over. The addictive sensation coursed through her body, making her feel more alive than she had ever felt before. She began to moan, unable to stop herself.

'Yes, Holly.' Michele smirked. 'Let's see if I can hear it now.' She sadistically took the remote over to her moaning hostess and caressed her cheeks with it. She turned the dial all the way to the right. After pocketing the remote, she grabbed Holly's skirt and with a casual twist ripped it off her, snapping off one button at a time.

She stripped her victim naked as Holly moaned and shuddered in the grip of a chain of humiliating orgasms. Her clit, her cunt, even the nipples on her breasts welcomed the return of life to the monstrous cock in her pussy and to the prongs pressing down and around on her clit. Her initial keening moans gave way to obscene, helpless mutterings, the repetition of Becky's lines from the recording.

'Oooh, Michele, fuck my cunnie pweeease ...' she moaned, rolling around on the couch and landing in a heap on the floor, right by Michele's feet.

Michele giggled and turned off the device.

Holly screamed and tried to grab the remote, but the tanned blonde shook off her weakened, shaking hands.

'You were right, baby,' laughed Michele. 'Working together, we did find the panties.'

'But ...' sobbed Holly. 'I'll buy it, OK?'

'Maybe I'll let you rent it,' said Michele, deep in thought. 'You're still really worked up, aren't you, uppity little Holly.'

'Please give me some more,' she begged. She gained inspiration from the video. 'Please fuck my cunnie, Michele!'

'You do have a nice body,' conceded the blonde. 'Turn over so I can get a good look at you.'

'I'm not – I – I meant use the remote,' sobbed Holly.

Michele turned the dial a quarter of the way to the right.

Holly emitted a gasp of delight and flopped over, displaying her panty-clad ass. She was so immersed in the dubious joys produced by the device that Michele's actions on the couch registered only as shadow images on the surface of her conscious mind.

The stripper opened her kit-bag and pulled out another pair of shiny black panties. She shed her thongs (red lace) and put them on, ignoring the moaning, crumpled form of Robert's girlfriend. These seemed identical to the ones on Holly, with one all-important difference: the big vibrator was sticking outwards. With a triumphant giggle, she once again turned off the vibrator in Holly's thoroughly addicted, drenched cunt.

'Please, you promised!' howled Holly. 'Why . . . Why're you doing this to me?' she sobbed.

'I don't remember making any promises – Holly. I don't like that name, you know.'

'It's my name,' cried Holly. 'It's my name, OK?'

'I think your name is . . . Trixie.' Michele laughed.

'You're sick!'

Michele casually grabbed the video camera and trained it on Holly's shivering, sobbing body.

She was still arching her feet and pressing her shoulders back; her ass was moving back and forth and she kept crossing her legs every few seconds. 'Please turn it back on!' she begged.

'Take it off, sweetie.' Michele laughed. 'Look what I have for you!' She trained the remote on the strap-on dick she was wearing and pressed the button. A familiar (albeit much louder than what she had heard thus far) buzzing filled Holly's ears – the big fake penis was vibrating and the odd little prongs of the clit stimulator at its base were rotating, squeezing, rotating, squeezing . . .

Holly gasped – she couldn't seem to look away, despite the fact that it registered in her mind that she was being filmed.

'What – what are you doing?' she stammered.

'You want it, here it is.' Michele smiled. 'All you have to do is just fuck yourself, just slide my big, fat black cock into your little Trixie pussy.'

'Please turn it on, please . . .' sobbed Holly. 'The one I have on, please turn that one on . . .'

Michele ran her manicured fingers over the shiny black surface of the big rubber cock. It swung back and forth, vibrating. She stroked it with her fingers, smiling. 'But it's on already, Trixie.' She pouted. 'Just come on over here and take off those ugly panties. Take them off so pretty Michele can shove this nice vibrating cock into the wet little Trixie pussy.' Her tone was beyond condescending. 'Go on, I'll wait a minute. After that, no more buzzing vibrator play for sweet Trixie.'

Holly stood and took off the panties. She threw them clear across the room until they landed in a heap against the balcony door.

'Temper tantrums? I suppose Trixie has them.' Michele laughed. 'Can't really expect a girl named Trixie to act with maturity now, can we?'

Collecting the remaining shards of her pride and dignity, Holly faced the manipulative slut on the couch. 'Go away,' she somehow managed to say. 'I don't want you here, you hear me?'

Michele stroked her big black cock with a free hand. 'Come here, little Trixie,' she cooed. 'Come on, now!' She trained the remote on the vibrator and turned the dial to maximum. The bulges on the shiny black surface blurred. She put the remote down and raised the camera again, training it on Holly.

'My name is Holly,' she screamed. Now that her pussy was not being stimulated on a non-stop basis, the crimson fog began to lift from her mind. 'Now get out!'

Michele smirked. She shrugged and peeled off the strap-on panties. 'Your loss,' she said. 'You'll call again but I'll have to be convinced to come back.'

'When hell freezes over,' mumbled Holly. Michele's pussy was the same colour as Becky's on the TV screen, right before she pushed the vibrator in . . .

Michele put the strap-on panties in her kit-bag. She picked up the panties that Holly had thrown away and placed them on top of the TV. The vibrator was sticking straight up; the prongs of the clit stimulator seemed to point directly at Holly, accusatory magic fingers. With a satisfied little giggle, Michele placed the remote inside the shiny black cave of the semi-hard rubbery material that formed the panties, leaning the controller against the huge phallus.

'Take that – *thing* – with you,' said Holly. She was feeling weak; the room seemed to fade in and out of focus. Yes, that was definitely the remote control from the video. It was right inside the panties, leaning against the shiny black bulges of the vibrator.

'Oh, I wouldn't dream of depriving you of your toy.' Michele smirked. 'It's a custom job, after all. You can't buy something like this in a simple sex shop; you have to know the right people.' She put a business card on the mantelpiece and glided out of the apartment. Holly followed as if in a daze, slamming the door shut behind her swaying, undulating ass. The dry, metallic click of the closing door jarred Holly out of her odd trance.

She was exhausted. Sleep – yes, what she needed was good old-fashioned sleep. She walked into the bedroom and fell on the sheets. A ghost of the body rub from the strippers still lingered. The apartment felt so empty now. After a moment her loneliness became a palpable thing. She hesitated for a few seconds then picked up the phone and dialled Robert's cell number. It went straight to voicemail.

'Robert – I don't know where you are, but I miss you. I'm back at the apartment. Please call.' She hung up before she realised she was actually being nice to him – the cheating bastard, she was actually nice to him on the phone! He would listen to her and think everything was all right. Serves him right – he would think he had gotten away with murder and then she would confront him with the evidence of his crime. She couldn't wait to see his face as she peeled out of her skirt and displayed the obscene black of those panties, to see the startled fear in his eyes . . .

She sighed and turned over. Despite her fatigue, sleep eluded her. Should she take a sleeping pill? Did she even have something that would put her to sleep? After a moment she remembered she had a bottle of antihistamines in the nightstand. They always made her drowsy. She opened the nightstand – it opened with some difficulty – and . . .

'What the hell?' she gasped. She lifted the magazine with two fingertips as if it were decaying meat. Two practically naked women wearing heavy makeup were fondling one another on the cover. What little they wore consisted of shiny red and black latex.

Holly threw the magazine on the floor and lifted out another one – the nightstand was jammed full of them. She checked the date: it was this month's issue! She went through them all – all the magazines were the most recent issues, some of them apparently from the future, since it was still September – although some of them looked *used*. She picked up the one on the bottom and sniffed with disgust – it smelt like garbage, the stale smell trash gets when it's left in the can too long.

'Who are you, Robert?' she whispered and sighed. 'You deserve everything that's coming to you, everything!' She sobbed and threw a handful of the magazines against the wall. Some fell apart. The staples were too weak. Glossy pages of naked girls covered the floor. Some of them fell on her bed. Her pillow was covered by a picture of a girl with blonde pigtails and enormous fake tits. She was sucking on a striped lollipop. Holly shuddered with revulsion and ran out of the bedroom, slamming the door behind her. She would show him! She marched to the TV and grabbed the panties and the remote, practically hammering the obscene device into her pussy. She was dry and it would not go in immediately so she rubbed herself for a few minutes – she wanted to forget, to feel pleasure, to wear this disgusting, evil thing so when Robert came through that door he would see what he had done to her.

After a minute or so it began to feel good. It felt very nice. It felt very nice to touch herself. The panties were up to her knees and the vibrator kept bumping against her inner thighs as she pleasured herself. Her masturbation was making her wet. The promise of the big fake dick in between her legs made her wet. By the time she pushed it inside – it slid into her drenched cunt without any trouble – she was moaning with gratification. Her cunt welcomed the intrusion; she gave a helpless little gasp when the

124

prongs settled around her clit. She licked her lips and pushed the button on the remote, squirming with delight as the pathways leading to her pleasure centres lit up – once again – with wave upon wave of addictive joy. She was coming! She was coming! Moaning, she turned the dial all the way to the right.

After she came three times she calmed down enough to turn the device down to a bare minimum. Robert could be home any minute, she told herself. There was simply no point in taking off the panties. She picked up the remote and caressed it, randomly pushing some of the buttons. A few minutes later she knew just the right combinations. When the dial was all the way to the right it was nearly too much; still, she ended up doing just that in the end. It took longer this time; the intensity of the vibrations seemed to have diminished. The prongs or the clit stimulator weren't moving as fast either.

After she climaxed (she had lost count of how many orgasms she'd had) she tried to get some rest.

I guess I'd better turn it off, she thought reluctantly. Still, a few minutes after she had turned off the device she became restless and once again decided to turn it on. She put it on the minimum setting. It felt so good, she closed her eyes, and somewhat to her surprise sleep finally came. The only sound remaining in the bedroom was the infinitesimally low buzzing of the vibrator inside her drenched pussy and the sound of her legs, subconsciously sliding and rubbing up against one another.

When she woke it was still dark. What happened? Why did she wake up? Was she thirsty? Did she have to go to the bathroom? She peered into the darkness and sat up, feeling the fullness of the rubber cock inside her. It was very quiet. It took a moment for the import of her observation to permeate her mind: the vibrator was not on!

Panicked, she flipped on the light, scrambling around for the remote. She gasped with relief when she saw it at the foot of the bed. Eagerly, she aimed it at the panties and pushed the button.

Nothing happened.

She pushed it again. She pushed them all and turned the dial – no, the dial was already turned as far to the right as it could go. What had happened?

She sobbed and sat on the edge of the easy chair, squirming. Without realising it, she was steadily grinding her clit against the prongs that surrounded it while trying to gather her wits about her at the same time. Maybe the thing – maybe the battery was dead? Dreading the act of parting, she wriggled out of the panties. She unscrewed the vibrator, examining the power leads on the bottom. She picked up her cell phone (noticing that she hadn't got any messages from Robert but not really able to feel anger) and looked at the power leads on the back. Sure enough, the leads on the two devices were similar, but definitely not identical.

She took the vibrator into the living room and tried to make the leads on the vibrator match those of the phone charger. They simply wouldn't fit. Maybe she could connect the charger with some wires? She was no electrician; even if she managed to connect it, how was she to know that the current from the phone charger was compatible with the vibrator? What if she – what was the word – made it melt down? She shivered with imagined loss.

Maybe she could get her own charger, or her very own vibrator. She stroked the quiescent black cock with her fingers. 'Please work!' she begged, sobbing.

The dead black rubber refused to move. Its motionless surface seemed to mock her.

She kept trying the buttons on the remote but nothing was happening. Suddenly she had an idea: maybe it wasn't the vibrator that was dead after all. Maybe it was the battery in the remote that needed to be replaced!

She ran to the kitchen and looked through the drawer for fresh batteries, but there weren't any. She would have to go out to buy some. Frustrated, she screwed the obscene black rubber dick back on to the panties and pushed it into position, gasping with pleasure as the monstrous phallus again filled her drenched pussy. 'Must get batteries,' she muttered, standing up. She had to go outside to get batteries, but she was barefoot, she needed shoes. Arching her feet, Holly strutted to the closet. She crawled over her other shoes, all sensible flats, to get to the sadly scuffed high heels she had discarded earlier. She took the elevator down to the lobby. 'Don't you dare talk to me,' she snarled to the janitor, the same black man who had ogled her feet earlier. 'Don't you dare!'

She glided out of the apartment building, moaning every couple of paces as the jarring shock of each high-arched step travelled up her feet and straight on to her clit.

Some immigrant manned the gas station. He wore a turban, for God's sake! 'Batteries,' she gasped, jogging in place. 'Give me double-A batteries!'

The attendant gaped at her. 'I am sorry,' he said, shaking his head. 'You want what?'

'Look, can't you people learn English?' screamed Holly, her tits flopping as she switched to little squirmy jumps to maximise the jarring. She somehow grabbed the remote and popped off the plastic lid (not an easy task in constant motion), and showed the man the two batteries within. She tried to speak clearly, enunciating each and every syllable. 'These are called bat-te-ries! They are used for e-lec-tric devices!' When the man still didn't move to give her what she wanted, she popped out the batteries and slammed them into the metal tray. 'These. I'm sorry all this advanced technology confuses you, I'm sorry we're not, you know, still living in the dark ages with cows and . . .'

'4.97,' said the attendant. He shoved a package of batteries into the tray.

'Oh, OK,' muttered Holly. She pulled out her wallet and paid the (Indian? Pakistani? Was there a difference?) man, feeling his eyes track her swaying ass as she ran off. The nerve of the man!

At the edge of the gas station she halted and replaced the batteries in the remote control. She closed her eyes and hit the central button.

Nothing?

Nothing. She felt nothing.

She turned the dial.

127

For a moment she thought she felt something, and she arched her feet even more, anticipating the wave, but then she realised she was fooling herself. Nothing. The big dick in her cunt and the prongs around her clit were completely dead.

'Oh no,' she whimpered. 'Why me?'

She strutted back to the apartment. There was still no sign of Robert!

Her feet ached and she took off the shoes, but now her ankles were even more sore and tired. Keeping her feet arched like this was exhausting work.

It took two hours before the absence of pleasure drove her to the phone.

'This is Michele.'

'Hi,' whispered Holly. 'Look, it's Holly.'

'What a pleasant surprise!' Michele's voice was heavy with irony. 'So what do you want?'

'Uh . . . You forgot to leave the charger,' sobbed Holly.

'Oh yes – how could I forget? I can be so forgetful sometimes! Can't really expect anything from a bimbo airhead like me, right?'

'Can I have the charger, please?' begged Holly. 'I'll come and pick it up. You don't have to come here.'

'I don't know. Maybe I'll let you play with the other one. Would you like to play with the other one, Trixie?'

'My name is not Trixie,' cried Holly. 'My name is Holly, OK?'

'I only have toys for Trixie.' Michele giggled. 'Not for Holly. Holly sounds too – goody two-shoes to fuck herself with a big black vibrator. Now, Trixie gets to stuff her pussy full of nice buzzing toys whenever she wants.'

'Can I have the charger, please?'

'Trixie says "pweeease",' said Michele. 'Say "pweeease". Bimbo Becky says "pweeease".'

Holly was crying.

'Trixie, say "pweeease".'

'Pweeease,' whispered Holly.

'I can't hear you, Trixie.'

'Pweeease!' Holly screamed into the receiver. 'Pweeease, let me have the charger!'

128

'Now we're getting somewhere. I knew you could learn to co-operate. I'll come by.' She laughed. 'Don't you go anywhere, Trixie baby.'

Unable to stay motionless, Holly went out into the lobby to wait for Michele. She kept pacing the length of the lobby, ignoring the irritating black man mopping the floor.

'Stop staring at me!' she snapped once, rotating her hips to maximise the rubbing in and around her helpless wet cunt. 'Just do your stupid job and wash the floor, OK?'

'Yes, ma'am,' growled Kevin. 'Whatever you say, ma'am.'

She was about to give him a sound tongue-lashing when she saw lights come up in the driveway. It must be Michele! She strutted to the doorway, oozing tip-toed frantic attention. The car halted in the driveway. It was a burly, gleaming SUV, hunter green. A wave of relief and excitement flooded through Holly's taut nerves as she recognised the slutty six-inch heels emerging from the car. The black stilettos bore their haughty owner to the door. She was carrying the kit-bag.

She was walking so slowly! Holly could have screamed. Michele was putting one foot in front of the other in a casual, uncaring strut – Holly could have choked her! How could she be doing this to her? She opened the door, holding it open for Michele. The stripper glided in like she owned the place.

Kevin stopped mopping and glanced at the newcomer with undisguised curiosity.

'Why don't you just do your job?' snarled Holly. 'This is not the theatre; not that you would even know what the theatre was ...'

'Thanks for coming.' She turned to Michele, smiling with relief. 'I'm sorry about the staff ...'

'I expect him to look.' Michele giggled. 'You like to watch?' she asked the janitor.

'I just do my job, ma'am,' answered Kevin calmly.

'So do we all,' answered Michele. 'So do we all. Trixie throws little temper tantrums sometimes, doesn't she?'

Stunned rage replaced the expression of relief on Holly's face. 'I'm not ...' she began, and Michele turned around and began to walk away, in the direction of the front door. 'I came to see *Trixie*.' She smirked.

Holly stared straight ahead for a long moment, panic etched into her face. 'OK, OK, I'm sorry, I do get temperamental sometimes.'

Michele halted with her hand on the door. 'You mean you have stupid little temper tantrums?' she asked.

'Yes, I have stupid little temper tantrums. I'm sorry,' said Holly. She sounded as if each word was drawn out of her with red-hot pincers.

'I thought your name was Holly, ma'am,' said Kevin in a guarded tone. 'I apologise if I've been calling you the wrong name.'

'It's OK,' said Holly in a near whisper. Why was Michele doing this to her? Didn't she do as she'd asked? Why was she being punished?

'Just make sure you call her by her name from now on.' Michele giggled. She tapped the kit-bag with a manicured finger. 'Let's go, Trixie.'

Holly strutted ahead to open the apartment door, already anticipating the avalanche of pleasure she was going to receive from the rubber cock in her cunt. 'Thanks for coming, Michele,' she said as the stripper waltzed in.

'Trixie, I'm thirsty,' said Michele. 'Bring me something to drink. Champagne will be fine.'

'But ...' sobbed Holly. 'Can I put it on the charger first?' The words burst from her lips.

'Trixie, I am thirsty *now*,' explained Michele patiently. 'Trixie is a petulant, selfish little girl, but she has to learn how to be a gracious hostess. I can leave if I don't feel like I'm wanted.'

Holly nodded and skipped into the kitchen, only stopping to squirm a little when she got to the refrigerator. When she opened it she saw at once that it was empty. The memory was unwelcome: of course it was empty – after all she had drunk both of the remaining bottles the other night.

'We're out of champagne,' she reported.

'You'll have to stock up, Trixie,' said Michele, shaking her head. 'I mean, how can you expect to have people over

130

when you can't even offer them a drink?' She moved into the living room.

'Yes, you are right,' said Holly, watching her retreating back. The stripper really had a great body; she envied those long legs, that great tan, those high heels ... With those heels it would be easy to arch her feet all day long.

Holly poured a glass of water and after a moment's hesitation took it over to Michele. 'Will you have a glass of water for now?'

'Why don't you ask one of your neighbours for a bottle of something nice?' asked Michele. 'You don't want to be – inhospitable, right? I mean it. If I feel like I'm not wanted I think I'll just leave.'

'I guess so,' stammered Holly. Confused, she offered the glass to Michele again. 'Will you have the glass of water while I go and ask?'

'Why not, Trixie. Ice and lemon, please.'

Holly went back to the kitchen to bring Michele her ice and a slice of lemon and went out into the hallway. She hesitated a second before knocking on Gordon's door. At least he and his wife had always been nice to her. Maybe he could ask Irene for a bottle of wine, explain to her that she had unexpected guests.

The door opened. It was Gordon. He was wearing a thick white terrycloth robe and black wide-rimmed reading glasses. In his left hand he was holding a book.

'Oh, hi,' he said, startled. He just stood there. It was obvious that he was surprised by her visit.

'Is Irene in?' asked Holly. It was hard to stand still. Unaware of how it looked, she aimlessly paced a little in front of her neighbour, rubbing her thighs together, feeling the sensation of the monstrous phallus and those prongs.

'Uh – Holly?'

'Oh, yes?' She felt herself blush. God, she must look like an absolute weirdo!

'Irene is not in tonight,' said Gordon. He looked nervous. He looked at her and swallowed. 'No, Irene is *not* in.'

Why was he repeating himself? 'Gordon, I have an unexpected guest and I don't have anything to offer her with dinner. Can I borrow a bottle of wine? I will replace it tomorrow.'

'Why, but of course. Come on in.'

He stood aside and she entered. She turned to ask him which way the kitchen was and encountered an unexpected and most unwelcome sight – Gordon was staring at her ass.

He flinched and blushed. Avoiding her gaze, he led her to the kitchen. There was a rack of wine bottles. He randomly picked one out and pressed it into her hand. 'Enjoy,' he mumbled.

She decided to pretend that all was well. 'Thank you.' She felt relieved when she got back into her own apartment.

'You look upset, Trixie.'

'I'm sorry.' Holly fidgeted. 'I borrowed a bottle of wine from the neighbour and he – he . . .' she blushed. 'I think he may have thought I was trying to flirt with him.'

'Let's see what you brought.'

Holly passed over the bottle.

Michele held it up against the light. 'So who is this neighbour?'

'His name is Gordon Parks.'

'What does he do?'

'He's a prosecutor or something,' sighed Holly. 'I don't really know. He is some sort of a government lawyer. Assistant district attorney . . .'

'I see . . . I don't drink Chardonnay, Trixie. Take it back to Mr Gordon and bring something better. Something dry and red.'

'But . . .'

'I guess I'm just not good enough to be offered a simple drink,' said Michele. 'I guess you're trying to make me feel unwelcome.'

'No, I will . . . Just wait here, please. I'll be right back.'

She pirouetted, ran back to Gordon's door and rang the doorbell. He took a while to answer. His robe was dishevelled and his glasses did not quite sit right on the ridge of his nose.

'Holly!'

She flinched. That was a man's guilty voice. What was he doing?

'Gordon, I'm sorry to bother you again. The wine . . .'

He took a deep breath. 'Would you like to come in, Holly?'

She squirmed and crossed her legs. 'I mean, I just have to have red wine. Good dry red wine. It's an important guest and I'm serving . . . veal.' She handed him the bottle of Chardonnay.

He took it. His eyes flickered. Was he looking at her breasts? 'I love veal.'

'So can I – can I have something red? I noticed you had a lot of wine.'

'I do, it just piles up. Irene doesn't drink. Feel free to pick out the one you want.'

She felt compelled to enter and hurried past him. Gordon's foyer had a marble floor. Each step caused a shockwave that travelled up her legs, hammering pinpricks of pleasure into her delirious clit.

'God, yes,' she moaned. She felt something.

Her eyes snapped open – Gordon was groping her ass! Her married neighbour was fondling her butt with both hands!

She slapped him. 'No, Gordon!'

'I'm sorry, I thought . . . I'm sorry.' He backed away and rushed into the kitchen. He reappeared a moment later with two bottles of wine. He thrust them into her hands. He kept looking down at the floor. 'I just . . .' He opened the door and held it for her.

'Thank you,' she said automatically as she left.

'Good girl!' Michele took a last sip of water and set aside the glass. She examined the bottles. 'These will do. Open them and pour me a glass of each.'

She seemed to relax completely, resting her arms on the sofa's back. Her skirt was longer than the last time Holly saw her, but when she sat it still rode up on her thighs until it revealed . . .

Holly gasped.

Michele followed her eyes and laughed. 'What is it, Trixie?'

133

Holly swallowed hard. 'Are you – are you wearing, are you wearing it?'

'Wearing what, Trixie?'

'Wearing the strap-on, Michele.'

'Why, Trixie, I *am* wearing it.'

'Can I . . . can I have the charger, please?'

'Where is Michele's wine? I know that she would really like to have a little wine.'

Holly squirmed her way to the kitchen and opened one of the bottles. She poured a glass half-full and brought it to the lounging stripper.

She sipped it and rolled it around her mouth. 'Not bad. Now the other one.'

Sobbing, Holly opened the other one and served her. After Michele had a taste she dared bring up the topic of the charger again.

'I forgot to bring it.' Michele laughed. She pulled up the hem of her skirt with both hands, parting her legs at the same time. The huge black rubber vibrator shone under the blazing lights of the chandelier. She pulled out a remote from the kit-bag and pushed the central button. The buzzing began; the prongs started to move and the bulges began their characteristic dance. 'You don't need it, Trixie, not when all you have to do is fuck the nice big cock that pretty Michele has on.'

'I'm not a lesbian,' said Holly, turning bright red in the face. She could not keep her eyes off Michele's tempting offering. 'I'm not bi either,' she sighed.

'The panties you have on, *that* doesn't make you into a lesbian,' said Michele. She stroked her big fake cock. The crimson nails were an almost shocking contrast against the black rubbery material.

'No, but if you were – if you were doing anything, you'd be having sex with me,' said Holly miserably.

'Well, you know, Trixie is bi. She is really an absolute slut, little Trixie. All she wants to do is fuck.'

'I – I can't,' sobbed Holly. 'Please don't make me . . .'

'I really don't have to make Trixie do anything. Not when she does everything on her own.' Michele giggled. Her voice assumed a tone of amused condescension. 'Tell you what ... There is a solution. I'll stay completely motionless. All you have to do is get on all fours and just push yourself on the nice vibrating cock. You can even wriggle! I promise I won't move an inch.'

'This is – insane,' mumbled Holly. 'How can you – can't I just have the charger?'

'I only have one,' said Michele. 'and I didn't bring it.' She removed her hand from the vibrator and let it hang between her legs, a perpetually stiff, shiny black rod of mind-numbing pleasure. 'Go on,' she cooed. 'Here it is, waiting for you!'

Holly peeled off the panties; the vibrator slid out of her cunt. The void inside her was not just unpleasant, it was unbearable.

'I can't!' she sobbed.

'I'm not a lesbian!' she wailed.

Holly lowered herself to the carpet. She lowered herself on to her hands and knees. 'I can't do this!'

She used her fingers to part her glistening, starving pussy lips and allow the tip of Michele's shiny buzzing cock unhindered access.

'I'll not let you fuck me,' she whimpered as she shoved herself up on the stripper's addictive, monstrous phallus.

'There's a good Trixie,' cooed Michele as the petite brunette's ass bumped up against the base of the panties. Those prongs slid right over her clit and Holly began to moan from the bottom of her lungs.

Michele laughed and lowered the dial until it was at the minimum setting.

'More, more,' cried Holly. 'Please!'

'Would you like me to fuck your wet pussy, Trixie?'

'Yes please. Yes, pwwweeease,' she begged. 'Fuck my wet pussy, pwwweeeease.'

The blonde pushed her down and began to fuck her, shoving the fake cock in and out of her eager victim's pussy. At the end of each thrust she turned the dial two-thirds of the way to the right; when she withdrew, she turned it back down to minimum.

'Please fuck me faster, Michele,' begged Holly. 'Please fuck me more, please, please.'

'What a good little fuck slut you are, Trixie. Are you a fuck slut, Trixie?'

'Yes, I am your fuck slut Michele.'

'Are you a bi fuck slut, Trixie?'

'Yes, Michele, I am a bi fuck slut – please fuck my cunt faster, please!' she sobbed, for Michele had stopped.

Smirking, Michele turned the dial two-thirds of the way to the right again and rammed it into Holly's pussy. She ran her hands over the petite brunette's body, fondling her legs, her ass and her back. 'You have a nice body,' she said to the squirming, sweat-drenched, moaning mound of orgasmic flesh that used to be Holly. 'Trixie likes it when I finger-fuck her ass while I fuck her pussy.' She added this almost as an afterthought, and inserted a manicured finger into Holly's anus.

'She likes it a lot.' Michele turned the dial all the way to the right as her finger began the degradation of Holly's previously virgin ass. 'You like that?' she asked, so innocent.

'Yes . . . Yes!' screamed Holly, gripped in the throes of multiple orgasms. It felt like they went on for hours; it felt like they went on for less than a moment. She finally collapsed on the carpet and her beloved toy slipped out just as sleep blissfully claimed her.

8

Holly

Holly halted her incessant pacing to stand on tip-toe next to the full-length mirror in the foyer. She spoke into the receiver.

'Please, come anytime. I bought some champagne and some strawberries too. On weekdays I can be home as early as five thirty.' After leaving the message she hung up, feeling rather unhappy with it. Why would Michele come over at all? It's not like she needed to come over; she had her own vibrator, she had the charger, she had the remote ... Why would she want to fuck Trixie when ...

Holly gasped and looked at her image in the mirror, mortified. Did she just call herself Trixie?

She lifted her hands and watched the tips of her fingers. They were trembling. She was really freaking out; she needed to break free of this cycle of addiction. She needed to get out of here; this apartment was choking her. It was transforming her. She had to just break out of this prison she was forging out of her own wanton lust.

'I've got to get out of here,' she muttered. 'I've got to get out. I'm Holly, I'm Holly. I'm an educated, upper-class woman of taste and distinction. *I'm Holly.*'

She peeled off the panties and stuffed them in the garbage, shuddering with unexpected revulsion. Her name was like a talisman: it gave her strength. Somehow, she knew the other one had the opposite effect: under no circumstances was she to think about it, to focus on it. 'Holly, Holly, Holly,' she chanted.

137

She grabbed a couple of her shoes – all sensible flats – a few blouses, a pair of pants and a knee-length skirt, and packed everything into a carry-on bag. The bag reminded her of the kit-bag that ... 'Holly, Holly, Holly,' she repeated, her voice firm. 'I am Holly. I am not ... I am Holly.'

She slipped out of the apartment and ran down the hallway. Holly didn't arch her feet; she made damned sure of that. She called the elevator. Running down those stairs would be a jarring experience and she did not want to engage in any jarring movements.

She walked to the front door, slouching on purpose, luxuriating in the absence of that self-imposed, absurdly feminine posture. Holly put her hand on the door, already imagining the crisp, clean air outside.

'Hello, Miss Trixie,' said Kevin. 'I mean, hi, Trixie. Miss Michele told me to just call you Trixie. She said you don't mind at all.' The janitor wore an odd little smile. 'She said if I see you down here that you're – well, in her own words, she said that little Trixie's to go right back up and put on her panties and then she's to call Miss Michele at once.'

'Call me a cab,' demanded Holly. Her voice sounded weak and shrill to her ears. Holly felt her toes curl up as she raised herself on tip-toe. She nearly swooned with pleasure. Oh, how Trixie would love to put the panties back on! Those wonderful black panties with the stiff cock in the middle, it would feel so good!

She shook her head with desperation. Holly, her name was Holly! Still, the thought of acceding to the humiliating demand of an – of an expensive whore (delivered via the agency of a black janitor!), and returning to a state of squirming, mindless masturbation – well, the idea made her wet. *It made little Trixie's slutty pussy really wet.* Her nipples grew hard underneath her blouse. 'I'm Holly,' she mumbled and leant against the cold glass of the door – it felt like freedom but the cold excited her nipples even more.

She couldn't arch her feet any more, so she thrust her ass out. What if the janitor felt up her ass? What if he just put his hand in between her legs? It would be so foul, so disgusting!

'Are you OK, Miss Trixie?'

'Stay away from me,' she said, gasping. She knew that his disgusting fingers would slip underneath her panties and slide in between her thighs; they would rub up against her pink pussy and tease her clit. He would laugh and tell her that she was one horny little bitch . . . Holly took in a shuddering deep breath. 'What – what did Michele say again?'

'What she said, exactly, well, you know, what she said was that if little Trixie showed her tight little butt down here she was to go back up, put on her pretty panties and give her a call right away.'

The humiliating command enraged her. How dare this stupid black janitor talk to her like this! She stomped her foot on the marble petulantly. If his fingers were inside her she would have leant into the disgusting caresses of his fingers. And then the janitor would tell her not to throw a hissy fit or he would spank her.

This was so unfair! Reluctantly, Holly broke away from the fantasy. But she still imagined his eyes lingering on her ass as she ran to the elevator, so she ran with extra grace to make him realise what he was missing.

She was crying while she dug through the garbage for the pleasure panties. She washed them with frantic energy, using anti-bacterial soap, and put them on while they were still dripping with water. Where were her shoes? It took another few minutes to find the heels; even those were definitely not high enough to help her keep her feet in the required arched position.

What else was she supposed to do? Oh, of course . . .

'Michele, I had to call. The janitor downstairs told me that Trixie was supposed to put on the panties and then call you right away,' she gasped. The humiliating surrender of her statement, coupled with the rubbing caused by the jarring impact of each step – and the idea of the janitor's coarse black fingers on her clean pink pussy – caused a lightning-fast but somewhat satisfying orgasm. 'Please come as soon as you can,' she sobbed, the humiliating phone call inducing another flash-like climax, nearly on top of the first one.

She greeted the doorbell with exuberant joy, strutting to open it. She had two visitors, not one! And Michele had her kit-bag! She recognised the other woman with the bleached-blonde hair and gigantic breasts at once. 'Becky!' She smiled.

'And you must be Trixie!' Becky giggled. Her breasts jiggled in the confines of her leopard-print top. 'We're gonna have so much fun!'

'Trixie, why did you try to run away?' purred Michele. She was wearing silver platform sandals and a very short silver dress. The bottom half-moons of her ass actually showed.

'I . . .' She found it hard to answer. She felt – unclean. So unclean it made her dizzy. What were these people doing here? 'I don't feel good,' she mumbled.

'Don't you worry, Trixie,' purred Michele, smiling. 'How pretty you are! Pretty girl! Go on now, go inside and take off all these silly clothes!'

Holly was drenched with anticipation. Barely able to stop herself from making a beeline for the edge of the easy chair, she sobbed, 'I – I don't know . . .' She leant against the wall, feeling weak.

'Trixie, wanna play with me first?' cooed Becky. She was holding the wonderful black rubber cock in her hand. 'This one is not like the others. It's like – this one is special!' She moved her hand to reveal the entire device. 'Look, there are two of them!' Sure enough, there were two vibrators attached in the middle to one another. 'We can both have fun at the same time!'

'I don't know,' said Holly, looking at the toy with an equal mix of anticipation and dread.

'We can fuck each other with the same cock,' explained Becky. She licked her lips. 'You're very pretty, Trixie.' The bleached-blonde stripper ran her hand over Holly's arm.

'Take off your top, Trixie,' purred Michele. 'Bimbo Becky wants to play with your little titties.'

'I'm not a lesbian,' said Holly weakly.

'Of course not,' said Michele. 'Just because Becky plays with your little titties doesn't make you a lesbian, Trixie. After all, you'll have a big cock up your pussy. A lesbian doesn't like big cocks, isn't that right?'

That certainly seemed to make sense. 'A lesbian doesn't like big cocks,' she said in a near whisper.

Becky lovingly caressed the tip of the big double vibrator.

'There are maybe three of these in the entire world. You've got to know the right people to get one,' said Michele.

Becky put her pink lips around one end of the black rubber and sucked it into her mouth. 'I like to make it nice and shiny before I put it in.' She giggled. 'Trixie, put it in your mouth and suck on it.'

'Maybe Trixie doesn't want to take off the panties she has on now.' Michele smirked cruelly. 'But look what I have for you, Trixie!' In her hand she brandished a piece of hefty anodised metal with two gold leads and an electric cord.

Oh my God! The charger! Maybe Michele could be persuaded to part with it. 'Thank you, Michele!' sobbed Holly. With the charger maybe she wouldn't have to humiliate herself by bending over and getting fucked from behind with the strap-on version ... The image flashed through her mind and centred itself on her clit.

'Oh God,' she gasped. Using frantic, jerky hand movements she peeled off the panties. Without them the yawning void in between her legs grew into an overwhelming yearning that simply had to be satisfied. She turned to Becky and her offering. 'Why are you doing this to me?' she asked pathetically.

'Just lie down, Trixie,' said Michele. 'Just lie down and have fun with bimbo Becky.'

'I don't want to,' she said, her lips curling down in shame; as a matter of fact she did want to, more than anything in the world; she just did not want to say it out loud.

'Of course not,' cooed Michele. 'I mean, it's not like I don't know that you didn't really have a choice, Trixie. Not with the two of us – overpowering you ...'

Taking turns, they stripped her clothes off. When her sobbing grew too great for them to continue, one or the other stroked her now exposed, naked flesh, rubbing it in a steady stream of calculated, manipulative caresses.

'I tried to resist,' sobbed Holly, weakly flailing against the hands that stripped and fondled her. Michele tore off the last cumbersome button of her expensive, conservative shirt, baring her perky B-cups to Becky's greedy fingers.

'Yes, you're so virtuous.' Michele smirked, caressing Holly's ass. 'You can't really be blamed for being forced to beg for some dirty lesbian licking. I mean, Trixie is such a bimbo slut, isn't she, Becky?'

'Mmm, she sure is. I *like* Trixie.'

'Good. Do you like Becky, Trixie?'

Holly lifted her eyes and inspected the bleached blonde. 'She is very pretty,' she admitted. Comparing the colossal mounds against her own breasts, she was forced to add, not entirely without a trace of envy, 'Her chest is so big!'

'Little Trixie doesn't have big titties,' said Michele, shaking her head. 'It's a terrible shame, isn't it?' She began to fumble around with something in the kit-bag.

'You know, you should get big titties, Trixie!' Becky giggled, pushing her tits against Holly's. Her nipples pressed against Holly's flesh.

'Yes, Trixie, you should get bigger boobs – but there is really no point in getting bigger boobs unless you're willing to show them off.' Michele's finger began to tweak and tease Holly's clit. 'Isn't that right, Trixie?'

'I don't know,' gasped Holly, closing her eyes. Michele's touch felt like chocolate. 'Yeah, I guess – right . . .' She began to squirm harder in response to the fingering. She was almost there!

But the pervasive debasement unfortunately came to a halt. Holly's eyes snapped open and blinked in the strong glare of the chandelier.

Michele sat on the couch and motioned towards the spare bedroom. 'Becky, go through the closet and the drawers and throw her stupid clothes on the floor. I want to see everything.'

'You can't do that! How dare you!' The words escaped

her lips before Holly's eyes had finally readjusted to the light; she turned to address Michele as soon as she could see clearly, but the planned continuation of her righteous rage remained unspoken. The stripper was wearing the strap-on panties. A low-level buzzing sound permeated Holly's addled consciousness.

'Why're you doing this?' sobbed Holly. 'Please leave!' Her demand was in truth the last thing she wanted; it was revealed as such at once. She bent over, eagerly parting her pussy lips to allow the obscene device immediate access.

The couch where Michele lounged faced the hallway, allowing her to see the spare room and her clothes; she watched as Becky rampaged through her neatly folded wardrobe. The bleached-blonde stripper grabbed piles of muted beige, grey and off-white shirts and tossed them on the floor. She blithely walked over them in her high heels; one stiletto caught in one of her expensive cashmere turtlenecks (white with grey stripes) and tore the fabric.

'No,' whimpered Holly. 'She has to stop, she has to!' She squirmed harder, shoving herself higher on the big strap-on.

'I suppose you'll just have to stop her. I mean, all you have to do is just tap her on the shoulder and Becky'll stop.' Michele laughed. She pulled the set of anal beads from the kit-bag and began to insert them into Holly's anus, one at a time. Every time she pushed one in she gave Holly a jolt of mindless pleasure with a humiliating click of the remote.

'Go on, get moving,' Michele urged. 'Just slide off my big stiff cock – and tell her to stop.'

Becky picked up a pair of Holly's favourite panties and shook her head with obvious distaste. 'I haven't found a single thing for Trixie to wear,' she yelled out. She tossed the panties in the pile on the floor and threw a designer dress (a conservative original piece Holly was desperately proud of owning) in a crumpled heap on the floor.

Holly moaned in desperation. She crawled in Becky's direction until she felt the fat head of the vibrator at the very edge of her pussy lips. If she moved another quarter of an inch the device would slip out of her entirely. Bitterly crying, Holly stopped.

143

'Oh, Trixie, don't you want to stop Becky from trashing all those nice, conservative outfits?' Michele giggled. 'If you don't do something about it I'll just assume you want the bimbo stripper with the strap-on to fuck little Trixie's pussy, mmm?'

'I . . . I . . .' Tears streamed down her face. She should move, she thought. Yes, definitely – she should move and stop Becky.

Michele gave Holly's ass a condescending slap and began to fuck her in earnest, thrusting the strap-on into her quivering, helpless cunt. 'Yes, Trixie, we're just going to have to go shopping!' She petted the sobbing, orgasming girl on the head, forcing the largest of the anal beads into her ass at the exact apex of her climax. As Holly came Michele scratched her behind the ear. 'Bring all your credit cards, you hear?'

'Oh, Miss Childress, it's so nice to see you again.' Trish smiled. 'I've been her personal consultant for several weeks now,' she informed the two women (embarrassing, distant cousins?) who accompanied the client.

'She has exceptional taste.' These other – women – who accompanied the client, wore revealing, cheap outfits; definitely *unrefined* clothing. One of them actually carried a remote control in her hand as if she had just come from watching her soaps on the couch of her trailer! It was preposterous, all too obvious that they never had the benefit of – or been able to afford – a personal shopping consultant.

'Trixie is working on a new image.' The tanned blonde giggled. 'She would like to show off her figure a touch more – she wants more revealing clothes. Hot pink, for starters.'

'Trixie? I'm sorry, I thought . . .'

The client squirmed and crossed her legs. 'Trixie,' she practically moaned. 'It's Trixie, OK?' She squirmed some more, gasping for breath. The tanned blonde giggled with amusement.

'Uhm – yes – Trixie,' said Trish with distaste. 'Hot pink –'

'Money is no object, right, Trixie?' The woman with the stiletto heels smirked. 'No object at all.'

'Really?' Trish gaped. Maybe these women were just – eccentric!

'Yes. We also want some nice, pretty things. Trixie would like to treat us to some pretty things, right, little Trixie?'

'Oh my God, oh my God, ohmygod, ohmygod I'm c–'

The tanned blonde flicked a switch on the remote and put it into her gold sequinned handbag (a designer knock-off). She offered her hand to Trish. 'My name is Michele.'

The client (Trixie or Holly, Trish was confused) suddenly looked severely distraught. She tugged on Michele's lace top. 'Please turn it back on, plea–'

'I warned you not to talk unless I asked you a question, Trixie,' said Michele. 'Now just be a good girl and come along, you hear?'

Trish shook Michele's hand. 'Nice to meet you, Michele.'

'Trixie wants to make sure she is attractive to the men around her,' said Michele. 'Like Becky here.'

Trish glanced at the obvious stripper with the big fake tits. 'Oh. I see.'

'Yes. Let's start with some nice push-up bras, and then we'll move on to shoes. You won't have to arch your feet all the time; won't that be nice, Trixie?' Michele put her hand inside her cheap purse and the client began to nod her head up and down in an anxious parody of agreement. 'Yes, Michele,' she gasped. 'Trixie needs some high-heeled whore shoes.'

'Good girl! Now we mustn't forget the makeup counter either. After all, Trixie barely has a touch of lipstick to her name!'

The client had hitherto refused Trish's numerous attempts to cajole her into cosmetics purchases; Trish smiled broadly and offered her arm to Michele. 'Please, let me escort you!'

After a long and lucrative stop at the lingerie department, they went to Ladies Formal and Ladies Business Wear.

'This looks boring!' Becky pouted. She picked up a sedate green sweater and dropped it in a crumpled heap on the display unit. She stomped her platform heels, exasperated. Her breasts shook; an old man escorting his wife stared at her giant mounds, mouth agape, until his wife dragged him away.

'Don't you have a department with, you know, *hotter* clothes? I mean, it's not like Trixie wants to look thirty!' Conspiratorially she leant closer to Trish, although she did not bother to lower her voice. 'Trixie wants some really hot, slutty clothes she can – you know, she can look good in, if you know what I mean.'

'Well ... We do have the Young Casuals Department,' hazarded Trish. 'It's normally not – I mean, it's not really business wear ...'

'Trixie doesn't need business wear.' Michele laughed. 'Trixie wants to show off her tits, not sign stupid, boring papers!' She put her hand in the little purse. 'Isn't that right, Trixie?'

'Yes! Yes! I'd like to show off my tits,' moaned Holly, gently swaying in place. 'Trish, just please help Michele ... OK?'

'Of course, Miss Childress.'

'Trixie doesn't insist on formality, Trish. All this Miss Childress and stuff ... Just call her Trixie. Little Trixie will be OK too.'

'OK, little Trixie.' Trish chuckled. 'Let's find some really hot little outfits so you can show off your boobies, hmmm?' It was really easy to slip into Michele's way of speaking about the client; Holly (Trixie, she corrected herself) definitely did not seem to mind.

'This little top is darling,' said Michele, giggling. 'I really love what it does to Trixie's tits, don't you, Becky?'

'Yeah, it's great. Just imagine the whole outfit, with the shoes and everything!'

'It's not perfect, you know ...' said Michele, critically examining the pink top with the little white heart, just below the enormous, deep slit of cleavage. 'I know!' she exclaimed brightly. 'We need it in extra small!'

146

'But – but it's a small already,' sobbed Holly. In the tight pink top, her breasts in the new push-up bra looked – well, not enormous, but definitely sizeable.

Trish looked at Michele – was she going to take lip from little Trixie?

'Becky wears a small, Trixie,' explained Michele as if she were talking to a wayward child. 'And she is a double D. Isn't that right, Becky?'

'I don't know.' Becky giggled. She put her hands over her enormous tits. 'I think they could be even bigger than double Ds!'

'Once you get tits like Becky's you can wear a small,' cooed Michele. 'Now, Trish, why don't you bring Trixie some extra small tops? Bring Becky a couple of them too, in a small – and bring me that darling little coat with the glitter I see over there.'

'Right away, Michele.' Trish smiled.

'But I don't have the mone–' The client (little Trixie) shuddered. 'Oh God, yes, yes, thank you . . .' she gasped.

'Credit cards are wonderful, aren't they, Trixie?' Michele herded Trixie into a changing room with the pile of fuzzy, lace-adorned and polyester outfits they'd already collected, only stopping by a rack of miniskirts. 'A couple of these, I think.' She picked up a few of the shortest ones (two of them advertised the wearer as being SEXY in large, glittering letters) and entered the booth with her, giggling.

Once inside the booth, Michele took the remote out and slid it in between Holly's legs. 'Trixie loves to shop, doesn't she?' She laughed. 'Trixie likes to show off her titties and her nice tight ass, isn't that right?'

'Why're you doing this to me?' sobbed Holly. 'I'm not like Becky or you, I'm . . .'

'Would you like to go back to wearing those drab ugly things?' Michele turned off the vibrator. 'Or would you rather put on this pretty little miniskirt!' She pushed some of the buttons in a random combination with savage, gloating cruelty.

'Oh, oh, oh . . .' Holly sank to the carpet, a shuddering, moaning pile of orgasming femininity. 'OK, I guess I can try it on,' she whispered after coming. 'I guess I can try it on,' she repeated without being aware of it.

'Good Trixie!' Michele smirked, dressing her like a doll. The miniskirt was so short that the shiny black of the pleasure panties was clearly visible by anyone who tried to take a look. 'It looks just darling with the new top and the push-up bra!'

'Thank you,' said Holly. She already wore the highest heels the store had – sexy, five inch stilettos, metallic red. In fact, they all were; Michele and Becky had both fallen in love with the absurdly expensive Italian shoes.

The cheap, hot-pink colour of the mini and the top clashed with the metallic red of the shoes, but somehow the lack of colour co-ordination made the overall effect even sleazier. Holly looked at her reflection in the mirror. 'I look like a slut,' she sobbed.

'Trixie *is* a slut,' said Michele. She put her hand on Holly's now practically exposed breasts and began to tweak her nipples.

Holly tried to push her hands off.

'Trixie gets the anal beads if she just plays nice,' said the stripper, laughing, and Holly stopped her useless flailing.

'The beads – that feels good,' she mumbled.

'Yes, it does!' cooed Michele. 'Anyway, you'll slowly get to like it, getting felt up. After all, Trixie loves getting felt up; it makes her pussy wet.'

'My pussy *is* wet,' whimpered Holly.

'That's because you're a slut, Trixie. Don't you worry, now, you won't have to wear those ugly drab things again. Won't that be nice?'

'I'm coming again, I'm coming, I'm com–'

'No, not yet,' said Michele, smirking as she turned off the device. 'Now you get a nice makeover! And then it's time to buy some more lingerie! I mean, you have to borrow panties, for God's sake . . .'

Trish hurried up to them as they exited the booth. She gaped at the woman who stumbled out after the tall blonde. The woman bore little resemblance to the uppity CPA who had come to shop here a few weeks ago; this incarnation wore red stiletto heels, a hot-pink miniskirt, a push-up bra, a tiny halter top that displayed her attenuated charms to their full advantage, and not much else. It did not take much effort to call her Trixie.

She coughed politely. 'Trixie, your card – it was declined.'

'You should get your limit raised,' said Michele. 'Give Trish another card right away.'

Holly trembled with a strange mixture of self-loathing and lust. 'We bought a lot of things . . .'

'Oooh, look at this!' cooed Becky. She was holding a little jacket, extremely short, with huge gold buttons. 'I bet this would look great on me! I wouldn't even need a top underneath!'

Michele rifled through Holly's new purse (pink polyester to match her new top and mini) and handed over Holly's remaining credit card (the platinum one). 'Becky'll have that – what is that – jacket? Yes, she'll have the jacket. Now let's go down to makeup. Trixie wants to slut herself up.'

'With your complexion, I definitely wouldn't go with that shade of pink,' said the saleswoman. She looked scandalised. 'In fact, I wouldn't go with pink at all. A muted red, perhaps, or something in . . .'

'Trixie definitely wants something in pink,' said Michele with authority. 'She doesn't have any makeup at all – we'll get everything today. But if it's not pink or . . .' Michele picked up an eyeliner and frowned. 'All right, eyeshadow can be blue, I suppose; anyway, everything else must be pink or it's a deal breaker.'

The saleswoman stopped protesting. 'Well, there is a colour you might like,' she said tentatively, picking up a nearly glowing shade of hot pink. 'It's new and it's a little more expensive than the others, but you'll find that . . .'

'Let's try it on,' said Michele.

The colour matched the miniskirt (although not the top, not exactly). Holly's lips looked shockingly pink against her complexion. 'Very nice.' Becky giggled. 'Those are some *nice* lips, Trixie. I bet you'll get some attention from men with those pretty pink lips.'

'We'll take it. Let's move on to some others,' said Michele.

They followed the same procedure with mascara, eye-liner, eyeshadow – everything she now needed. By the time they had finished with the counter she was fully made up, painted and scented, a pink, decorative toy strutting around on glorified red stilts.

Trish promised to get their bags delivered to the apartment tonight; without the delivery service they never would have been able to get all the stuff home.

'We're not done yet.' Becky beamed. 'Now comes my favourite part!'

'Yes, Trixie.' Michele ruffled her hair. 'Now we go to the salon!'

'My hair?' asked Holly. Her voice sounded very far away to her. 'What's wrong with my hair?'

'Everything,' answered Becky and Michele in unison. They broke out in laughter.

Michele petted her head. 'Don't you worry your pretty little head about it!'

'Blondes have more fun!' whispered Michele in her ear. 'Look at Becky! She has fun all the time!'

Holly glanced over at the large-breasted blonde. The stripper was giggling and swaying to the music coming from the overhead speakers. When she saw Holly's eyes on her she twirled a long bleached-blonde lock around one finger.

'I don't know,' Holly ventured, hesitating. 'Maybe a few highlights at most. Nobody would take me seriously at work if I came in with hair like hers.'

'But Trixie,' cooed Michele, 'don't you want to be pretty like Becky?' She began to play with Holly's hair. 'It's so drab and brown . . . Isn't it just ugly, Janice?'

The hair dresser – a girl in her early twenties – was chewing gum. She nodded, obviously bored. 'Yeah, it's like, you know, she looks dull. I could make her look pretty hot, you know.'

'Her name is Trixie,' Michele informed her.

'Uhm – she doesn't look like a Trixie.' The girl looked

Holly up and down, taking in the push-up bra, the *ultra-tight* pink *halter* top, the miniskirt and the metallic-red heels. 'But she dresses like a Trixie,' she admitted grudgingly.

'That's why we're here,' said Michele. 'Trixie here really likes the way Becky gets all kinds of attention. Don't you, Trixie?' Laughing, she trained the remote on Holly's pussy and turned the dial halfway to the right. 'Answer me, Trixie!'

'God, Michele, yes, yes, she is so hot,' moaned Holly. She shuddered with waves of pleasure. Her eyes roved over Becky's curves and the long curly strands of bleached-blonde hair.

'OK.' Janice shrugged. 'Just sit there, Trixie, and let me do my job, like, today, OK?'

Holly squirmed her way into the seat indicated and closed her eyes, only to feel fingers on her scalp and different fingers, those magic, electric fingers, massaging her clit and casting spells within her drenched pussy. She climaxed several times before her eyes drooped shut and her head lolled forwards.

'Oooh, Trixie, you look so fuckable!' Becky giggled and licked her lips. 'You look sooo hot! Ooh la la, baby!'

'What's happening? What happened?' said Holly, not quite sure about her location. Where was she? Her eyes focused on the tawdry slut sitting in front of her. She wore heavy makeup with a lot of blue eyeshadow, hot pink lipstick, mascara and very long fake eyelashes. Her hair was a cascading sensual tangle of platinum-blonde curls. She wore the skankiest hot-pink top Holly had ever seen and a matching – no, not quite matching – miniskirt. In fact, it was so short that she could see that the woman was wearing shiny black panties . . .

'Oh my God!' she gasped, seeing the painted lips of the woman in front of her repeat the words. 'What – what have you done to me?' She reached out towards the mirror with her hand, seeing her image mimic the gesture. Her new, long, fake, pink fingernails finally touched glass. 'I can't go to work like this!' she said in a sudden panic. 'I'll be fired!'

'We can't have you not working now, can we?' Michele smirked. She was standing behind Holly, admiring her new look. The stripper lowered the remote until it came right up against Holly's panties. She pressed the button and laughed as her new plaything began to moan and squirm. 'After all, Trixie is a high-maintenance girl. Trixie likes to shop for her new best friends. Isn't that right, Becky?'

'Yeah, it's so nice you bought us all this stuff!' cooed Becky. 'I mean, it's great!'

'I can't go to work like this,' sobbed Holly. 'I mean, I look like an absolute – you know.'

'Trixie doesn't like all that dull work in some stuffy office when she can strut her stuff in the clubs,' said Michele.

'But I have to finish my project,' moaned Holly, bucking and thrusting her hips. 'I've got to get my briefcase from work; I can finish it at home and email it in. I can say I'm sick.'

'I'll get it for you,' cooed Michele. 'I'm so nice!'

'You – you can't, you don't ... I mean, you wouldn't look like you fit – there, Michele,' whimpered Holly, her panicked soul locked in a mortal struggle with the filthy waves of pleasure erupting between her legs. 'You don't look very – corporate – oh my God – you know.'

Michele petted her on the head while thumbing the remote. 'You're so right, Trixie! That's why we have some more shopping to do!'

'You know; conservative business clothes. Very classy stuff.' Michele smiled.

'But I thought she wanted this new look?' asked Trish, confused. Obviously she was not seeing something. The client had successfully transformed herself from a conservative, upper-class executive into a trashy slut; was she now turning herself back into a conservative business-woman? Of course Trish was entirely in favour of switching back and forth, as long as she got her commission.

'Conservative, classy – but not for Trixie. I mean, just look at her!' She stroked Holly's face with a single finger, making her moan softly. For some reason she kept pressing buttons on that remote control. 'Nobody would take Trixie seriously in a business suit.' She laughed.

152

Trish glanced over at the cli– at Trixie. Her eyes were slightly out of focus but she looked happy. Trixie appeared entirely consumed by the act of manically agreeing with the tanned blonde's assertions. She was gasping for breath. 'God, yes! Yes, Michele!'

The woman was practically moaning!

'Well, sure, Michele. Would this be a new client? I am fairly booked, or . . .'

'Not exactly, Trish.' Michele put her hand over Trish's, smiling. 'It's for me! Isn't that wonderful? I mean, it's not like Trixie can go to some stuffy office with her tits popping out of her top.'

'Well, sure, Michele. All I need is a major credit card and . . .'

'Oh no, Trish.' The stripper laughed. 'I don't have to have my own account; we will just have a grand old time shopping with my girlfriend Trixie.' She petted the head of the strutting bit of slutty femininity swaying aimlessly on her right side. 'Isn't that right, Trixie darling?'

'Yesss,' said Trixie. She closed her eyes and leant against the wall. 'Oh God, yessss . . .'

Trish averted her eyes from the obviously unbalanced young woman. Her earlier assessment concerning her social class had obviously been mistaken. 'Absolutely, Michele!' She smiled brightly. Business suits – designer ones – were many times more expensive than the outfits sold in Young Casuals. Why, if only she could sell this woman two suits her commission for the day would . . . She performed a quick calculation in her head. 'You have a wonderful figure, Michele,' she gushed. 'I know just the suit that would go perfectly well with your body type. You do have the perfect body, by the way. Now this suit, it's a touch pricy, but . . .'

'Michele likes expensive things.' Becky giggled. 'Me too!' she pouted. 'I want to have suits too!'

'Oh Becky, how would you fit your hooters into a business suit?' Michele smirked.

Trish halted in mid-stride; could it be? These women could make her a small fortune! 'It's not difficult to alter some of the designs,' she said diplomatically. 'I'm sure we can arrange it.'

'Oooh, Michele!' squealed Becky, jumping up and down with excitement. Her enormous breasts jiggled up and down; the men who had not yet been staring acquired an immediate interest in the attractive threesome.

'But I ...' sobbed Trixie, looking dejected. 'I can't afford this!'

'Becky, why don't you play with Trixie a little bit while Trish helps me pick out a couple of new suits,' commanded Michele. She handed something to the other woman, who cooed with delight – it was the remote control. The bleached-blonde woman immediately began to push a couple of the buttons.

Trish looked at Trixie – after all, this was her account, her credit card – but the client – Trixie, she corrected herself – said nothing. She just stood there with her mouth open, squirming in place. Oh well – it was money in her pocket.

They went over to the department for business attire. Their entrance was tracked by incredulous eyes. Somebody recognised the sleazy bimbo in the stiletto heels.

'Ma'am?'

The four of them turned as one to look at a young woman carrying a pile of beige and white sweaters and ankle-length skirts.

'Miss Childress?' The woman's voice was an odd mix of stunned surprise, fear and condescension.

'Betty?' Holly – Trixie – looked blearily up at the girl, her eyes only half focusing.

'You know Trixie?' asked Michele.

'Ms Childress . . . She's my boss,' said Betty.

'What are you doing, Betty?'

She lifted her pile. 'I have to go and buy all these clothes for work. Ms Childress told me I didn't dress conservatively enough.'

Michele smiled. 'You look just about her size. There are all these clothes back at her apartment – she won't need them any more.'

9

James

'What have I done?' James groaned and leant against the counter. He rummaged through the cupboard until he had found a pack of Lucille's stashed cigarettes. He lit one.

'I thought you didn't smoke,' said Robert, sounding nearly as perturbed as James.

'Oh, Robert,' said James, taking a deep drag of the cigarette. 'I can't believe I've done what I've done. I mean, I cheated on Lucille!'

'You didn't *fuck* Becky.' Robert sighed. He looked wistful for a moment. 'You told me so.'

'No, technically – I guess I didn't, but . . .'

'So don't worry about it. It's not like Lucille will ever know.'

'I guess not.' James did not sound too sure of himself.

'James, promise me you won't fall to pieces when Lucille comes back. If you tell her what happened, it won't be just *your* relationship that falls apart.'

'I guess that's true. But I still feel guilty.'

Robert nervously raked his hands through his hair. He glanced in the direction of the front door. 'James, let's get out of here.'

'What are you talking about? We just got back. I have to go to work tomorrow. Lucille should be coming back from the mall any minute.'

'Exactly. Exactly my point. If she comes back you'll fall to pieces and confess. You'll tell her Becky gave you head or something.'

'She didn't give me head, Robert,' snapped James. No, *she* definitely hadn't given *him* head. Still, the idea of

155

getting head, the idea of those hot pink lips wrapped around his cock – well, the idea evoked yet another image and he didn't need any more of them on his mind. 'It wasn't like that at all.'

'OK, she didn't give you head – fine, whatever. I still think you should call Lucille and tell her an unexpected business meeting – or something – has come up and you need to get out of town for a few days. She'll understand.' Robert seemed to search for the right phrase. 'She is very supportive of your career.'

'You want me to lie to her?'

'Look, I assume you don't want her to call off the wedding, right? Not because of some slutty stripper who shoved her ass in your face for a few bucks.'

James swallowed and nervously licked his lips. 'Well, no, of course not. I don't want her to call off the wedding.'

'So give yourself a chance to calm down. Let's go somewhere for a few days and try to relax.'

'I can't leave town, though,' said James. 'I have some important meetings; I can't actually go away.'

'Does Lucille ever come to the office to visit?'

James pondered the question for a few seconds. 'Well, now that you mention it, no. She never came by, not once. She does ask a lot of questions about things like the annual bonus and what office I have ... And she made me give her a bunch of my business cards.'

'Then don't worry about it. Just tell her you have to leave and – it's Lucille we're talking about – tell her to go shopping.'

'Jesus, that's a good idea, Robert. She won't have any time to think about anything else. She loves shopping.'

'Good. Do you want me to call? Will you be OK when you talk to her?'

'Yeah, I think so.' In fact James did not think so. He thought there was a roughly 50-50 chance that he would mumble about like a terrified mouse until the truth came stumbling out. Still, there was not much else he could do.

He called and she picked up. Her voice filled the bay of silence like an incoming tide.

'Darling, I really don't have time to talk right now, I have an appointment with the curtains woman, she is ...'

156

James let Lucille's monologue wash over him. When the words finally ceased (it took a while) he spoke his carefully worded piece, two sentences combined into a single, quick burst. 'Darling, I have to go out of town for a few days; it's a business meeting, very important. I thought you could do some shopping for the living room.'

She responded immediately. 'But you insisted on having – how did you put it? – *input* on the living room.'

'I would, I did, I know, normally, but since I have to go out of town . . .' said James nervously. 'Just charge it; I will leave a credit card on the desk.'

'It's so nice of you to trust me with the living room, darling,' gushed Lucille. 'I will make sure it's something you can live with, honey.'

'Thanks, baby,' said James. 'I have to go, OK?'

'What do you think of a soft blue?'

'I'm sorry?'

'A soft blue. What do you think?'

James closed his eyes. Was Lucille even paying attention? 'Sure, sure: soft blue.'

'Bring me a present, darling!'

'Yeah, sure thing, honey.'

'The curtains woman is back. Must run! Love you, honey! Make sure you're back by Wednesday, we have dinner reservations.'

'I love you too.' James hung up. 'That went easier than expected,' he said slowly. He wiped the dewy beads of perspiration from his forehead. The few minutes of conversation with Lucille had wrung him out completely.

'Told you. Just wave a credit card in her face.' Robert laughed.

'Robert, come on – she is not like that.'

'No. Of course not. I mean – she is a touch materialistic, though, don't you think?'

'Yes, I suppose so. She is special, you know.'

'Yes, of course.'

James sighed. 'Well, I called . . . Where are we going now? I can't stay here now that I have a so-called out-of-town business meeting.' He raised his hands. 'And don't tell me to go back to your place. I don't want to go back to your place. It reminds me of the party. I feel dirty just thinking about it.'

'Oh, come on, James. It's not like you hated every minute of it.'

James blushed. 'That's exactly it, Robert. I didn't.'

Robert called Scott on his cell phone. James couldn't hear Scott but he could fill in the blanks.

'Where did you guys go? We came out and you weren't anywhere . . .'

'Oh no, you know we wouldn't . . .'

'Yes, of course we had a good time. I just hope you guys weren't pissed or anything, I mean it was meant to be a party.'

'Yes, I know it was meant for James.'

Robert winked at him. 'He did have a good time, he told me so, just a minute ago. He's a bit freaked about Lucille's reaction . . .'

Robert listened for a moment. 'That might be a good idea.'

He put down the phone. 'Scott thinks we ought to go somewhere where you and I can calm down without the women bothering us.'

'What did he suggest?'

'Let's just get some hotel rooms somewhere downtown. We can both go to work. I don't have to call Holly, thank God.'

James considered the idea. It definitely had some positive aspects. He did not feel ready to face Lucille; that was a fact. 'You know, that may be a good idea.'

'Any hotel you want?'

'Not really. Just some all-right place downtown.'

'Scott said Jefferson Suites is cheap and it's close to the hospital. Once we find rooms let's go and walk around. I think we could both use some fresh air. Get something to eat too. I'm starving.'

'I suppose so,' muttered James. 'I'll pack an overnight bag and we can go. Do you need anything?'

'I guess I should go home and get some clothes,' said Robert. He considered James's pale countenance, and James was all too aware of what he saw: the trembling lips, the unfocused eyes. 'But you know, I just don't feel like it. I don't really want to leave you alone, not now. Truth be told, you look a bit out of it.'

James nodded begrudgingly. 'There is a clothes shop on the corner near where I work. I guess you can get some basics there.'

'Good idea. Let's go there later. We eat first, find some hotel rooms and then buy some clothes. It'll be like a road trip in college.'

'Yeah.'

James threw some clothes in an overnight bag and they drove downtown.

'What do you know,' chuckled Robert. 'It's the club.' Hot Summer's loomed on the left side of the street. 'Look at the sign! Becky is working.' His voice became alarmed. 'Watch it! Watch it, man, you nearly hit that car!'

'Sorry,' mumbled James. They were at the address that Scott had given them in any case. 'I don't want to drive any more,' he said, exhausted. 'Just let's get some rooms. This is the place, anyway.'

'Oh yes, Jefferson Suites.' Robert examined the place from the bottom up. 'It looks like a dive,' he declared, laughing. 'But all right. We can stay here if you like.' He glanced over at the club at the same time James did.

'It's just for a night or two. We'll talk, order some room service. It's not like we're going anywhere close to that place.'

'We don't even know if they have any vacancies here.'

'Sure they do. I saw the sign. VACANCY, it said.'

'Isn't that supposed to be VACANCIES? or ROOMS TO LET?'

'I'm sure they didn't hire some English major to write up the signs.'

The hotel was seedy. The lobby reminded James of a late-70s sitcom. He could practically hear the laugh track. A greasy-haired old woman sat behind the counter. She was watching TV and drinking a coke. When she saw the two men come in she looked up without any obvious sign of interest, then unreeled words in a mindless monotone. 'What can I do for you gentlemen.'

'Uhm – two rooms, I guess, if you have them,' said James, already regretting the move.

159

'Major credit card please.'

James handed one over.

She ran the card while they filled out the paperwork. After James had signed, she passed them two heavy wooden slabs with their room numbers burnt on to them. The keys were anchored to the slabs at the end of thin steel chains.

James stared at the absurd design and shook his head. 'Wow. That could be used as a weapon.' He chuckled. His eyes scanned the wall behind the woman – all the keys seemed to be there. Could they be the only guests?

The woman did not share his amusement. She just stared at them like a gargoyle. 'Check-out is at noon,' she said after a brief pause. 'Two nights, right?'

'Yes, two nights at most,' said James.

She nodded and lit a cigarette. Pushing aside a large NO SMOKING sign with the ashtray, she turned back to her tiny television.

They walked to the elevator and took the rickety contraption up to the third floor. James's room was number 319, Robert's 323.

'I feel exhausted,' said James. 'This whole party ... I mean, I don't want you to think that I'm ungrateful or anything, but those strippers were just ...'

'Yeah,' sighed Robert wistfully.

James plunged on, not quite sure where he was going with it. 'I mean, they were very attractive ...'

'They weren't attractive,' Robert interrupted, laughing. 'They were sexy.'

'Yeah. They were that,' admitted James. 'You know, I've never cheated on Lucille. Not even with Pamela – you remember Pamela.'

'Hard to forget,' said Robert. 'I still can't believe Lucille made you fire your own secretary.'

'I was not exactly – *not* tempted, if you remember.'

'I remember. Here we are.' Robert stopped in front of 319. 'This is your room. Why don't you drop off your bag and come over to my room. We'll order room service and eat together.'

'Sounds good.' James held the huge wooden slab in his

left hand while operating the key with his right. The door opened to reveal the tackiest hotel room in existence. James just stared and stared some more – he'd had no idea such places still existed.

The room was dripping in pink and red synthetic taffeta. Even the bedding was an amalgamation of the two colours. No natural wood graced the space anywhere. Everything was white plastic or gleaming metal except for the overwhelming silky sheen of red and pink polyester. 'Good Lord,' gasped James. He plopped down on the bed, only to spring up at once. The soft sloshing sound under his posterior could only mean one thing.

He laughed and tossed his bag in a scarlet love seat. He walked over to 323. 'I have a waterbed,' he reported as soon as Robert let him in.

'I know – place is pretty slick, huh?'

Robert's room was essentially a twin of James's. 'I'm starving,' said Robert as he rummaged through the taffeta jungle for the menu.

James found it first and stared at it. It was the same stare mice give snakes after being placed in the reptile house. 'You're not going to believe this,' he said, passing it over.

Robert read it out loud: 'Catering by Hot Summer's?'

James groaned and sat on the edge of Robert's waterbed, shuddering a little as the sloshing sound kept on going for a few seconds. 'That place is everywhere.'

'Prices are not bad at all,' said Robert. 'They are really cheap, actually, if you do carry-out.'

'Are you kidding me?'

'We can call, pick up the food, and come right back. It's not like we're children.'

'I suppose so,' said James. He was not happy.

'You don't even have to go in,' said Robert. 'I'll go and get the food myself.'

'Why don't we go somewhere else? It's not like it's the only restaurant in town.'

'That's true,' admitted Robert. 'We could go somewhere else. This is so stupid, though. We're grown men. Why are we afraid of going into a silly strip club? I mean, are we that afraid of Lucille and Holly? As far as Holly . . . If she

161

even knew I was within a mile of a place like Hot Summer's she would be apoplectic with rage.'

'She's nearly as conservative as Lucille,' agreed James. 'I'm surprised you're willing to risk it.'

Robert had the grace to look embarrassed. 'I know I owe her one. I guess I'll marry her, eventually. This is my last chance to – how would Scott put it – grow some balls?'

'Yeah, grow some balls.' James pondered Robert's words. When all was said and done, they *were* grown men. 'All right, Robert. We order some food from the club.' He found a sandwich with a mouth-watering description. A brief scan of the ordering instructions revealed an additional item of interest. 'Look, there's a way to place orders online, directly from the club.'

'Really?' Robert's eyes seemed to glaze over for a moment. 'I do have my laptop with me.'

'But you don't have net access.'

Robert scanned the walls near the desk, to no avail. 'I can check if there is maybe wireless.'

'I guess so,' said James. 'Why don't we just call, though?'

Robert flipped open his laptop and turned it on. He tapped the wall with his fingers while he waited for his computer to search the airways for wireless service.

'This is great,' he reported after a minute. 'I have access. Somebody has an unsecured network.'

James shrugged. 'I guess we don't have to call if you don't want to, then. I'll have the roast-beef sandwich and fries,' he said. 'And a coke. And I'll have a . . .' His voice trailed off. The website had finally loaded. Becky's giant tits filled the screen, the nipples barely covered in the flimsiest leopard-print bikini top.

'Oh God,' groaned James. 'Look at that.'

'Yeah.'

Robert typed in their order and entered his credit-card information. The screen began to blink with the familiar insistent flash, prompting him to confirm his purchase. He was reminded of the last time he did just that and his member stiffened in anticipation. He eagerly clicked on CONFIRM but he was disappointed – no seductive images surfaced on screen besides Becky's top-heavy picture. Not even a 'good boy' – not even one.

'I booked the party on the website. When you click on CONFIRM they show you a bunch of pictures of the strippers . . .' He trailed off.

'Oh yeah?' asked James. His eyes roved over Becky's huge hot tits.

'Yeah.'

'I guess we should wait a while for the food.'

'Yeah.'

'So what kind of pictures did they show you when you booked the girls?'

Robert paused before replying. 'Really hot ones.'

'That's pretty slick.'

'Yeah, it was.'

James picked up the menu. 'I should have gotten some appetisers. I'm starving.'

'It's not too late, I suppose.' Robert peered over James's shoulder at the menu. 'Look, they have crispy chicken wings – a dozen for seven bucks.'

'Wish we had them to munch on while we waited for the sandwiches.'

They slowly looked at one another.

James glanced over at the laptop. Becky's mammoth tits beckoned on the screen.

'I guess we can have some wings while we wait.' He sighed. He was a grown man. He didn't *have* to tip these women. He didn't *have* to ogle them either. He would just go in with Robert, they would sit at the bar, have a couple of wings and come right back with the food . . .

'All right, let's go,' said Robert.

They walked across the avenue to the club. A heavy, sensual beat filtered out through the double doors. Black letters on a bright-yellow sign captured James's attention. He read the list of names with a sense of mounting arousal. Sure enough, Becky was working – and Michele was working as well.

The security man simply said 'Two' into his throat mike and stood aside as they disappeared into the scented darkness.

* * *

163

Black lights lit the central stage. Two strippers, attractive Asian girls (definitely not Becky and Michele) were seductively twirling around the pole, occasionally stroking themselves and each other.

A petite waitress with pigtails, in a skimpy miniskirt and a tiny red top, smiled at James as she delivered drinks to a table full of Japanese men in suits. As they watched her waltz past, two men stood and left one of the tables immediately to the left of the stage.

The hostess – a redhead in orange stiletto pumps and an ultra-tight white dress that exposed the bottom of her tight ass cheeks – escorted them to the newly vacated table. The chairs faced the stage.

The waitress with the pigtails came by. 'What can I get you, boys?' she chirped, smiling. She plopped down on the remaining chair and rested her elbows on the table, propping her head up on her hands. She smiled at James. Her mouth was very red and not very wide. When she opened it her lips formed a perfect O.

Her uniform was a cross between a normal server's attire and the slinkiest of lace lingerie.

'Well – we would like some buffalo wings,' he stammered. 'While we wait for our order.'

'You ordered food?'

'Yes, we ordered online.'

'Oh, I better check on that – but what are you having to drink?' She laughed. 'You have to have a drink!'

'Just a glass of water, I suppose.'

'Mineral water.' It wasn't a question.

'Tap water?'

'So sorry, we don't serve tap water.'

'I guess a mineral water, then.' What kind of a place didn't serve plain, old-fashioned water?

Robert ordered a light beer.

'Too early for me,' said James. 'I thought you said you had work later.'

'I do, but I can't really cope with this place sober.'

'I guess I know what you mean.'

The song concluded and the two girls on stage wriggled back into their flimsy outfits. The announcer's voice

164

crackled through the loudspeakers. 'Let's all give a big hand for Tina and Heather! And now, let's not waste any more time – put your hands together for – Becky!'

James swallowed the sudden rush of saliva in his mouth. Becky swayed her way up on to the stage, wearing a tight pink top with a white heart on it, an equally tight mini and five-inch metallic-red stiletto heels.

He drew back a little, hoping the shadows would hide him from her attention. He honestly thought his manoeuvre might have succeeded if it hadn't been for Scott. He was standing right behind James, grinning, his dark eyes gleaming with mischief. 'Hey, Becky!' he roared, waving his hand. Once he had her attention, he simply pointed directly at James.

The big-titted blonde smiled at him and waved the waitress over, then leant down – by God, those tits were huge – and whispered in her ear. The girl glanced over at James and nodded several times before disappearing into the stairwell that led up to the champagne room.

Scott sat down at their table. Tina came past and Scott tipped her a ten-dollar bill. She whispered in his ear and he whispered back.

James fidgeted. 'We should leave,' he told Robert.

'You *can't* leave,' said Scott firmly. He leant forwards and winked at James. 'Becky wants to say hello. She said she had a fantastic time at the party. Those were her exact words, I'm not kidding you.'

'I can't . . .' James started to say something but then the music started and Becky wrapped her legs around the metal pole. She stroked herself with her manicured fingertips, tweaking her luscious breasts one at a time. Each manipulative caress was like a stream of fingers over his straining cock until his member and the fabric of his pants formed a humiliating pop-up tent. He could not remember the words he had been going to say.

Becky traced the tip of her wet red tongue on her upper lip while maintaining eye contact with him. James found it difficult not to stare at her luscious body. The memories of the bachelor party kept intruding into his mind, despite his best efforts to deny them access. He swallowed again.

She turned away from him, seductively swaying her ass a few feet from his riveted gaze.

'I'll see you guys later,' said James and tried to stand up.

'Sit down, dude!' snapped Scott and pulled him back into the chair. 'Don't be such an idiot, she just wants to say hello! Anyway, look at her! Isn't she hot?'

Becky slid down around the pole until she was on her hands and knees. Her hands pulled up the hem of her mini to expose her entire ass, so round and smooth and tempting. She was practically aiming it at James's face.

'Oh God,' he heard himself moan.

'I guess you really ought to tip her.' Scott chuckled.

'Yeah, you really should,' said Robert.

'You're such a good boy, Robbie.' The familiar contemptuous voice came directly from behind Robert. Michele wore the same Catholic schoolgirl uniform that had graced them at the bachelor party. Behind her were the two Asian strippers who had been dancing as they'd come in.

'Hi,' he said without looking away from the show on stage.

'I brought something for Becky. I'm sure you'll like it,' said Michele mockingly, gliding around their table to get to the stage. By now, with the exception of the metallic-red heels, Becky was completely nude. She giggled at Michele as she took possession of her offering, a long, rainbow-coloured lollipop, more than suggestive in its shape. She began to tongue it while watching James. She sucked on the tip and licked it slowly, extending her tongue like a bitch on heat, then made her way right down to the lollipop's base. Once the lollipop was shiny from all those teasing licks, she circled her nipples with the tip, rolling the sticky rod against her skin. Crumbs of rainbow-coloured glaze smeared her skin, leaving a trail as she worked her way down towards her pussy.

Michele nodded to Scott. 'Tina and Heather are waiting for you upstairs, Scott.'

He grinned and stood up, holding the chair for her while she sat down. After he disappeared, Michele whispered in James's ear, 'You know, Jimmy, Becky'll be an absolutely sticky wet bitch after this.'

166

James nodded.

Michele propped her pretty head up with both hands until her crimson lips were just an inch away from James's ear. Her voice became a throaty purr. 'You like to watch her smear herself sticky, don't you? Bimbo Becky told me she wants you to lick her clean, Jimmy. She is making herself into the prettiest lollipop in the world. Isn't that nice? Wouldn't it be nice if she was *your* lollipop?'

'We're just here to pick up some food.' James realised how indescribably lame that sounded even as the words escaped his lips.

'Lollipops *are* food.' Michele laughed.

James willed himself away from the tawdry spectacle of Becky rubbing the oozing sweet against her inner thighs. The manipulative blonde was tracing the tip of the lollipop in an ever tightening spiral around her pussy.

Somehow he managed to look away from the addictive vision, hoping for some strength from Robert.

His friend was watching Michele with naked hunger in his eyes. He looked – yes, James figured that's what it was – jealous.

Michele followed James's look and laughed again. She put her metallic-red heels in Robert's lap. He stared down at the stilettos and swallowed hard.

She used a pointy toe to prod him in the stomach. 'Massage my feet, Robbie. I have to tell Jimmy what Bimbo Becky wants.'

Robert took hold of Michele's stiletto-clad feet. He fumbled with the straps until the shoes slipped off, then began to rub the stripper's naked foot, a slow, halting massage gaining strength with each tentative rub. He appeared oblivious to everything else.

Smirking, Michele turned her attention back to James. 'He's *such* a good boy. Are you a good boy, Jimmy? I mean, Becky's all sticky now, isn't she?'

He glanced at the stage. Becky was on her back. Her legs were wide apart and she was slowly rubbing the lollipop against her clit. There were at least four men in line to tip her but she was ignoring them. The pink mound of her pussy was covered with rainbow glaze.

'Yes, very sticky,' James heard himself say.

'Becky's expensive pink pussy will need a lot of cleaning,' purred Michele. 'You did such a good job licking her butt the last time, she thinks she might let you do it again.'

'I – what?'

'Look, James ...' Michele put her other foot on Robert's lap. 'Rub this one too, dear. Now, James, here is the deal. You're a very lucky man.'

'I am?'

'Yes, James. You're rich enough to keep Bimbo Becky's pussy happy. You're rich enough for Bimbo Becky to let you suck on her shaved pink cunt. All you have to do is give her lots of shiny pretties.'

James coughed up a nervous chuckle. 'You're kidding, right? I mean, I'm engaged to be married, you know, it's not like I ...'

'Becky is a high-maintenance slut, Jimmy. You don't expect her to let you lick her ass for free?'

'But I don't want to lick her at all,' said James in a near whisper. He lowered his eyes to escape the teasing torment on stage but the alternative was nearly as bad.

Michele's naked foot was rubbing up against the relevant part of Robert's pants. His friend was mindlessly massaging the stripper's foot, assisting in his own degradation.

'You're such a liar, Jimmy. Why don't you tell Becky you're not interested,' Michele teased. 'Go on, tell her.'

'Oh come on,' mumbled James. 'You're too funny ...'

'I think little Jimmy just can't wait for Bimbo Becky to milk him for all he's worth.' Michele laughed. She prodded Robert's erection, making him gasp. 'Put my shoes back on, puppy. It's time for my set.'

Indeed, the song ended and Becky climbed off the stage. Instead of coming over to their table, she joined the company of three businessmen on the other side of the club. Who were those guys? James wondered.

With her shoes securely back on her feet, Michele withdrew her legs from Robert's lap. She got up and petted James on the head. 'Don't you worry, Jimmy. She'll come by later, maybe. If you tip her well enough maybe she will let you beg her for a lap dance.' She leant over to Robert.

'Maybe if someone tips *me* well enough, I might let him beg *me* for a lap dance.'

She oozed on to the stage and a line of men began to form up immediately. Their table was close enough to the stage for James to take note of the denominations. Most of the men held twenty-dollar bills. One of them actually held a fifty.

'God,' croaked Robert. He seemed thoroughly flustered. 'I need a drink.' He waved to the waitress who was threading her way in between two other tables with a loaded tray.

'Hi, can I have another ...' began Robert, but the waitress was already putting drinks on their table. There was a bottle of champagne – the same brand as from the room above – champagne flutes and eight shots of tequila. Robert absently noted that here they did not forget the salt and lime.

'We didn't order this,' said James.

'Michele told me to bring it,' replied the girl, smiling. She really was very attractive in her revealing lacy uniform and her startled crimson O of a mouth. 'She must really like you guys. Would you really put me to all the trouble of taking it all back?' she purred.

'I'm afraid so,' said James. 'Sorry, but ...'

'Jimmy!' Yet another familiar voice giggled behind James. An avalanche of bleached-blonde hair cascaded over his head, a scented jungle that evoked sordid memories. Hands snaked around his chair, clasping manicured fingers around his arms.

He felt twin mounds of flesh, tipped with a familiar hardness, press against his back. All the blood in his head seemed to rush directly into his cock.

'What's wrong, Jimmy? Miss me?'

'I ... yes, of course,' he said quickly. It was only polite to say so.

Becky giggled and sat down in the chair vacated by Michele. She pointed at the champagne flute and the waitress poured, wearing an amused smile.

Becky put her hand on James's knee and leant her head on his shoulder. 'Have a drink with me, Jimmy, pweeease ...'

'I have work, I have to go to work,' he muttered.

'Pweeease . . .' She pouted and moved her hand higher on his thigh.

His arousal was so great her hand was actually getting near the tip of his engorged member. Indeed, she chanced upon it.

Her eyes grew large with exaggerated innocence. 'Oooh, Jimmy, what's this? Why won't you have a drink with pretty little Becky?' She rested her hand right over the tip of his cock, subtly pressing on the shameful indicator of his lust. 'Go on, Jimmy,' she cooed with encouragement. She put down her champagne flute – now stained with the hot pink of her lipstick – and prodded his closed lips with one of the shots of tequila. At the same time, her other hand began to softly rub the tip of his mindless, stiff member through his pants. 'Drink more, sweetie,' she purred. 'When you loosen up a bit I'll let you take me upstairs. Don't you want to help me with all the sticky candy I rubbed on my pussy?'

He shook his head vehemently to deny her victory and decided to push her hand away from his erection. He put his hand on hers, but his will lacked conviction, and his feeble attempt lacked strength.

She seemed to recognise the conflict between his morals and his arousal; her fingers gained strength and confidence, manipulating his member along with his crumbling will.

He gasped after a particularly pleasurable stroke, his lips parting without his actually intending them to. She used the opportunity to pour the tequila into his mouth. He nearly choked but eventually managed to swallow the entire shot.

'Good boy.' She giggled. 'Have some more!' She lifted another shot and raised it against his lips. In the gloomy darkness under the table her hand fondled his cock through his pants. She tilted the shot and he was forced to drink it down to avoid being doused with liquor.

'You're such a good boy,' she crooned. Her nipples pressed against him.

The tequila coursed through him like liquid heat. He glanced over at Robert and realised that his friend was not in his chair. Looking around, he noticed him by the stage, stuffing a wad of twenty-dollar bills in Michele's garter. The tanned blonde was petting Robert on the head and scratching him behind the ear.

'Have some champagne to wash it down,' suggested Becky. She poured his champagne flute full and pressed it against his lips. 'Champagne and lollipops taste so good together,' she purred. 'Sweet sticky lollipop . . . Drink up, Jimmy.'

Frazzled, he sipped some champagne.

'There you go! Just relax and have a good time.' Becky giggled.

'We're here to pick up some food,' he mumbled. Nothing seemed to make sense. His head reeled with desire and hard liquor.

'Why don't you give Jeremy a hundred dollars so I can sit in your lap – all alone?' purred Becky.

'But Lucille would kill me,' he croaked. He sipped some more champagne. The bubbles exploded on his tongue.

'Is that your little girlfriend?' cooed Becky. She pushed her tits together; he could see the sticky stains the lollipop had left behind on the smooth, vast expanse of her breasts. 'Does she have big boobies like mine?'

'No,' he said, staring at her offering. He felt dry-mouthed and sipped some more champagne.

'There you go, Jimmy.' Becky giggled again and refilled his glass. 'Go and pay Jeremy now, Jimmy, and maybe I'll let you help me with this awful sticky mess.'

She stood and pulled him to the cash machine. He paused next to a table where Tiffany was chatting with two men and Becky pushed herself against his back. The scent of her sweet body rub was heavy in the air, a cloud of cloying seduction. 'I loved your tongue in my ass, Jimmy,' she whispered, herding him forwards with a constant stream of manipulative caresses, until they finally stood in front of the ATM. 'Think about your cock in my ass, Jimmy,' she purred. 'Just stick that card in the machine like you would stick your cock in my hot tight ass.'

'You're – but Lucille . . .' he mumbled.

Becky stood very close to him, her breasts and hands

sliding and rubbing up against him every time his will grew strong enough to engage in an attempt to break free. Each soft, feather-light caress fuelled his growing lust. She pushed her breasts right into his face until they were just a few inches from his trapped gaze. Her hands entered his pockets, patting him down with professional skill until she had found his wallet.

'Just relax, sweet Jimmy,' she said soothingly. 'Just keep your eyes on my big titties and let Becky help you do what you want anyway.' She casually went through his wallet until she found his ATM card. She slid it into the machine slot until the words requesting his PIN came up on screen.

'What're you waiting for, honey?' She pouted, leaning against him, her perfect curves corroding his will like water on brittle black iron. 'I'm so sticky, Jimmy! A pretty girl like me shouldn't be so sticky!' She stomped her feet, making her tits jiggle. 'Put in your pin *now*, Jimmy!'

Desperate for help, James looked for Robert. He saw him back at the table. Michele's set must have come to an end, as the doctor was once again utterly absorbed in the humiliating labour of massaging Michele's feet.

'Go on, Jimmy,' cooed Becky. She stood next to him until her body blocked the view of anyone from the direction of the tables. She resumed the stroking of his erection through his pants. 'Put in your pin number, sweetie,' she purred. 'Put it in, Jimmy. Be a good boy!'

James stared at the ATM. Nothing else seemed to exist beside the manipulative strokes of his seductress and the machine with its hungry, blinking demand for his pin number. He put his hand on the keyboard and tentatively put in the first digit.

'That's it! Good boy!' Becky's long, delicate fingers maintained his member's steady, methodical manipulation. 'Keep putting it in, honey.'

James put in the second, then the third digit.

'Just one more to go and we can go on upstairs!' squealed Becky, jumping up like a cheerleader. 'Put it in, Jimmy. Just put in the last number.' She pressed herself against him and her fingers slid underneath his pants. She stroked the defenceless flesh of his rock-hard member for a fleeting moment before pulling her hand out.

Gasping, James entered the last digit and pressed ENTER, twice.

'Such a good boy! You'll want enough for a few dances, sweetie.'

'A few dances.' He nodded numbly. He pressed the button for QUICK CASH. There were options for 100, 200, 300, 500 and 1000 dollars.

'Five hundred would give you enough time to lick me soooo clean,' cooed Becky. 'If we had enough time, you might *really* turn me on – and who knows what you would get to stick in my pretty pink pussy!'

The waitress came by and handed Becky a shooter.

'It's a jello shooter,' she explained. 'To give you a taste of what's coming.' She leant against the wall next to the cash machine and planted the shot glass in the valley of her breasts. 'You won't need a straw, sweetie.'

Reeling a little from all the tequila, he shook his head. 'No, I have work tomorrow,' he mumbled. 'I can't drink any more, really.'

Becky smiled cruelly and simply put her hands on the back of Jimmy's head. She pulled him forwards until his world shrank to the enticing view of her tits, centred on the shooter. 'Slurp it down, honey.' She giggled. 'You either drink up or you'll be all smothered.'

He supposed she was right. It was a lesser transgression to have another drink than to wallow in the sensation of Becky's tits smothering his face. He dutifully sucked the jello shooter into his mouth, swallowing the burning, sweet alcohol in two hectic gulps. Becky's hot scented flesh pressed against his cheeks regardless.

'Good boy, Jimmy,' she said, laughing. Becky took his hand and put it on the keypad. She moved his finger until it rested on the button that was next to the 1000-dollar withdrawal. She pressed on the tip of his finger until the machine duly registered the transaction.

I really didn't do it, James told himself. It was Becky.

Hundred-dollar bills began to slide into the ATM tray.

'Ooooh!' cooed Becky.

He collected the money as if in a daze.

'Is that all for me?' she squeaked with excitement. She hugged James, clinging against him.

'I . . .' said James. He was feeling dizzy.

Becky pulled him to the staircase. The muscle-bound suit nodded to his manipulative escort and stared at him with absolute lack of emotion. 'That'll be a hundred dollars.'

Becky giggled with satisfaction as James pulled out the wad of hundreds and handed one over to the guy.

He stood aside and she whisked him up the stairs.

'Michele likes to tease her little boys on the stairs.' Becky laughed, stopping halfway up. 'She likes to wriggle her butt right in their faces. Like this!' She demonstrated exactly what she meant. Becky's skimpy little skirt did nothing to hide her charms. If anything, her thong accentuated her natural curves. Her ass cheeks were streaked with dried glazed candy.

'So sticky!' she cooed, taking his hand and pressing it against the dried trail of the lollipop on her inner thigh. 'It feels sticky!' she complained whiningly.

'It's very sticky.' He nodded, tight-lipped. Her flesh was smooth and warm; his fingers had been instantly covered in the lollipop's sticky residue.

Giggling, she pulled him the rest of the way to the room with the curtained alcoves. 'You liked touching the sticky, didn't you, Jimmy?'

'Yes,' he mumbled. He couldn't think straight. The room was barely lit. Some of the rich red velvet curtains moved once in a while, and not just to the beat of the music. Obviously they were not the only pair there. He wondered if Scott were behind one of them with the Asian girls. How could Scott afford this? He worked for the government, for God's sake.

'More bubbly!' Becky pouted, lazily waving her hand in the direction of the bar. Parting velvet, she slipped into one of the alcoves. The curtains closed behind her.

He took a tentative step towards the alcove.

Becky's hand re-emerged from behind the curtain. She extended a single finger, tipped with a useless long fingernail, and beckoned him to join her. 'But first, bring Becky bubbly!' she whined.

James's cock was straining in his pants. The liquor coursed through his veins. He felt feverish and his face was ruddy with desire. He went to the bar, randomly grabbed one of the bottles, and rushed to the alcove until he stood right in front of the dense velvet curtain.

There he stood, frozen with sudden shame. What was he doing here? Why was he – *serving* – a money-grubbing bimbo? He was a top-notch executive, for crying out loud! He had a girlfriend! No, not a girlfriend – he was engaged to be married! He had a fiancée! There was absolutely no way he could remain here. It was wrong, a filthy, shameful thing to do.

'Oh, Jimmy! I'm so sticky!' wailed Becky from within the alcove. 'What're you doing?'

'I have to go,' he muttered. Her voice invoked memories of glistening curves that were better left forgotten.

'Leave?!' She pouted. 'Come in here this instant! Silly boy! Jimmy gets a lap dance from Bimbo Becky!' She giggled. 'Come on, Jimmy!'

He shook his head again and entered the staircase. He nearly ran into Michele; the tanned blonde was standing right behind the curtains that separated the champagne room from the staircase. She was not alone. She was pulling Robert after her. He was trailing after the tall stripper like some dazed, obedient puppy.

Michele smirked and ran her free hand over James's erection.

He gasped.

'Leaving so soon?' she purred. 'Such a rude little boy. Bimbo Becky is waiting, Jimmy.' She laughed and pushed him back into the champagne room. Her arm was surprisingly strong. 'Go on, Jimmy,' she commanded. 'Bimbo Becky's wet pink pussy is waiting.'

Becky parted the velvet of her alcove. She had shed her costume, all of it except for her heels. She was lusciously naked, her skin covered in patches of sticky candy.

Seeing James being herded back into her manicured clutches, Becky smiled. She caressed herself, sliding her pink-polished nails over her tits.

175

'He tried to run away!' She pouted. 'Just when we were about to play! He's rich, Michele! I let him play with me!' She giggled and softly caressed James's face, then pulled him into the alcove, her ass swaying from side to side.

The curtains slid into position behind them and suddenly they were finally isolated, alone.

Becky pressed herself against him, stroking his arms, his stomach, working her way down to his aching, impatient cock. 'Would you like a lap dance, my little tent-popper?' she cooed.

'I – no, I have to – I . . .'

James shuddered with an equal mix of mindless lust and trepidation as Becky's fingers skilfully pulled down his zipper. She freed his cock and began to stroke his exposed, addled flesh with soft, insistent caresses.

'Why don't you just lean back and enjoy, Jimmy?' she cooed. 'You know you can't say no.' She smirked. 'You loved licking my ass and pussy at the party. You were such a good boy, you licked them until they were all nice and shiny.' She pulled his face against the sticky mounds of her breasts.

He could barely breathe surrounded by the expanse of her tempting, gorgeous flesh. He felt sticky crumbs on his cheeks.

'Lick, Jimmy.' Becky giggled. Her fingers tightened around his cock and she accelerated the pace of manipulation.

James groaned. He had to leave, now, before it was too late.

Becky slid a slender finger to the base of his member.

James sobbed within the quivering walls of Becky's tits, a custom-designed prison constructed of her warm flesh and his own lust. His tears fell on the sticky skin of his seductress, smearing the remnants of the lollipop still further.

'There you go, Jimmy!' cooed Becky. 'It's OK to cry!' She giggled with obvious contempt. 'Go on, now! You know you want to lick Becky's big titties clean!' She squirmed against him, her curves goading him into action.

He realised he might as well admit it to himself – he wanted to lick Becky. God, he wanted more than that – he wanted to fuck Becky. He wanted to shove his cock in the stripper's gaping pink hole. 'Oh my God,' he sobbed, feeling weak. The sleazy stripper with the big fake tits was manipulating his cock and his will, one lazy, calculated stroke at a time. Tentatively James felt his lips part. Like a dog in the window of a moving car, his tongue slipped out and he experienced the flavour of Becky's sticky-sweet, salt-stained skin. The aroma was a mixture of the lollipop, the stripper's pervasive sweet body rub, perfume, champagne and his own salty tears of shame and humiliation. His surrender reinforced his arousal. Somehow, the idea of mindlessly, pathetically worshipping the body of this manipulative, expensive whore wormed its way into his subconscious and fuelled his lust in a vicious circle of addiction.

As soon as he began to lick her in earnest, Becky leant back and giggled, satisfied. 'There you go, Jimmy!' She stopped playing with his cock, letting the quivering, rock-hard member fall back against his thigh, the slap of flesh on flesh an audible representation of his surrender.

Desperate for the resumption of her manipulation, he redoubled his efforts. He sucked on her nipples, swallowing the sweet mixture of his own saliva and the lollipop stains.

She reclined even further until she was nearly lounging on her back. He followed the twin globes of his now shiny prize, slavering over her exposed flesh.

'The song is over, Jimmy.' She laughed. 'Would you like to play some more?' She giggled, parting her legs slightly. The pink flesh of her pussy glistened wetly in the subtle lighting of the alcove. Here and there it was stained with the rainbow colours of the lollipop.

'Yes, please, please,' he gibbered, a dazed expression in his eyes.

Becky began to stroke her clit, watching James with eyes half hidden behind long fake lashes. 'It's a new song, Jimmy,' she warned him.

He frantically fished out his wallet and peeled off a crisp hundred, pressing the bill in her hand.

'Oooh, Jimmy, are you sure you want to pay me for the honour of licking my cunnie clean?' She laughed and

177

slowly pushed a finger into her gaping hole, fucking herself to the heavy rhythm of the music.

'Yes, please,' he heard himself say. 'Please let me – please let me lick you clean.'

She frowned. 'Ask me nicer! I mean, it's like anybody can give me a hundred dollars. I don't let just anybody lick my pretty clitty.' She giggled. 'I mean, look at me, Jimmy. Don't you think I'm worth more than one lousy hundred?' She cruelly closed her legs, trapping her subtly moving hand – and his gaze – in between her thighs.

'I said look at me!' She pouted.

He raised his eyes and looked her over, starting from the sexy tangle of her bleached-blonde hair all the way to the metallic-red stilettos on her feet. From the movement of her lower arm he could tell she was still fingering her perfect shaved hole. Her enormous breasts were glistening with his oral worship.

He stepped closer.

'No, Jimmy.' She petted his head, laughing. 'Answer the question, Jimmy! Don't you think I'm worth more than a single hundred?'

'Yes,' he muttered. Without taking his eyes off the promise of hidden paradise between her legs, he peeled off a few more bills and shoved the crumpled cash in the stripper's outstretched hand.

She petted him on the head again and slowly opened her legs, exposing his reward: the yawning pink of her shaved pussy. 'Such a good boy!' she cooed. 'You get a treat! Get on all fours now, Jimmy! Come on, boy!'

James dropped to his feet and scrambled in between Becky's legs. The stripper raised her left leg and rested the stiletto heel of her metallic-red shoes on James's shoulder. Her foot slid further down his back as he crawled forwards and assumed a position of subservient pussy-worship.

'Still want to leave?' She giggled.

The tip of his tongue reached out for his prize. She tasted like melting candy.

'Suck on my pussy,' she demanded. 'I want you to suck my pussy, Jimmy.' Becky lifted the bottle and poured an avalanche of sparkling wine over her lower stomach. The champagne thoroughly soaked James's head. He began to slurp and suck on the mixture of lollipop, champagne, pussy juice and body rub.

'Yeah, good boy.' Becky laughed. 'Suck on my pussy and drink up, honey. It'll make you feel good.' She pushed her pussy into his face, straddling his head with her legs. 'Almost forgot, song is nearly over, lover. Show me how much you love eating cunt.'

Without lifting his face from its degrading labour, James tried to find his wallet, but was unable to locate it with his questing fingers.

'Let me help you there, Jimmy.' Becky smirked. She closed her legs enough to rise a few inches, then leant forwards, pushing her drenched pussy flush against James's shiny lips. Now she was close enough to her target. She picked up the dazed executive's wallet and leant back against the wall, parting her legs all the way again. 'Go on Jimmy.' She laughed. 'Jimmy boy was a good boy, Jimmy boy gets to play with the pretty pink cunnie!'

She leisurely looked through his wallet while its owner worshipped her drenched pussy. She examined the receipt from the ATM, checking the balance. She smiled, softly stroking James's head. 'You're such a *good boy*, Jimmy!'

She poured more champagne down her stomach until the bottle was empty. A puddle of sparkling wine formed a pool of gold around her metallic-red heels. She pushed his head into the puddle.

'Slurpy slurpy!' She giggled. 'Slurp it all up!'

The humiliating command fed his arousal to astonishing heights; he nearly came right then and there, with his face resting in the centre of that puddle, slurping on champagne filtered through the pussy of his seductress.

Becky tapped him on the head with his wallet. She was holding a photograph. She casually pulled his head from between her legs so he could get a good look. 'Is this your little fiancée?' she asked, holding the picture of Lucille a few inches from his addled eyes.

'Yes,' he mumbled and licked up the last few drops of champagne from the ground.

'What's her name again?'

179

'Lucille,' he whimpered. 'Her name is Lucille.' He began to sob with the shame of it all. 'I can't believe I'm . . .'

The bleached-blonde stripper prodded James on the cheek with her stiletto heels. 'Jimmy, you're a pussy-whipped bitch,' she said, laughing. 'Look at you! Lick my heel up and down like a doggie, Jimmy!'

'I . . .' he cried. 'I . . .'

'Jimmy, I'm going to turn you into my very own ATM!' cooed Becky. 'Isn't that nice?' She reclined on the couch and spread her legs wide. 'If you make me happy you get to spurt.' She giggled. 'Isn't that nice?'

She raised a long, perfect leg and slid a metallic-red heel against his lips. 'Suck on it, Jimmy!'

10

James

The sun was coming up. Faint white light coated the rooftops.

'I'm hungry,' said James.

'Me too.'

'We should order breakfast.'

'From the club?'

'I suppose that's the only place to order from.'

'That's true – but it's not like we got food the last time we ordered.'

'Do they even have a kitchen? If they do, is it open this early? I mean – you never got the food either, I assume.'

'No.' James laughed with the irony of it all. Or was it something else? His befuddled brain tried to come up with the definition of 'irony'. Did the concept even apply to their situation?

Robert glanced over at him. He shook his head slowly. 'Man, hate to tell you this, but you're drunk off your ass.'

'So?' James frowned. 'So what? Cast the first stone . . .' He collapsed on the bed, still muttering. 'Kettle black – shit, I don't know . . .'

'Exactly my point.' Robert took out his wallet and turned it over. It was empty. 'I have to get more cash,' he groaned.

'Me too,' said James. 'I'm all out.'

'At least the girls aren't working tonight,' said Robert. 'I don't think I can afford to go back there for a while.'

'They're not working tonight?'

'Well – no. You seriously wanted to go back tonight? What happened between you and Becky, man?'

'Hey, what happened between you and Michele?' snapped James. 'We – we had some champagne, that's all.'

'In the champagne room you had some champagne!'

'Damn, you're just too funny,' drawled James. 'Yeah, we had some champagne in the champagne room. Want to make something of it?'

Robert raised his hands in the air. 'James, relax! I was there, remember?'

'I wonder what the girls are doing tonight. I mean, they're not working.'

'They're not working at the club, that's true. Maybe they're doing another bachelor party or something.'

'Or actually resting?'

'Maybe resting, yeah.'

'Maybe we should check the website.'

James nodded eagerly. 'Good idea. Let's check the website.'

The site loaded. The men jostled one another for the perfect viewing position.

'Check out the gallery,' said James. 'See if they have some pictures of Becky.'

'They do, but they only show the good stuff if you order something. I know that a bunch of really hot shots come up if you hire them . . .' Robert trailed off. 'I think I told you about this already.'

'Does it say if they're working some party tonight?'

'I don't think so. Let me check.'

Robert clicked on the 'Special Event' links until the familiar, seductive teaser came up. 'This is all there is,' he said, disappointed. 'There is just no way to check if they've been booked already.'

'Unless we try to book them for tonight.' James laughed. 'Wow, we would sure have a problem if we did that.'

'Yeah, we sure would.' Robert walked to the mini-bar and popped a beer. He gulped it down. 'I was thirsty,' he said.

'Pass me one too,' said James.

'Sure, it's good for the hangover.'

'I agree.' James popped the proffered can and drank. He swallowed more of the beer as the procession of sensual images on screen insinuated themselves into his subconscious. Abruptly he realised that he had gotten hard.

'These chicks are so hot,' he declared.

'Yeah, sure are . . .' Robert got up from the chair. 'I'll be right back.'

James heard Robert shut the bathroom door. He focused his attention on the monitor. He entered his name, today's date, 8 p.m., and his hotel room as the site of a hypothetical bachelor party. The pace of images quickened; his cock strained with approval. A stream of filthy images was followed by stills of the strippers.

He selected Becky and Michele; feeling expansive, amused, he also clicked on the redhead, Tiffany.

James practically came in his pants as a short video of Michele and Tiffany filled a small window on screen. Tiffany was on all fours, moaning as Michele felt her up from behind. More images followed, one of them of Michele and Becky. The tall blonde was wearing a bitchy, condescending expression. The leash in her hand was connected to a collar around Becky's neck.

Becky's mammoth tits were dangling low, pushed against the floor, the nipples hidden by the sheer expanse of her flesh. She wore shiny black panties that covered her pussy.

Suddenly, the pictures disappeared. Blinking words instructed James to enter his credit-card number.

'I just want to know if they're working somewhere tonight . . .' he muttered under his breath. 'That's all.'

He picked up his wallet and entered his credit-card information.

The screen flashed, 'Good boy! Good boy!'

James groaned with need; more videos and still shots flooded the screen, along with more pictures of Becky's glistening, enormous tits, more shots of Michele in her schoolgirl uniform, and shots of Tiffany dressed up as a cheerleader. She was bending over and giving the photographer a sultry look.

The images faded. The blank screen began to fill up with promises of more to come, concluding in two words, repeating; 'Press Confirm! Press Confirm! Press Confirm!'

James was too focused on the images to notice – or care about – the amount. He clicked on CONFIRM.

'Good boy! Good boy!' The screen filled with pornographic filth starring the strippers: Tiffany and Michele playing with dildos, a video of Becky being fucked in the ass with a monstrous, shiny black cock, followed by yet another video showing Michele. She wore the shiny black strap-on. It was vibrating and she was ordering some sleazy blonde bimbo named Trixie to suck on it before she would deign to fuck her.

Sobbing, the girl wrapped her hot-pink lips around the vibrator. She looked vaguely familiar. She wore the same metallic-red heels as Michele and Becky. Maybe it's Amber or Heather 2, thought James. He must have seen her at the club.

He had to get off. He just had to. He picked up the laptop – Robert was still closeted away in his bathroom – and went back to his own room. He locked the room door and unzipped his pants. Fingers trembling, he managed to pull out his stiff red cock. His pants were down to his ankles by the time he had made it to the crimson-pink edifice that was the bed.

Not wasting any time, he put the laptop on top of the bed and collapsed in a heap next to it, wrapping his fingers around his member. The screen with its tawdry content was just a few inches from his face. He gasped as he finally felt his balls contract. He spurted come all over his lower stomach and thighs, falling asleep nearly at once.

He woke up in a few hours. Pink and red light streamed in through the curtains. He wasn't sure where he was, but came to after a few moments. The absurd interior was less of a clue than the dried mess on his stomach.

He took a long hot shower. The laptop was still open, although at some time during the night the battery had run down. He carried it back to Robert's room, walking in without knocking.

Robert was on the phone. He looked agitated. His wallet was lying on the nightstand. It was open and his credit card had been pulled out, a silver rectangle resting against the shiny brown leather.

He raised an admonitory finger as he spoke into the receiver. 'Look, just raise my limit, OK?'

He must not have liked what he heard because he raised his voice and practically snarled, 'Look, I'm a plastic surgeon, I have to entertain – I have to entertain clients.'

After a moment's pause he continued: 'Oncologist? No, plastic surgeon. Yes. Yes, yes, just change it. So what'll it be? Yes, that'll be good.' Robert hung up the phone. 'I'll have to go home for a few minutes,' he said.

'What's up?' asked James, putting the laptop on the bed. He felt drained.

'Nothing,' said Robert. 'Just dealing with shit. Let's go catch a movie tonight.'

'I'm staying in,' said James. 'I'm staying in.' Those three simple words gave him an immediate erection. He had a triple date, a triple *hot* date.

'No clubbing for you tonight?' Robert laughed. He lifted his credit card like a teenager with his first backstage pass. 'I might go back for a set or two.'

'Go ahead.' James smiled, thinking of Becky's mammoth tits in his face as his tongue lapped up the sweet crumbs of the lollipop. 'I'm sure you'll have a good time.'

'If I see Becky I'll tell her you said hello.' Robert chuckled, his eyes twinkling. 'Maybe I'll tell her in the champagne room.'

James grinned. 'I'll tell *Michele* you said hello.' The tall blonde had great legs.

'Yeah, right . . . What's on your plate today?'

James nearly did a little jig of gloating triumph before deciding that discretion was the better part of valour. He concentrated on Robert's choice of words: 'On your plate *today*'. Today meant daytime hours. He didn't have to lie.

'I have to go to work. I'm totally exhausted but there is a meeting I have to attend and there is . . .' He closed his eyes, trying to concentrate. He knew he was forgetting something. 'Jesus, I'm out of it.'

'Me too,' sighed Robert. He leant against the headboard. The words came with obvious reluctance. 'I actually have to operate at noon.'

James gaped at him. 'You can't! No offence, Robert, but

185

you look like hell. What's the operation? Hold out your hand!'

Robert held his hand out in front of him; the trembling was immediate and noticeable. 'Damn,' he muttered. 'It's technical. Kind of experimental. No point in talking about it, though. I've been so busy with – one thing or another, that I've been missing some work. Can't give any more excuses. Wayne would get too pissed off, even with his stupid schoolboy crush on Holly.'

'He has a crush on Holly?'

'Yeah, every time he sees her he stares at her like some besotted puppy. I've been getting sort of irritated about it but he's my boss and now that I missed some stupid operations I just have to tell him Holly said hello or some garbage and he stops being a pain.'

'Oh . . . Still, you have to do it? What about your hand?'

'It'll be OK by the time I go.'

'You sure?'

'Yes, of course. Don't worry about me.'

James glanced at him uneasily.

Robert's eyes were bloodshot and surrounded by dark, unhealthy circles. His lips were pale and his chin was heavy with stubble.

'Well, if you say so – but make sure you take a long shower, and don't forget to shave.'

'I will.' Robert laughed. 'Then I'll go and get something to eat. They serve lunch at the club. They even have mimosas and – what do you call the drink with vodka and tomato juice with the thing – the celery . . .'

'You mean a Bloody Mary? Are you serious? That's nuts, Robert. You're operating in something like five hours!'

'I'll be all right.' Robert smiled, looking vaguely preoccupied.

He really should not do this, thought James. Of course, there was no way he was going to get a refund – he was not a complete fool. He had paid his money (he wasn't really sure how much it was, and he was absolutely certain he did not really want to know) and now he might as well enjoy himself. Once he had married Lucille, he was not likely to have too many opportunities to cavort around with a trio of go-go dancers.

The appointed time had come and gone and the girls were still a no-show. James was getting irritated. After all, he had paid for a service! He turned on the television and sat down on the edge of the bed. One of the channels was a pay-per-view porn thing.

He clicked his way to a movie that looked promising (the headline implied a lot of girl-on-girl action) and pressed the button to confirm. Why not? he reasoned. In any case, he didn't have much of a choice. Just pressing 'confirm' turned him on. He clicked on 'confirm' two more times. Where were they, damn it?

Was that a sound from the corridor? He rushed to the door and opened it.

His ears had reported the girls' arrival accurately. The three women stood in the hallway. Michele stood front and centre, with a raised hand ready to knock. Flanking her on either side stood Becky and Tiffany. Tiffany wore a slinky maid's uniform with black lace gloves. Her long red hair spilled over her bare shoulders. She was carrying two kit-bags, one in each hand. Michele and Becky wore expensive looking, originally conservative suits, although they had obviously been altered: their cleavage – particularly Becky's – had been cut low enough to display their enhanced charms to their best advantage. The two blondes also wore matching metallic-red stiletto heels. Michele smiled and lowered her hand.

'Oooh, Jimmy.' Becky giggled. 'You're staring at my titties!'

'Please come in,' he mumbled.

'I see you're watching a naughty movie, Jimmy!' Michele laughed. 'You're a good boy, yes you are! Where is little Robbie?'

'He's – he's out,' said James. 'He is out, having fun.'

'Is he now?' purred Michele. 'You didn't tell him about this little party, did you, Jimmy?'

Becky smiled and sidled closer to him, taking his arm. 'You want pretty Becky all to yourself, don't you, honey?'

'Answer Bimbo Becky, Jimmy,' said Michele. 'Tell her how she makes you feel.'

During this exchange Tiffany was laying out a cornucopia of sex toys on the coffee table.

'Why did you ask for Tiffany, by the way?' asked Becky petulantly. 'I thought you liked *me*!'

Tiffany tossed her glorious red hair back and smiled at James. Her smile was all too knowing.

'The maid is flirting with my man,' complained Becky to Michele. 'She's such a whore, you really ought to punish her.'

'Well, Jimmy? Be a good boy and tell Bimbo Becky why you just had to get some exotic red pussy. Is it because you're an insatiable little boy?'

'I don't know,' whimpered James. 'She's – she's pretty, I guess.'

'You guess? Tiffany, Jimmy here "guesses" that you're pretty. You think you can seduce him, maid Tiffany?'

'Michele, he's mine.' Becky pouted. 'He's my very own, you know?'

'Is that true, Jimmy?' Michele pointed at Tiffany, asking the obvious. 'Why does he want a new toy, then?'

'She is pretty,' admitted Becky. 'I like to play with her too. She is fun to play dress-up with.'

'Thank you, Mistress.' Tiffany curtsied, then turned to James. 'Thank you, sir, for asking for me. Would you like to play with me, sir?' She inserted her manicured index finger in between her luscious red lips and sucked on it.

'She's a sleazy tart, Becky. I can't believe your man finds her attractive. She has no class at all.'

Becky frowned. She gave Tiffany a lazy slap on her ass, making the redhead squeal. Becky faced her. 'Why're you trying to fuck Jimmy?'

'He's easy.' Tiffany giggled. 'He gets hard looking at me. He's rich. He's got a nice place . . .'

'You're a gold-digging slut,' said Becky. She slapped her ass even harder. 'He gets hard looking at *me*.'

Tiffany gasped and bent over a little. Her flimsy uniform rode up until it showed off her frilly white lace garter belt and panties. 'He wants to stick his cock in my pussy,' she said, giving James a sultry side glance. Becky slapped her ass and she moaned softly. 'The second we're alone he'll be on his knees begging to eat my red pussy.'

Enraged, Becky slapped her on the butt, hard. Tiffany fell forwards, gasping. Becky slapped her again, and again. Tiffany sobbed and collapsed on to her hands and knees on the floor. 'Her ass's getting so red.' Michele laughed. 'Doesn't her ass look red?'

'Not red enough,' hissed Becky. She opened the kit-bag and brought out a long piece of rectangular leather. 'Such a whore, she needs to be disciplined.'

11

Wayne

'Doctor Waverly.' Rainer's voice was anything but friendly. 'This is not a disciplinary hearing in a formal sense yet.'

'What?' snarled Robert. 'So some – mistakes, minor mistakes – were made. There were no complications.'

Rainer got up from behind his desk and leant over to sniff the air around Robert. 'Doctor, you've been drinking.' It was a statement, not a question.

'I don't know what you mean,' said Robert uneasily.

'I think you know exactly what I mean, Doctor Waverly. You've been neglecting your research. What's even worse, what's absolutely inexcusable, is that you've been neglecting your work, you've been coming in late – or missing days completely, forcing others to cover for you, others who have their own research, their own patients, their own responsibilities – and you expect special treatment. I am leaning towards convening a formal disciplinary hearing.'

'That would destroy my career!' gasped Robert.

'Hardly. You seem to be doing that all on your own, Doctor Waverly.'

'Holly and I . . .'

'Doctor Waverly, I am most fond of your fiancée. She is a woman of the highest calibre. I wish the best for her. However, a patient was in serious jeopardy of losing his life because you made some mistakes, some *avoidable* mistakes. That is my professional opinion as a surgeon. The only reason the man survived and the operation was a success was that I was standing next to you, Doctor Waverly, and took over after it became obvious that you were unable to do your job.'

'I can't believe that after all this time . . .'

'Oh please, Doctor, you know full well you messed up and messed up bad. For a moment forget that I am your boss and tell me what the hell is wrong with you? You're falling apart, man!'

Robert sighed. 'I'm not sure . . . You're right, Wayne. I'm having a problem.'

Rainer leant back in his chair. 'Robert, I'm not trying to be a jerk. You just don't do some things in medicine, that's all. Like drink or do drugs, particularly when you are operating. Are you on anything, Wayne?'

'No, no way. Wayne, I am sorry about what happened. Let me make it up to you. There is the Periwinkle project – I'll volunteer for it. I know you can't find enough people to do that.'

The Periwinkle project was quite conceivably the most boring job anyone with a PhD – or even a high school dropout – could conceive of. The theory was intensely complicated but the practical lab work simply involved going through 200,000 samples in minute detail. If one of the slides turned a faint periwinkle green, the cell culture supposedly contained the mythical super-cell that would cure cancer. The project had become famous in oncology circles as the last refuge for failed researchers. If someone joined the Periwinkle project they had pretty much admitted to themselves that they were incapable of serious research. It was a modern search for a microscopic grail in an ocean of chaos. The likelihood that they would find something that obvious – that mythical periwinkle colouration – was close to nil, but a trained scientist could possibly see something in the jumble of cellular debris that could be worthy of further study. This was why they couldn't use interns or trained monkeys for the work.

'I guess you can't really make any mistakes there,' said Wayne. 'Your participation in the project will be considered a mitigating factor, I'm sure.'

'That's not why I'm doing it,' said Robert. 'I'm doing it because it's important.'

'Of course. Very well. I will assign you a range of cells to look at.'

'Thanks, Wayne. You won't regret this.'

Robert examined three slides in total before he realised there was no way he was cut out for the Periwinkle project. The way it worked, the computer put up a cell on the monitor. It logged that he was looking at it and loaded the next one into its memory. He had to left-click with the mouse over the cell to move on to the new one. If he spent less than 45 seconds on a given cell, it remained marked as unexamined in the computer's memory. Right now he was looking at the electron microscope image of cell 83622. 83623 had already loaded into memory. 83622 was just a useless grey heap of cellular debris.

Robert yawned. So boring! He peered at his open door and closed it. He needed privacy for serious research. Yes, that would be a good excuse if someone questioned him about why he had closed his door.

He opened a new window and typed in the URL for the club. He unzipped his pants and wrapped his hand around his member. He redirected the image of the cells on to the small screen so he could use the large one to display a teaser video of Michele and Becky.

Robert's eyes were slavishly locked on Michele's long tanned legs. The stripper was wearing her slut nurse Michele uniform. She was stroking Becky, who was dressed in a doctor's labcoat. He recognised it as one of his own. Michele was looking at the camera.

'Good boy,' she said and giggled. 'Now take it out and play with it!'

He replayed the video while taking his cock out. The annoying Periwinkle program kept beeping at him to move on to another slide and he clicked forwards to the next cell, not even bothering to glance at the small monitor.

The blazing periwinkle green of cell 83623 disappeared and was replaced by the dull grey mess of cell 83624.

Wayne had a lot of work to do over the next few days. On Thursday, he had some visitors. His secretary, Dawn, announced them.

'Sir, you have visitors,' she said over the intercom. Her normally calm, steady voice sounded a touch strained. 'It is two women. One of these women – she says her name is Holly Childress. The other one's name is Michele – just Michele, she says.'

He sat up ramrod straight in his chair, flush with excitement. Holly had come to see him? Why? For a moment he thought maybe she was here because she had noticed – but then he gave himself a figurative mental slap. The answer was obvious: she was here to plead on her boyfriend's behalf. He played with the idea of not receiving her. Certainly he would not have hesitated to do so if she had tried to make an appointment by phone. In person, she was more difficult to get rid of.

He smiled a bitter smile. As early as yesterday, he could not have imagined an occasion when he would have preferred to get rid of Holly Childress. Just thinking about her made him weak-kneed.

What about this Michele person? For an unpleasant moment he thought that maybe she had brought a lawyer with her. The more he thought about it the more likely that scenario appeared to him; some hard-nosed feminist, no doubt doing a favour for her bridge partner. He had a vague recollection that Holly played bridge. It was something that just fitted her.

He couldn't even tell his secretary that he had a meeting. Holly and the lawyer were probably sitting next to Dawn's desk up front and they would hear his voice on the intercom.

He sighed and told her to admit them.

Wayne quickly checked his reflection in the window. His thinning hair was sprinkled with liberal doses of silver. He kept telling himself that it made him look distinguished but he couldn't fool himself; he was getting old. He nervously smoothed his labcoat with both hands and sucked in his modest gut.

Two women entered the room.

Wayne gaped at them. The one who entered first was wearing a very short, very tight polyester miniskirt of hot pink and white stripes. She wore at least five-inch-tall metallic-red stiletto heels and an undersized hot-pink halter top with an embroidered white heart just below the astonishingly revealing cleavage. Like some schoolgirl in her mid-teens, her hair was done in pigtails, bleached to a near-white platinum blonde. Her lips were hot pink and she wore a lot of blue eyeshadow. The woman behind her was much more respectable; she wore those metallic-red stiletto heels as well and a revealing top, but at least she was wearing a suit – looked expensive too.

'I am Doctor Rainer. Maybe there has been some kind of mistake,' he said firmly, although he had trouble keeping his eyes off the obvious call girl. Somehow she looked familiar. 'Can I help you?' he asked, polite but in a tone that indicated that his time was valuable.

The golden blonde who wore the suit – very attractive, with long, tanned legs – smiled at him. 'I'm Michele,' she said. Her voice had a subtle, seductive quality to it, like the persuasive purr of a kitten. She gently petted the slutty blonde on the head. 'Ask Doctor Rainer how much he likes your new look, sweetie.'

'Do you like my new look, Wayne?' squealed the bleached-blonde accessory. She religiously maintained a ridiculously affected body posture, pressing her tits forwards and her ass back. It was absurd.

But her voice was like a hot knife slicing through the butter of his consciousness. 'Oh my God!' he gasped. 'Holly?'

'She is getting the name legally changed today.' The woman in the suit smirked. 'It will be Trixie forever and ever!'

'What – what happened?'

'Wayne – I hope you don't mind if I call you Wayne,' said the woman (Michele, he reminded himself). 'I hear little Robbie made a boo-boo.'

'That's one way of putting it,' he said. 'If I hadn't been there ...'

Holly leant against the wall. Her breasts were nearly exposed in the tiny top. She kept squirming in place and Wayne found it difficult to focus on the matter at hand. What was it? Oh yes – they were talking about Robert's malpractice, about the nearly botched surgery, about ...

'Trixie is here to ask you to be nice.' Michele laughed. 'Robbie will leave this silly research hospital and move on to boob jobs and facelifts instead. He'll be out of your hair and you won't have to worry about him making a boo-boo.'

He felt his eyes bulge with the sheer impertinence of the monologue. 'I'm not some kind of child,' he began. 'Holly, you know that I'm the head of this department and . . .'

Holly sat down on the edge of the sofa. She was quite obviously rubbing herself against it. It was incredibly – distracting. She arched her feet until she was a near caricature of feminine grace. 'Trixie, dear Wayne,' she moaned. 'Call me Trixie, pweeeease.'

Wayne could not keep his eyes off the vision of tawdry sleaze that the love of his life had been turned into. His cock strained against the prison of his boxer shorts. He had sort of expected Holly to plead for Robert's career but never in his wildest dreams had he expected an attempt to seduce him.

'All you have to do is give Robert a raise and a nice recommendation when he leaves,' cooed Michele. 'Give him a good bonus too and little Trixie will suck you off a few times a week. Give him that grant he was whining about as well. Oh, and he doesn't want to look for green on those stupid slides any more.'

'A raise? The grant?!' gasped Wayne. 'That's preposterous! There will be disciplinary hearings at the very least, and maybe the family will bring an action against the hospital. He was drunk, I smelt the liquor on his breath! And he *begged* me to let him do the Periwinkle project. He deserves to . . .' His words trailed off and he stared at Holly – inexplicably responding to the humiliating name Trixie – because she had just begun to moan. She slid long, fake nails against the flimsy pink polyester covering her chest until the fabric peeled off, exposing her beautiful breasts. She discovered her nipples with a delighted squeal.

'Go ahead, Trixie,' purred the tall blonde with her. 'Pinch your nice hard nipples, show the good doctor what an obedient pretty slut you can be for some lucky man with a little – shall we say, flexibility?'

195

Holly pinched her nipples. She whimpered with obvious, mindless pleasure.

'She can be your little secret,' promised the tall blonde. She moved closer until she was practically crooning in his ear. 'You can make her into your ... *private* secretary. She'll be your very own sex kitten. Ever fuck a girl in the ass? You can fuck her in the ass all you want. Trixie likes it up the butt, don't you, Trixie?'

Wayne gaped at Holly. He did not see Michele, wearing a contemptuous smirk, reach into her jacket pocket.

Holly's moans gained in strength; she practically ran over to Wayne, at least as much as she could run in those ridiculous stiletto heels. She turned, an over-exaggerated, seductive twirl, until her butt bumped against his crotch.

Wayne was frozen with shock. This sleazy bimbo was nothing like Holly. But she looked a little like Holly – at least a slutty stripper version of Holly – and no woman who looked this good had ever even looked at him, much less promised to – promised to, well, have sex with him.

Holly rubbed her ass against his rock-hard erection. 'Yes, Michele, yes, yes, yes!' she moaned.

'Tell the good doctor that you want his fat cock up your ass,' ordered Michele.

'Please fuck me in the ass, Wayne,' Holly begged. She leant her head against Wayne's chest and gazed up into his eyes, a seductive, demanding vixen on heat. Her pigtails rested against his labcoat. She glanced over at the tall blonde. 'Is this what you want, Michele?' she gasped. 'Am I doing good?'

'You're doing just fine, Trixie.' Michele laughed, then turned to smile at Wayne. 'All you have to do is be a little – reasonable.' Michele put her free hand – the one not in her purse – on top of Wayne's, and moved his hands, one at a time, until he was cupping Holly's exposed tits. 'It feels nice to feel her up,' she cooed.

'Yes, it does,' whispered Wayne. His member was oozing pre-come. The tawdry slut and her keeper made him feel so ashamed – ashamed yet excited at the same time. Despite Wayne's success as a professional, he had never been a hit with women, particularly pretty ones. In high

196

school and college he had been in the chess club and on the debating team. He had never been athletic and he'd had terrible teeth that had not been corrected until his early thirties. He was not a virgin but he had only two girlfriends and they had both left him for the same reason: another, more exciting, taller man. The sleazy, gorgeous bit of fluff rubbing herself against his almost virgin member was an irresistible lure.

Still. 'The patient – what Robert did . . .' he mumbled. It was difficult to come up with coherent sentences. All the blood in his brain had collected in his happy, raging hard-on.

The tall blonde woman – Michele – walked to his office door and turned the key.

'Why don't we give the good doctor a demonstration?' She smirked knowingly at Holly.

'I don't see how that would . . .' began Wayne, unable to take his eyes from the seductive vision before him.

'Put the doctor's cock in your mouth, Trixie.'

Holly quickly turned and knelt in front of Wayne.

Her movement forced his hand to part from her exposed breast. He felt a nearly elemental longing for the touch of the flawless, beautiful flesh.

She unzipped his pants and he felt her fingers latch around his member. Without hesitating, she wrapped her lips around the tip of his cock.

'Go ahead, Doctor,' urged Michele. 'Slide your dick into her mouth. I mean, that's what she's for, you know.'

'No,' he gasped. 'I don't . . .'

'You've been jerking off to photos of her for years now, Wayne.' Michele laughed. 'I bet you've been looking at her tits and ass on pictures you took at cocktail parties. Cock-Tail parties.' She giggled, amused by her little joke. 'You played with your prick all the time, moaning her silly little name. Don't let it bother you, Doctor Rainer. Live a little, spurt your load into the mouth of your *perfect woman*.'

Wayne glanced down; from his vantage point overhead, one of Holly's nipples was completely exposed. Her new hair was incredibly tawdry-looking with those bleached, silky blonde pigtails on either side. Holly smelt as if she'd slept in a tubful of cheap perfume, but given the circumstances – and her appearance – it somehow worked for her; the cloud of cloying scent made him even more excited.

'What about Robert?' he asked weakly. She did have a boyfriend. This boyfriend was his colleague. He thought about removing his member from Holly's lips. 'Are you still with Robert?' he mumbled. He really ought to pull his cock – he really ought to remove himself from this shameful situation.

He heard a faint sound – buzzing? – And Holly's lips tightened around his member.

There was no point in rushing . . .

'Trixie's pretty pink lips are wrapped around your stiffy, Doctor.' Michele giggled. 'And you worry about some other guy? Come on, Doctor, don't you want to fuck some hot bitch like Trixie?' She patiently draped his fingers, one at a time, around Holly's pigtails. He was holding on to both of them now. 'I know you do . . . Trixie, suck on the good doctor's prick for a minute.'

Holly slid her lips higher on his cock.

He felt like a prisoner being force-fed addictive drugs. 'This is unethical,' he moaned.

'It is,' purred Michele. 'Completely. I'm using your stupid adolescent crush on this little slut to turn you into a pitiful pussy-whipped bitch.' She reached out and pushed against his hand, still locked on Trixie's pigtails. Her head bobbed and his cock slid deeper into her mouth. 'Go on,' she urged him. 'Fuck her in the mouth, doctor.'

He just stood there, frozen with indecision. Michele giggled cruelly and casually pushed the back of Holly's head with her knee, until her lips slid all the way to the base of his rock-hard member. 'It's nice, isn't it?' she asked with a contemptuous smirk.

It felt so good, he withdrew a little and then pushed it back in – there was just no way around it.

'That's it, Wayne!' cooed Michele. 'Fuck her in the mouth, get a taste! Feels so nice, fucking little Trixie in the mouth!'

He stopped but felt Michele guide his hand. His fingers were made to pull on the pigtails. Wayne felt his cock slide in and out of Holly's hot-pink lips. The feeling of pleasure was intense. After the first two strokes he could not help himself and took the initiative again. He began to fuck Holly's head with mindless, debased strokes, pumping his cock in and out of Holly's painted lips.

Suddenly, Michele's hands slid off his own. She watched his frantic thrusts with amused condescension as she pulled a digital camera from her purse. She recorded the sordid tableau while addressing him. 'Little boy likes to fuck pretty Trixie's lips, isn't that right?' She laughed. 'There you go,' she said, grinning. 'It just happens naturally. You see, Doctor Rainer, Trixie is a bimbo slut. If you want to plug her cunnie in the future you'll have to co-operate with me, and for now that means you'll have to be nice to Robbie.'

With a stifled moan, Wayne lost control. His balls contracted and he spurted his come inside Holly's mouth. She swallowed with a desperate eagerness.

Michele petted her on the head. She put the camera away, took a remote control from her purse and trained it on the come-stained form of the former accountant. She pushed a few of the buttons and Holly collapsed in a heap of moaning, sweat-drenched flesh.

Michele faced Wayne. 'She is a hot little number, isn't she, Doctor Rainer?'

Wayne collapsed in his chair. He pulled up his pants. 'Oh my God,' he muttered. He felt dirty. He *was* dirty – his own come was drying on his lower stomach.

'Don't worry about it, Wayne,' said Michele in an amused tone. 'You'll be horny again in an hour at most ... and suddenly all this moral anguish won't matter at all.' She picked up one of Wayne's business cards from the desk. 'I'll email you a couple of pictures, just you and the love of your life with her lips wrapped around your cock. You can look at them when we leave. It'll help you when you're all alone and you need to relieve some tension.'

The details of the sordid event kept surfacing in his conscious mind about an hour after they had left but he managed to retain the semblance of scientific detachment. He refused to read any suspicious emails. It struck him that it would be a good idea to set his email filter to auto-delete anything unfamiliar. He sent a message to the researchers to use an alternate address.

He coped with what had happened by refusing to acknowledge it. It was kind of an ostrich with its head in the sand trick but it was working.

A few days later, recruiters began to call about Robert. He had been half expecting it. He had managed to schedule Robert for the absolute minimum amount of work, and he still managed to turn up late or screw up half the time.

Poor Holly!

Despite his antipathy towards the incompetent drunkard, Wayne knew that he would still be listed as a reference on Robert's CV. He would have to be; this research hospital and specifically this lab had to be listed as Robert's primary job reference. In fact he had Robert over a barrel. He derived some satisfaction from this state of affairs. He told the first two headhunters exactly what he thought of the useless lump of liquored-up fool.

He reflected on what had happened to Holly. He had been thinking about her a lot lately. Poor girl! That Michele woman had somehow brainwashed her – that was a certainty. Not that he hadn't enjoyed the results – he still blushed when he recalled the scene.

Barbara came in with his morning mail. He had a routine with the mail – he always went through each item with mechanical precision, in the order received. Letter opener, notebook, pen, glass of water . . . Yes, all was in order. Invoices, research materials, journals, a draft article, CVs from med students, a manila envelope presumably containing a CV – he lifted it from the pile. There was a stiff sheet inside. Maybe a CT scan or an MRI?

He cut the envelope open. Inside was a laminated photograph. He pulled it out and stared at it, aghast. His face looked like a caricature of himself, red, drooling – the eyes were halfway closed but it was obvious that he was enjoying himself. Holly's face was not visible, but her tongue was, and she was licking his – well, what she was doing was blatantly obvious.

So Michele hadn't been lying after all! She had taken pictures.

What would happen if she sent this photo to his colleagues? Or to his family? He dismissed the family angle immediately – his parents had passed away, his only sister was half a world away, in Kenya of all places – but the professional angle ... Why, Holly's breasts were uncovered and her hot-pink lips were leaving blatant smudges on his member. She certainly looked good. No, good was not descriptive enough. She looked phenomenal. That blonde hair, the pigtails, that sleazy little outfit and those high heels, yes, she looked incredible. He supposed she looked cheap, yes, that was a good word – slutty, even, but so what? Not everyone could wear a suit like that lawyer Michele.

He looked around nervously and put the picture in his briefcase. The last thing he needed was his secretary getting a good look at the photo. Now, why had they sent this picture? Obviously because he refused to check his email, he reasoned. Was this an attempt at blackmail? A moment's worth of reflection returned the distressing conclusion that yes, it definitely was. What could he do about it? Could he claim that the picture was a fabrication?

He'd better look at it again. Maybe it was a fabrication. After all, his recollection was fairly jumbled when it came to the scene of his filthy seduction.

He pulled out the picture again. By God, Holly looked appetising. He put it back in the envelope when he heard his secretary approach with his coffee. He would have to look at the picture somewhere safe, like the bathroom, inside a securely locked stall.

Yes, that was a good idea.

He had inspected the photograph thoroughly in the bathroom and a few times at home. He was forced to conclude that it was most likely genuine. In any case, it wouldn't matter even if it weren't. People would *assume* that it was. He should inspect it again, maybe at lunch, to make sure he hadn't missed anything. He pulled the picture out. Barbara was coming into his office again. She really ought to knock, he reflected. In any case, she deserved a day off!

'Barbara, why don't you take tomorrow off,' he told her when she came in and dropped off the Oncological Convention File. It's not like the convention couldn't wait, he thought resentfully.

'I don't understand, sir,' she stammered. 'You want me to take a sick day?'

'No, no.' He smiled through gritted teeth. 'Just take a day off, see family or friends. I don't have anything important scheduled tomorrow, I'll be fine all by myself.'

'That's very kind of you, sir,' she said. There was doubt in her voice.

'No trouble, no trouble. And feel free to take a long lunch too, I'll be busy here with this –' he raised the file she just brought in '– file.'

When she left he locked the door and checked his email. It was ridiculous to keep the filter on. He was sure that by now they would have stopped sending the pictures.

When he came in the next day he checked his email immediately. There were no pictures. At noon, right before he was about to lock his office door so he could inspect the picture in the solitude of his office, he had one more phone call. It was the managing director of a top-notch plastic surgery clinic uptown. He leant back in his chair, anticipating another gruelling session where he would be forced to torpedo whatever remained of Robert's career. Poor, deluded, corrupted Holly . . .

'Robert Waverly? Yes, he still works here,' said Wayne. 'I mean, yes, he works here.' The questions were always the same.

'What is my opinion of his skills? Well, let me tell you . . .' His voice trailed off, his heart skipping a beat. Holly had appeared in the doorway of his office. As she came in she shed the long raincoat that covered her from delicate neck to slender ankle. Underneath she was completely naked except for stiletto heels, metallic-red daggers digging directly into his soul.

Wayne's lust rose like a tidal wave. He stared at the receiver in his hand for an endless moment. 'He's – he's an – an exceptional surgeon,' he mumbled.

Holly pulled the door shut.

12

Lucille

The phone rang. Lucille frowned with exasperation. What now? She had too much to do as it was; she didn't need yet another phone call from her mother or the florist . . .

'Lucille White,' she purred into the receiver, thinking how delicious it was going to be when she could finally say her new married name in a few weeks. The sisters from the sorority would just die with envy!

'It's Holly.' Her friend's voice was strained.

'Oh darling, I'm so glad I got you on the phone, you just have to come over and take a look at these lovely patterns, really never expected to find them again, it's quite . . .'

The girl cut her off! 'Lucille, I'm in trouble . . .'

Lucille paused. What was it that people said when someone said something like this? 'Darling! Is there anything I can do?'

Holly sobbed. 'I – I don't know who I am any more, Lucy. Things have gotten very strange . . . Please help . . .'

What was this girl thinking? 'I'm not sure how much help I can be, sweetheart – with the wedding and all I really have my days full, you know how it is. Just the other day I got this call from the florist, you wouldn't believe what . . .'

Holly screamed into the receiver. Lucille was forced to hold the phone away from her ear. 'Lucille, I'm a blonde! I'm a bleach – bleached – platinum blonde!'

'Oh my God!' exclaimed Lucille. 'You're one of my bridesmaids, Holly! I can't believe you would do this to me!' She could already see the wedding pictures – she would be forced to discard *hundreds* of them if one of the bridesmaids became persona non grata.

'Lucille, for a second, for one crying second stop thinking about the goddamned wedding!'

Lucille gasped. 'I can't believe you just said that! For your information I was not thinking about the wedding. I'm your friend, you know that.'

'Lucille, if you really are my friend, then I need your help! Please come and get me – I'm getting so weak . . .'

'Are you sick?' If she was sick she could certainly be replaced without any repercussions.

'Not sick, it's something a lot more complicated. It's not something I can explain over the phone.'

'Well – I have a lot of . . . OK. I guess there is still enough time to get you to a hair salon. Seriously, darling, I can't believe you di –'

The girl hung up on her!

'I did it,' moaned Holly. She got on all fours, spreading her pussy lips wide, and looked up, pleading. 'She's coming here now.' Holly licked her lips. 'You said that if I called her over you would – you would . . .'

'Good girl!' Becky giggled. She slowly pushed the vibrator into Holly's drenched cunt. She crooned to the helpless, moaning young woman as if she were some small child who had eaten all her vegetables. 'You've been a good girl, yes, what a good little girl you've been . . .'

Lucille couldn't believe the nerve of the woman. It wasn't enough that she had become an unwanted house guest for weeks – particularly when all of Lucille's time was taken up with the wedding preparations – she also had the nerve to be, well, attractive.

Oh yes, she'd seen James look at her occasionally. She was not going to lose her Fortune 500 executive to some little skank!

She should have known that of all her friends it was Holly who was going to become a problem. How could she have dyed her hair blonde? Was she trying to become *more* attractive? Men were too easy to manipulate for a pretty fluff like Holly. She always knew the woman was just putting on a show with those conservative suits and that no-makeup routine; Lucille was looking forwards to discussing her lack of class – with a touch of sorrow in her voice, of course – at the next sorority get-together.

If it weren't a mere three days until the ceremony she would definitely replace her in the wedding party. It was too late now; in any case, Robert was a groomsman of James's and they had to walk up the aisle together. Of course, James could pair him up with a suitable girl. There were still a few single girls from the chapter who would welcome the opportunity . . .

She shook her head, annoyed. There was simply not enough time to get someone prepared and outfitted. Not to mention that a new girl would have had to do the wedding without the benefit of a single rehearsal!

She breathed in deeply, trying to calm herself. It wasn't easy. To think that she had actually considered Holly Childress as a potential Maid of Honour!

She drove her brand-new BMW convertible to Holly's apartment building. Of course, once she was married, she would also have to get a nice SUV – maybe something from Britain? She nodded to herself: yes, a Land Rover would do, a very classy car (automobile, she corrected herself; no point in sounding like she grew up in the Bronx) in anticipation of ferrying the children about. She would keep the roadster for fun, of course, or have it replaced with something better once James's career *truly* took off.

She pulled up to the entrance.

A young black man, an ebony tower of muscle, stood there in a tuxedo. He flashed her a blazing smile.

She averted her eyes from the servant.

'I haven't seen you here before,' she told him in a peremptory tone.

'I'm only here tonight,' he answered. His voice was so deep, so powerful, she was actually startled.

He had the manners to hold the door and bow to her as she exited the car.

The man was just huge, rippling with muscle. He was the best-looking black man she had ever seen.

'Want me to escort you upstairs, ma'am?' he asked. His voice thrummed with power.

'No thanks.' She did not see the man's eyes on her body but she felt his gaze traverse the length of it regardless. The sensation made her blush to the roots of her hair.

He nodded and kept smiling. 'See ya later, then,' he said.

She did not answer him. She was thinking. Maybe Holly had dyed her hair blonde to appeal to this hulking ebony god.

She passed an old black man sweeping the lobby. He leant on his mop and looked at her.

'Can I help you?!' she shrieked.

'No, ma'am,' he said simply. His voice was deep as well.

The elevator arrived with a smooth, nearly inaudible hum. Lucille stepped inside immediately, and turned around to keep an eye on the suspicious-looking janitor. The enormous, muscular black man had entered the lobby and now stood alongside the old man. They were not talking, just looking at her inside the elevator. She pressed 2 and backed up until she hit the back wall. Lucille saw the valet stride towards the elevator and her breath caught in the back of her throat. Why was he coming to the elevator? Were the doors closing? Yes, they were closing. The visible slice of the man narrowed with each passing moment until the door finally closed and the elevator began to ascend.

She walked to Robert's apartment and checked her makeup before ringing the doorbell. Robert had some rich, influential colleagues; if they happened to come by, she couldn't possibly look like some orphan who'd just been dragged off from the street. She was James's fiancée; she had to represent him as much as herself.

The door opened.

It took a moment for Lucille's mind to process the image. By the time she managed it and turned to flee, the hulking valet from downstairs was already standing behind her.

He was grinning. She whirled around again and came face to face with the huge black man who had opened the door. He was practically a twin of the valet, except that this one was wearing leopard-print thongs and cowboy

206

boots. That was *all* he was wearing. His muscles were gleaming, rippling mounds of defined masculinity.

'Lucille! Lucille!' It was Holly's voice.

Lucille tore her eyes from the outline of what had to be an absolutely enormous member and managed a feeble croak of a response. 'Yeah – yes, it's me. What's going on?'

'Come on in, pwease – please – I organised your very own bachelorette party!'

The stripper stood aside and bowed. The valet grinned at her and motioned in the direction of the door. 'After you, ma'am.'

'I really – I mean . . .' she muttered. He really looked exactly like the stripper. Maybe they were twins. 'Do I have to?'

'I have the video of James's bachelor party,' yelled Holly, still inside the apartment. 'I think you ought to see it . . .'

Lucille marched into the apartment. 'What do you mean?' she demanded. 'He had a bachelor party? Here? You have a video? *You* took a video of *my* husband's bachelor party?'

There were practically no lights on inside the apartment; the only illumination within was provided by a couple of bright-red candles. Some song with a sensual beat was playing on the stereo. A woman was sitting on the edge of the couch. Her hair was platinum blonde. She wore a long, shapeless dress, nearly a smock, and very high, metallic-red stiletto heels. It took a few seconds for Lucille to make the connection.

'Holy cow,' she gasped. '*Holly?*'

The woman squirmed on the edge of the couch. 'Oh Lucille, I'm so glad you came!' She stood up and tip-toed closer, heels clicking on the hardwood floors.

Even in the dim candlelight Lucille could make out the change on Holly's face. She was wearing lipstick, eye-shadow, eyeliner, mascara, fake eyelashes – there were so many artificial enhancements to her appearance that after a momentary effort Lucille simply gave up trying to catalogue them.

'Holly – you don't look . . . You look different.'

207

Naturally, she would never do as a bridesmaid. She would just have to find someone else. In two days. Get them fitted with the bridesmaid dress, somehow get them to a rehearsal so they wouldn't mess up the ceremony ... Suddenly she realised all the printed materials had Holly listed as a member of the wedding party. She was listed right after her sister, the maid of honour! She could never withdraw Holly's name from the wedding, there was simply no way to do it without having to engage in uncomfortable explanations. She could already see it. She could hear her mother's incessant questioning, she could hear the reporter from the *New York Times* 'Fashion & Style' section asking, 'Why isn't Holly Childress in the wedding? Wasn't she supposed to be one of the bridesmaids?' She could not see herself responding with the truth: Holly Childress had turned herself into a bleached-blonde whore.

Lucille began to sob. How could Holly do this to her? 'Holly, what happened?'

'I think you've met Kevin Junior and Jake,' said Holly, motioning in the direction of the kitchen. 'Michele and Becky ...' She began to squirm with a little more intensity and her voice abruptly changed in timbre and inflection. 'I mean, *I* hired them to do your bachelorette party. Darling, the men have done a terrible thing ...' She lifted a remote control from the coffee table and turned on the television.

The light from the TV monitor was an almost painful shock in the mellow, candlelit darkness. When her eyes adjusted, she saw a luxurious leather couch and a large breasted, bleached-blonde woman, completely naked except for stiletto heels. A man was on his hands and knees in between her legs. The slut giggled and lifted his head from its shameful position, positioning it so the identity of the obscene pussy-licker was undeniable.

It was James.

The woman picked up a bottle of champagne and poured some foaming, sparkling wine over her shaved pussy.

James lapped it up with obvious eagerness. He was using his tongue like a dog would, leaving eager, shiny, worshipful trails. He finally put his mouth right over the slut's cunt and began to – slurp. The sound was exactly that – he was slurping on the big-titted wonder's pussy, sucking on the flood of champagne.

Holly squirmed closer to her and put a friendly hand on her shoulder. 'Oh, don't worry, Lucille.'

'How can you say that?' Lucille cried out in a tone that was half grief and half rage. This was intolerable! Holly had seen this – transgression – this *serious* transgression. What if she told someone? She could never look her in the eye again. And what if Holly told one of the other sorority sisters? She would be the laughing stock of the entire chapter! What was worse, maybe some of those – bitches, yes, that's what they were – maybe they would now think James was free game! Holly's hair practically looked like the hair of that sleazy whore on the TV monitor. How could James have done this to her? He'd never seemed interested in going down on her, so how come that woman appealed to him so much? Who was she, anyway?

She began to cry.

Holly poured her a drink and pressed it in her hand.

She sobbed and drained it. 'How could he do this to me?' she whimpered. 'I can't believe he – cheated on me!' She became almost nauseated by the word. 'Cheated! On me! The mother . . . the future mother of his children!'

'Oh sweetie . . .' Holly gently petted her on the head, then hugged her.

Her perfume was very heavy but right now Lucille welcomed the sensation of being hugged. It felt good being comforted.

'Men are evil!' she cried.

'Yes, they are!' agreed Holly. 'James hired some strippers and had a good time at his bachelor party and he thought you would never know! Have another drink, darling . . .'

Lucille drank and held out her glass for a refill. 'Oh no,' she wailed, thinking of the worst possible scenario. 'You think he won't want to get married now?'

Kevin Junior – or maybe it was the other one, Lucille

couldn't remember his name – began to massage the knots in her shoulder.

Holly snuggled closer, leaning her head on Lucille's shoulder. 'Oh sweetie,' she sighed. 'Do you still want to marry him? I mean – he cheated on you!'

Lucille nodded. 'That may be true but – but I love him!' she insisted, sobbing. Kevin Junior – or Jake, yes, that was the name – had magic fingers. Despite her frazzled state, she had to admit that it felt good. She sipped from the glass, feeling warm. 'What is this?' she asked, quizzically examining the off-pink, slightly sweet concoction.

'It's champagne, tequila and pomegranate juice.'

'Oh my goodness,' said Lucille. It was getting so warm in there. On screen, the picture shifted to a tall, tanned blonde in red stilettos. She was getting her feet rubbed by – Robert!

'Oh my God,' she gasped, shocked. 'Robert?'

'Yes!' Holly sobbed. 'It's horrible!'

There was something else.

'Are you wearing the same shoes as that woman?' asked Lucille, scandalised.

'I – yes. I found them and thought Robert would feel guilty if he saw me in the same shoes as Mi –' Holly was stammering but Lucille figured she was feeling as confused and betrayed as she was herself.

Jake (by now Lucille was pretty sure this was the one called Jake) was doing a masterful job on her back and shoulders. Despite her shock and displeasure, the cocktail and the massage had really loosened her up. Lucille thought about telling him to rub Holly's shoulders too, but it felt so good – and she deserved something special, going through all this pain. She sighed.

Jake called out to the other man. 'Kevin!' The other man – his twin, he had to be, thought Lucille – came into the room from the kitchen. He was carrying a bucket of ice in one hand, and a pitcher in the other, full of the transparent pink stuff that she had been drinking.

'Oh Lucille . . .' sighed Holly. 'Let's just have a good time and not think about those evil men!'

'But . . .'

'There is nothing we can do right now. They went out of town anyway, both of them ... I wouldn't be surprised if they left together.'

Lucille vaguely recalled the telephone conversation with James. The curtains! She could – the living room ... She drank again. It tasted good.

She leant further back, driving her shoulders against Jake's fingers. 'Rub them harder,' she pleaded.

In the meantime the action continued on the monitor; Robert's seductress pushed him down on a couch of his own. She sat in his lap and began to gyrate on top of him. The woman was wearing a satisfied, gloating smirk.

'It's horrible,' gasped Holly. She couldn't stand still for a second; as she was watching the disloyalty of her boyfriend unfold, her agitation grew. 'They cheated on us,' she cried.

'Yes, they did,' replied Lucille. 'Cheated on us, yes.'

Jake's hands slid lower. She felt the rippling muscles of his forearms against the middle of her back. It was quite obvious that his hands had found their way underneath her dress. He could not advance any lower unless she made space for his hands between the couch and her back by moving forwards.

'They'll be fucking any second now,' panted Holly, squirming. 'Any second now Robert'll be fucking Michele.'

'What're you saying?' asked Lucille. 'You watched this already, I guess ...' Her head lolled forwards; she leant over the table to pour herself another drink. She *had* to lean forwards to reach the bottle.

Jake's huge hands slid lower, until they were over her lower back.

Lucille furtively glanced over at Holly. The former brunette was – well, she was rubbing her clit against the edge of the couch. How disgusting! Lucille saw a bowl of chips on the coffee table. She picked one up and her hand brushed against the bowl as she withdrew her fingers. The whole thing just fell on the floor, spilling dozens of crisps on the carpet.

'Oh no,' said Lucille. She rose slightly and bent over to pick up the chips.

Jake's monstrous hands slipped lower until they were cupping her ass. He squeezed her cheeks, hard. Lucille gasped; she felt the man's massive erection pressing against her bottom.

'Yeah, there it is,' moaned Holly. She rubbed herself against the edge of the couch and gave a running commentary for the filth unfolding on screen. 'There, Michele is riding his cock. She is fucking Robert with her pretty shaved pussy . . .'

Lucille stood there while that enormous rigid cock pressed against her drenched panties. After a moment of indecision she whirled around and shoved Jake hard on his massive, rippling chest. 'How dare you!' she screamed, although not too loud. Someone might hear.

'Fuck her hard, she likes it,' moaned Holly. 'She likes being forced a little.'

Those huge hands reached out like an elemental force of nature and tore her dress off. She felt like a toy doll in his gigantic hands.

'How dare you!' She sobbed and covered her breasts with her hands – her nipples were so hard she thought they might poke through the bra. 'I'm engaged,' she squealed as he roughly bent her over. His fingers checked her panties. 'So wet.' He laughed, then slapped her hard on the rump. 'Tight, too.'

'I'll scream!' she squealed. She raised her eyes and saw Holly fumble with the pants of the valet. Her bridesmaid freed Kevin Junior's enormous member.

'Will she scream?' Jake asked Holly.

'She has been fantasising about a gang-bang for years. Ever since her freshman year in college. She wants one from behind and one in her mouth,' moaned Holly. 'Years ago, but . . .'

Why was she squirming? Why was she betraying all Lucille's secrets?

Kevin Junior walked over until he was standing in front of her. 'Suck on it, bitch,' he ordered, laughing and pushing his cock against her lips. 'Suck on it!'

'You're forcing me!' she whimpered. It was right in her face; enormous, black and veiny. She put her lips around the pulsating member. She took it in as deeply as she could. After all, she was being forced. Who knows what they would do to her if she didn't accede to their every whim?

Her cunt was so wet. So fucking wet. When were they gonna fuck her?

She felt Jake's enormous dick slide into her. She thought she was going to split for a moment, but then the sensation turned into a nearly excruciating wave of non-stop pleasure. She tried to moan but the cock in her mouth turned it into a stifled cough.

'Don't try to speak, Lucy.' Holly squirmed her way over until she was kneeling next to Lucille's prone, bent-over body. 'Just suck on the big black cock . . . I know you like it, you told me – suck it good . . .'

'Mmmmm . . .'

'That's it, Lucille. Suck it, suck it . . .'

Holly stood up, teetering from side to side in the heels. She took off her shapeless dress; underneath she wore the sleaziest lace lingerie Lucille had ever seen. It was all transparent pink lace. A corset squeezed her waist until even her normal-sized breasts appeared huge. The fabric permitted her nipples to poke through unhindered. Holly tore her dress and used a strip of the fabric to blindfold Lucille.

Lucille now felt completely helpless. Those monstrous cocks were skewering her from both directions. She wanted to scream out loud about how good it felt, when she felt hands over her tits, squeezing them, pinching her nipples. Those fingers had long sharp nails. It could only be Holly. The skank fondled her breasts and moved on to her ass.

Lucille moaned.

An unfamiliar female voice came from behind. 'Tell her what you told me, Trixie.'

'I . . .' Oddly enough, Holly began to sob; the sobs turned into moans; the moans slowly resolved into coherent words. She was crying, but it was obvious that the former brunette was somehow getting off on every single word of the confession. 'I've been wanting to touch you for a few days now, Lucille. You're such a hot – oh God –

bitch, yes, yes, I like – I love your body. I want to – I want to lick your pussy . . . Oh God, yes, yes, thank you, thank you!'

'Mmmmm . . .' Lucille was just too aroused to care what she was hearing; she sucked on the enormous cock with frantic energy, sucking down each drop of pre-come with relish.

More hands joined the ones on her breasts and her efforts were finally rewarded by a sustained spurt of come directly into her mouth.

She eagerly swallowed every single drop. She felt the spent cock withdraw from her mouth, only to be replaced with another one. This one was nearly as large as the first; perhaps it was the other man? No, it couldn't be; *his* cock was still pumping in and out of her pussy. She wrapped her lips around it and used all her skill to pleasure the new man. The cock in her pussy withdrew and she felt him ejaculate all over her ass. She wriggled her bottom, desperate for something – anything – to substitute for the pleasure received from the valet's enormous member.

Something hard pressed against her pussy lips. A dildo?

'Go ahead, Becky,' came the voice of the mysterious woman. 'Fuck little miss Lucille, she wants it bad. You do want it bad, don't you, Lucy? Lucy is a nice, slutty name – almost good enough for you. But not quite. Let me think of a new name . . . How about . . . Kitty?'

Lucy did have a vibrator at home; still, the *thing* that entered her was as much a mere vibrator as the Hope diamond was a simple pebble. Someone – some woman named Becky, apparently – was fucking her from behind with the toy. It was horribly shameful and humiliating. Lucille couldn't help wanting more. She rammed herself back until her pussy lips rode up the rubber member, her pussy now no more than an insatiable mouth of drooling pink, desperate to gobble more cock. Only some of her muffled moans escaped the thick member plugging her mouth.

The man with his cock in Lucille's throat suddenly withdrew and came all over her face. She screamed with the pleasure of the device in her cunt, screamed like a bitch on heat. The blindfold, already loose from the rhythmical movement of sex, came off.

Lucille's eyes adjusted to the light.

A contracting member was dribbling droplets of come on to her face. Her eyes focused on the face of the owner – it was Kevin, the janitor from the lobby. She opened her mouth in horror. He grinned at her and stroked his cock with his hand, forcing another drop of come to ooze from the tip. It fell straight in her open mouth. She choked and spat it out just as she saw Robert. He was only a few feet away from her. Even though he wore his labcoat, he was not a sight for sore eyes. Doctor Waverly wore a collar, a shocking-pink, rhinestone-studded number that looked like something very expensive pets were given for Christmas by very old ladies living in trailer parks. His zipper was open and his cock was peeking out. It was fully engorged. The doctor was on his hands and knees, busily licking the metallic-red heels of the tall blonde from the video she had seen earlier, except that this was no movie. As Lucille watched, the tall blonde attached a no-nonsense-looking leather leash to Robert's collar.

Robert seemed to sense Lucille's eyes on him; his licking faltered. He had the grace to look ashamed. The tall blonde prodded his cheeks with the pointed toe of her shoe and he responded with a nearly helpless moan.

'I have to, I'm sorry . . .' he sobbed and resumed his task.

Lucille tried to look over her shoulder. She managed to turn quarter of the way around before the woman who had been fucking her – Becky – shoved the vibrator all the way into her cunt. Some sort of prongs slid right over her clit and began to rotate.

Lucille experienced a gorgeous, perfect, sustained orgasm that burned directly into her soul. 'Yes, yes, yes, oh God, yes!' she panted, sensing more come dribbling on to her face from the janitor's spent cock. She wrapped her lips around his member and sucked on it, desperate for more. The sensations from her clit just kept coming on and on and on and Lucille felt astonishingly alive and filthy. She

215

felt like a dirty whore in love with her work. By the time Lucille felt the big fuck toy slip out of her she was sobbing with the pain of parting. The avalanche of pleasure simply ceased. Its absence was sheer torture.

'Please don't stop – please ...' she gasped. She flipped over on to her back to get a good look at the source of her pleasure, to get a good look at Becky.

The big-titted wonder from the video, the one with the bleached-blonde hair, stood outlined in the flickering candlelight, tall in those familiar metallic-red stilettos. She wore a strap-on vibrator, shiny black, covered with odd protrusions along its entire length. There was a man in a familiar, expensive-looking navy-blue power suit behind her. It was an incongruous picture because he was on his knees.

The tip of the monstrous fake cock was swaying back and forth. Becky was gyrating her ass and the length of the vibrator magnified the movement until it was obviously noticeable at the tip. The light from the candles reflected off the shiny black material. Lucille looked at it with longing.

She sobbed. Was she being teased with the treat?

No, impossible. Becky's eyes were closed, and she wore a satisfied smile.

It took a moment for Lucille to realise the reason for her satisfaction. The man in the suit was licking her panties, worshipping her encased ass and pussy with doglike devotion.

As Lucille looked on she saw one of the man's hands reach out and unzip his pants. He took out his cock and began to jerk off, matching his strokes to the rhythm of his degraded ass worship.

The man wore a ring. Specifically, he wore a shiny gold promise ring. The man's penis was familiar. It was James.

'How could you do this to me!' shrieked Lucille. The janitor's come dribbled down her chin as her entire body shook with inner turmoil. 'You cheated on me!' she whimpered. 'How could you?'

Becky giggled and pushed down the strap-on panties. She leant back, smothering James's face with her newly naked ass. His face got caught in the triangle formed by her ass cheeks and the pleasure panties. Becky cooed with pleasure and ground her anus on to the tongue of Lucille's fiancé.

Michele laughed. 'So sad. Becky's pussy-whipped sugar-daddy just can't get enough ass to lick.'

James groaned; the pace of his degraded, pathetic licking intensified, along with his frantic masturbation.

'Good boy!' Michele smirked and strutted over to join Becky. Robert followed her on all fours, obeying the tugging on his leash. His face was shiny with the stripper's pussy juices.

'You've been a naughty little slut, Kitty!' Michele said teasingly. She put a hand on the strap-on that Becky wore, now pulled down to mid-thigh, and held it in place. 'Come here, Kitty!' she crooned. 'Here is a yummy little treat for your wet little pussy!' She picked up a remote control from the coffee table and trained it on the vibrator, then punched the central button. The prongs at the base began to rotate.

Becky giggled. She grasped the base of her artificial prick as Michele let go of it. 'Come here, kitty kitty!'

Lucille heard a stifled gasp.

Holly had tip-toed over. Her eyes were glazed with longing as she stared at the monstrous fake cock. 'I'll do it,' she begged. 'Please, please let Becky fuck me, Michele.'

'After Kitty, if you behave – maybe then.' Michele petted Holly on the head. 'You've become such a naughty whore, Trixie.'

'Go on. Please, just do as she says,' Holly said to Lucille. She sobbed. Her eyes were locked on the bopping vibrator. '*Please* hurry up, Lucille.'

Michele sat down on the love seat. She spread her legs wide and Robert crawled between them. The fabric on the back of his labcoat bore little holes, the marks of stiletto heels. He stared at her pussy for a moment. Lucille could see the internal conflict raging within him. With a pathetic sob, Robert lurched forwards, extending his tongue to lick the stripper's shiny shaved slit.

Michele did not even bother to acknowledge his drooling, pathetic service. She frowned at Holly. 'Her name is

Kitty, little Trixie. Try to remember some simple things. Dumb blonde slut!'

'Yes, Michele,' whimpered Holly. 'I'm so sorry. Please forgive me. Pweeease . . .'

She returned to face Lucille, sobbing softly. 'I beg of you, Kitty, please . . .' She moved closer. 'Please, Kitty, just bend over – you'll come so fast – and then it'll be my turn . . .'

Lucille glanced at the shiny black toy. When it was inside it certainly felt phenomenal, astonishing, wonderful. It was pleasure incarnate. Still, she was not going to turn into the same run-of-the-mill nympho bitch Holly had evidently become.

'I can't possibly,' she protested.

Michele turned on Becky's strap-on with her remote. She turned a dial until every single prong and protrusion seemed to be in motion.

Lucille stared at the monstrous device. 'I would have to be forced,' she finally squeaked.

Michele smirked. 'The sleazy little bitch has to be forced.' She roughly hauled Robert up by his leash. 'Hold her down, Robbie.'

Michele turned to Becky. 'Tell your ass-licker cash machine to go and help his friend.'

Becky nodded. She grabbed James by the hair and removed him from the smothering embrace of her bottom. 'You can go back to licking my butt soon, sweetie,' she cooed. 'First, I want you to hold Kitty down while I fuck her.'

'No, James, you can't!' wailed Lucille. 'No! Don't you love me?'

She stood and stumbled towards the door. She had to flee at once, before Becky had a chance to shove that buzzing wonder into her cunt, until she couldn't think any more, until all she could do was writhe and moan with pleasure over and over . . .

There was a chair in the way. She really couldn't take the risk of leaping over it; she might trip and fall. She ought to go around it. Oh no, she was going too fast; she stumbled on the chair and fell, just as she had feared. The men were too dazed to catch up with her, even now; Lucille stood and felt the blood rush into her head. Why, she was feeling suddenly weak. She *must* have been drugged. That would definitely have slowed her down.

Finally James was close enough to grab her wrist. His weak, pussy-slick fingers slid off her skin.

Robert stumbled up to her and brought her down from the other side.

'No, stop it, stop it!' she wailed. She kept pushing their hands away from her. They could not get a good grip. Where were the hulking twins? Where was the janitor? Had they left already? They most certainly wouldn't let her get away!

Eventually she saw Michele reach into her kit-bag and pull out a pair of fuzzy pink handcuffs.

She walked over. James was inexpertly trying to hold on to her arm.

'I am so angry!' screamed Lucille, ignoring the approaching blonde. After all, why should she pay attention to her? She was being manhandled by her own future husband! How shameful, how humiliating! Michele was almost in a position where she could handcuff her.

Lucille slapped James and spat in his face. Obviously she was too angry to think logically; if she had just used her brain, she would have broken free of his hold and made a run for the door. It was too late now, of course. Michele used the moment of her hysterical attack on her fiancé to slip the handcuffs on her.

With her hands immobilised, it was a simple matter for the men to push her down to her knees. She was squirming so much they had to bind her legs as well, using restraints from the kit-bag.

'No!' she moaned. 'Don't rape me, don't rape me!'

Michele fondled her between her legs. 'So wet, Kitty's pussy is just drenched,' she cooed. 'Must be so shameful to be so wet just when Kitty's about to get raped in every hole.'

'Please don't rape me,' squealed Lucille, writhing, exposed, defenceless. 'Please don't rape my wet pussy!' The fuzzy handcuffs were not very high quality; if she really

219

tried she probably could snap one of the links and free her hands. She was surrounded by the domineering, manipulative whores (Holly included) and their mindless drones, including her fiancé. Who knows what they would do to her if she tried to escape? Better to bide her time. It was definitely better not to try anything, at least as long as they didn't brutalise her. She would just have to take it, however they chose to use her.

'We will start with the other holes, then.' Michele laughed. 'I sent Kevin and his nephews out for some more drinks. When they get back they'll fuck pretty Kitty until she's just covered in cream, yum yum!'

Michele turned to Holly. 'Trixie, honey, here is your chance to lick some fresh pussy,' she cooed. 'Give the little kitty a good tongue lashing!'

Holly's pretty red tongue on her sopping wet clit . . . 'I'm not a lesbian,' cried Lucille. 'I'm not a lesbian!'

Holly eagerly positioned herself between Lucille's legs. She licked her way up from her pedicured toes, caressing her every once in a while with her hands.

'Not fair,' whined Becky. 'It's like, how come Trixie gets to play with the new toy?'

'You're a spoiled bimbo, Becky. Now get on all fours and lick Trixie while she eats Luc . . . Kitty's pussy,' ordered Michele.

Holly squealed with delight. She wiggled her bottom in anticipation of Becky's efforts just as her own lips descended on Lucille's pussy. She sucked her friend's pussy lips into her mouth and moved higher, teasing her clit with the tip of her tongue.

'I'm not a lesbian!' moaned Lucille. She *could* thrash around and make it difficult for Holly, but they would just – obviously they would just beat her into submission. That's right, they would probably overpower her. Anyway, she seemed to be frozen with fear. She had read something about that in a magazine. She was 'frozen with fear', stunned into immobility by what Holly was doing with her tongue and fingers and magical lips to her sopping-wet, quivering, defenceless pussy.

Holly's tongue circled her clit. She pushed two, then

three fingers into Lucille's drenched cunt and began to rhythmically finger-fuck her.

'I'm not a lesbian!' groaned Lucille, pushing her insatiable whore pussy on to the useless bitch's fingers. Why wasn't she using more of them? 'I'm not a lesbian!' she wailed and squirmed until her clit rubbed against Holly's lips just so.

She was going to come! She was going to come!

'Oh, you're not into girls!' said Michele, sounding surprised. 'In that case, stop playing with her, Trixie. She's not a lesbian!'

Holly obeyed at once. Now that her friend was, unfortunately, no longer doing what she had been between Lucille's legs, Lucille could marshal enough of her frustrated faculties to register the rest of what was happening in the room. Holly was giving off tiny moans of satisfaction as she ground her pussy into Becky's face. The big-titted stripper was on her hands and knees and doing something to Holly, much to her friend's delight.

She could also make out a shape in a navy-blue suit behind her, servicing Becky in a similar fashion. James's pants had fallen all the way down to his ankles. His member was erect and his hand was draped around it again.

'I'm – I'm not a . . .' she whimpered tentatively. Why wasn't somebody paying attention to her? She would have stomped her foot and thrown a temper tantrum if she hadn't been tied up.

'I guess if Kitty is not a lesbian she would hate the shiny black strap-on too,' the tanned blonde said. 'We bi bitches'll just fuck and lick all night while straight little Kitty's all tied up. Yeah, I think that's exactly what we'll do.'

'Don't leave me like this!' begged Lucille. 'Please!'

'Kitty-kitty-kitty,' purred Michele. She squatted next to Lucille's head. She wasn't wearing any panties.

'Lick my cunt, Kitty,' said Michele. 'Lick it right now. If you do a good job, I'll let Becky fuck you with the vibrator.' She rose slightly and lowered herself on to Lucille's face.

Lucille was gasping for air. The stripper's pussy was smothering her face; the tip of Lucille's nose pressed against Michele's clit. She needed to breathe! She struggled beneath the warm, gorgeous flesh, shaking her head from left to right. She managed to suck down a breath of air along with some of Michele's pussy juices.

It was obvious that unless she obeyed the tall blonde's instructions she would be smothered to death. She would have to obey. Yes, she would have to. It was very hot being smothered like this. As she began to lap Michele's cunt, she spread her legs a little wider. After all, it was very hot; spreading her legs helped her keep cool.

'Good kitty!' Michele laughed. 'I knew little Kitty would be licking pussy in no time!'

Finally! A hard, vibrating object pressed against Lucille's pussy lips. Still, whoever was holding it was making no effort to put it inside her. She was so wet! Why, if she just struggled a little, the thing might slip right inside!

'She is one horny slut, Becky. Only fuck her if she makes me come.'

'Yes, Michele.'

Lucille intensified her efforts. She thought about all the things that made her excited when someone went down on her, and used all of them. She licked the shaved pink slit, teased the clit with her tongue; she did anything and everything she could think of.

'Very nice,' said Michele. Her voice sounded strained with effort. 'Keep . . . Good Kitty. Good Kitty!'

Lucille shoved her tongue as deep into Michele's pussy as she could. She french-kissed the stripper's spasming, orgasming cunt.

'Good Kitty,' gasped Michele, sliding off her face. 'You can fuck Kitty, Becky!'

'Yes, Michele,' said Becky. She pulled the panties all the way back up, pushing James's questing face away. 'Later, Jimmy,' she said and laughed.

Lucille spread her legs as wide as she could.'Yes, fuck me, please, please,' she moaned.

Becky slid the vibrating strap-on toy all the way into Lucille's desperately wet fuck-hole.

222

'Thank Becky for fucking your worthless pussy, Kitty,' said Michele, frowning. 'Show some gratitude.'

'Thank you, Becky, for fucking my worthless pussy,' groaned Lucille in the throes of a phenomenal orgasm. 'Thank you Becky for fucking Kitty's worthless pussy.'

'Tell Becky you're a pussy-licking lesbian whore, Kitty,' said Michele.

'I'm a pussy-licking lesbian whore,' screamed Lucille. 'Please fuck my worthless pussy, please!'

'Bimbo Becky's marrying Jimmy ATM.' Michele laughed. 'But she doesn't have a ring yet. Stop fucking her, Becky. Stop fucking little wet whore Kitty.'

Becky pulled out the shiny black strap-on.

'Please don't stop!' whimpered Lucille. 'Please don't stop!'

Michele explained the situation slowly, contempt radiating from every single word. 'Kitty, the thing is – Bimbo Becky is sad. She doesn't have a pretty diamond engagement ring for when she marries Jimmy ATM! If she was happy, maybe then, maybe, just maybe she'd fuck little Kitty some more.'

'Please fuck me!' sobbed Lucille. 'Please fuck my wet pussy!'

'No ring, no big vibrating prick in pussy, Kitty!'

Lucille raised her handcuffed arms and held her hand out to Becky, pleading. 'Please take it,' she begged. 'Please take the ring and fuck me, I beg you!'

'You're so nice!' crooned Becky. 'You really want to give me your nice diamond engagement ring?'

'Yes, fuck, yes. Please fuck me. Please, please . . .'

'Are you absolutely sure?' Michele smirked. She opened the handcuffs. 'You're giving your ring and your man to Bimbo Becky in exchange for a lezzie fuck?'

'Yes, yes,' moaned Lucille. 'Please turn it on, please . . .' Now that her hands were free, she used her newly won freedom to tug frantically at the ring until it slid off her finger. She held it up to Becky, desperate to reach her.

'You're so nice, Kitty!' cooed Becky. She greedily grabbed Lucille's hand and slid the three-carat diamond engagement ring on to her finger. She giggled triumphantly and crawled on top of Lucille, driving the strap-on into her. The prongs slid over Lucille's clit, rewarding her humiliating surrender.

Wearing a gloating smile, Michele aimed the remote and pushed the centre button.

13

Wedding Bells

'Oh honey, of course you just must have a bachelor party.'

'Really?'

'Absolutely!' cooed Michele. 'You must invite *all* your new colleagues from the clinic!'

'But – I really don't have the cash right now ... I'll have two more facelifts and a couple of breast implants coming up the next weekend; I'll have some more money then.' For a moment he looked worried. What if he couldn't keep her happy?

Michele leant into him. Her curves pressed against his body. 'Don't you worry, Robbie honey! Pretty Michele'll give little Robbie a quick loan!'

'I can't even afford to buy you the new car you asked for,' muttered Robert. 'I'm so sorry ...'

'Oh Robbie, don't you worry about that.' Michele giggled. 'I'll make do with *your* car. But you should sign over the title, honey. All the girls say you're just using me. I mean, if you give me your car it'll mean I'm more than just some nice shaved pussy.'

'You want me to sign over my car?' asked Robert. He shook his head, feeling confused. He loved that car ...

Smirking, she unzipped his pants and began to stroke his straining, overworked cock. 'Doesn't that feel good, honey?'

'Yeah, yeah,' he gasped. 'But – my car ...'

'Don't worry about hiring girls. I'll talk to some of them at the club. They won't mind. They want to party with a bunch of plastic surgeons.'

'Good . . .' Robert stared at the humiliating display of the stripper's crimson nails sliding up and down on his erect member. The manicure had cost him a hundred dollars earlier that day. 'I – I'm sorry, what – I can't think.'

'You don't have to think, sweety,' purred Michele. 'I bought you a nice new pen and I brought your organiser, too! Look, there is the title, all filled out. I even put my itsy-bitsy name on it, so all you have to do is put your important Doctor Robbie signature on it.' She sat in his lap and wriggled her way around, inserting the stiff engorged joystick to Robert's soul into her pussy. 'Isn't that nice? It feels sooo good!' Her cunt was tight and wet and it fastened upon his member like a velvet vice.

'Yes, very nice . . .' he moaned.

She placed his fingers around the pen – forefinger, then thumb, one at a time. 'I like fucking you, Robbie.' She pouted. 'But I really want your itsy-bitsy, pretty red car. You understand, Robbie baby?'

Martha was beaming. She had used the key Lucille had given her to visit – she didn't want to spoil the surprise. She sat in an easy chair (she made a note of telling Lucille to have the thing re-upholstered as soon as possible. The silk of the rigid, narrow arms was frayed) and faced the door.

It was well past midnight by the time the door creaked open. Oddly enough, Lucille was wearing bulky sweats and very high heels.

'Honey, I have something to tell you!'

Lucille screamed. 'Mom, you nearly scared me dead!'

'Sweetheart, I'm sorry, I just had to come in person to give you the good news.'

'I'm so tired,' mumbled Lucille. She gingerly hobbled over to the refrigerator and pulled out a carton of milk. She took a few fevered gulps and threw the empty carton in the trash. 'Can't it wait, Mom?'

'You won't be so tired when I tell you the big news!'

'Yes?'

Martha grabbed both of her arms and spoke with ringing pride. 'We got the cathedral!'

It had not been easy. Pastor Baines believed that only the most dedicated members of the flock could be granted the honour of entering the blessed state of holy matrimony at the cathedral. It had taken considerable research and a box of girl-scout cookies to Mrs Barristan, the church secretary, to learn of his likes and dislikes. By grace, he did have an Achilles heel. Apparently Pastor Baines was a sucker for a certain good cause. His pet charity had something to do with mentally ill mothers and babies – or was it just insane mothers? – Martha wasn't really sure. She cared, of course – that was the reason for her more than generous grant – still, they really needed to have a little chat about the cathedral. Yes, her daughter was a devout member of the flock. Yes, her daughter shared her mother's love of the church and she was just dying to make this same grant next year. Yes, yes, of course, annually. Who was she marrying? Why, James Ballantine, an up-and-coming young executive. Yes, *once married*, James would be inclined to recommend the church to his company's charity committee! Martha wasn't really sure if there was such a thing, but it certainly sounded good and Pastor Baines did not look the type to know any better.

Even with his support one did not get the cathedral, of course. There was a list. It was long and it contained couples who had been waiting for years. Some of them probably weren't even together any more.

She had pleaded and cajoled and twisted some arms and called in some old favours. And she had *won*! She had won and Lucille was going to marry James Ballantine in the wedding of the year. The wedding of the *decade*, she corrected herself.

To say the least, her daughter's reaction was a disappointment. Lucille smiled tentatively. 'That's great, Mom,' she said. 'Absolutely wonderful. Do we have any more Vaseline around the house?'

'I went through hell getting you that cathedral, young lady. The least you can do is show a little appreciation.' She sniffed and walked out into the kitchen for a snack.

She remembered something. 'We have to have another rehearsal, of course. At the cathedral. I know it's the third and your father will refuse to come, but it's a new site and we have to . . .'

'Fine, Mom!' Lucille snapped. She was speculatively eyeing a tub of margarine.

Before this third, final rehearsal, her daughter's fiancé threw a party – no, Martha corrected herself, he gave a reception. It was 'give'; that was the word, she was almost sure of it. He was giving a reception to the wedding party and some select friends.

Martha looked around the restaurant with considerable pride. Using every last bit of influence she could muster, she had managed to secure the cathedral for the ceremony. She nearly rubbed her hands together again. They'd got *the cathedral*! Her daughter was about to marry an eminently suitable young man *in the cathedral*! Why, she would be able to show off the wedding pictures to everyone, meaning everyone who was anyone. Speaking of everyone . . .

'Where is everyone?' she asked. She was obviously nervous. Being a woman of considerable girth, in her green dress she looked like an enormous shambling bush. 'I can't believe she didn't let me help her get ready . . . It's very unusual, don't you think? I mean, I am her mother. When is she coming?'

The wedding planner shrugged and rolled her eyes. 'Why don't you have some appetisers?' She gestured in the direction of the side table. 'There is a cheese platter over there, I think. I'm sure you can find it. I know your daughter, ma'am – I'm pretty sure she's coming just about now.'

Subtle attacks had little chance of permeating the layers of ignorance that coated Martha's mind; still, she couldn't shake the notion that she was being bribed with cheese. Who was this cheeky blonde anyway? She did not like all these changes.

'Where is Lucille? I mean, even her sister hasn't seen her yet and she will be the Maid of Honour.'

Pamela walked up. Her lavender bridesmaid's dress was slightly rumpled. She was crying!

'I can't believe she's done this to me!' s

Martha looked at her daughter, scandal
going to ruin her makeup! 'Honey, honey – w
mean?'

'Didn't she tell you? I was told –' Pamela point
the wedding planner, '– I mean – I mean she told me
Lucille told Holly Childress she would be her maid of
honour!'

'What?' Martha shook her by the shoulders. 'What did
you just say?!'

'Oh yeah, I forgot to mention it.' The wedding planner
smirked, stifling a yawn. 'Last-minute jitters, I'm sure.'

'That's preposterous! I mean, we can't change it now.
Look at the invitations, everything is ready . . . What about
the embossed stationery?' Martha gaped at the insouciant
wedding planner in shock.

'What?'

Martha ripped an invitation from a passing guest. The
poor man was a distant cousin, irrelevant.

'Now you look here,' she told the wedding planner,
brandishing the invitation like some amulet against evil.
She stabbed a fat ring-encrusted finger at a line on the
header. 'It says here "Pamela White – Maid of Honour"; it
doesn't say "Holly Childress"; do you understand? We
have stationery – thousands of sheets of goddamned
stationery – and every single goddamned one of them says
"Pamela White – Maid of Honour". We *can't* change it
now. Where is my daughter?'

'You're right, it shouldn't say Holly Childress.' The
woman laughed. 'It should say Trixie – Trixie Pixie? There
is something to think up on a rainy night . . .'

'What're you talking about? Where is Holly, anyway?'

'She'll be around, I'm sure.' The wedding planner
snapped her fingers and a waiter materialised with a tray
of cheeses. She picked up a toothpick kebab of blue cheese
and popped it in her mouth. 'Tasty – have some. It'll calm
you down.'

Martha tried to get a hold of herself. 'Look, I mean to
clear this up with Lucille immediately.'

'Go ahead.' The woman pointed at the basement stairs.

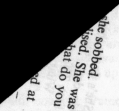

k she's trying to relax before her
/Might want to slim down some
etty narrow.'
cille doing in the basement?
ur sister at once!'

slowly negotiated the stairs. She
the uncomfortable high heels if it
ding planner. Michele was keeping a
tight grip on her arm. 'Thanks,' she said. The blonde was
sort of a bitch but it was sure nice of her to keep her from
falling on those stairs.

'No problem,' she said. She pointed at a door. 'Your
sister is in the laundry room with some old friends.'

Pamela opened the door and stormed inside. 'Lucille,
what's . . . OH MY GOD!'

Lucille's wedding gown was a matted ruin. Gobs of
white gummed the folds of antique lace. Her sister's hair
(400 dollars at a downtown hair salon) was also dripping
with the same lotion. She was on her knees with six black
men lined up in a row, all tall, all muscular, all drinking
beer. Pamela's brain catalogued the brand – it was a cheap
domestic. The men had not bothered to take off their
clothes; they had simply unzipped their pants and dangled
their members within reach of Lucille's questing lips and
fingers. One of them finished his beer. He put the can on
Lucille's back – it fell over her side with a loud clang – and
his cock in her mouth.

Lucille looked like a gang-bang victim but she certainly
didn't act like a gang-bang victim.

'Little Kitty is a slut,' Michele whispered in Pamela's
ear. 'Little Kitty can't go through the rehearsal looking
like this.'

'Oh my God,' groaned Pamela. She had never expected
to see a gang-bang orgy in real life. Never. 'Oh my God.'
One of the men walked behind Lucille and lifted Grand-
ma's wedding gown to finger her sister's ass. Lucille
squealed with delight.

'Mother is going to kill her,' declared Pamela.

'Maybe there is another way,' said Michele. 'What if you

230

said she had come down with a sudden case of – stomach flu?'

Lucille choked on a monstrous cock. Instead of spitting it out she somehow controlled the spasm and worked her lips higher on the enormous black member.

'Maybe she swallowed something that didn't agree with her?'

'Oh my God . . .' Pamela's brain was simply not able to come to grips with what she was seeing. It retreated to mere mechanics. She processed Michele's words and spat out some kind of an automated response. 'I guess. I guess we don't have to do the rehearsal. But James missed the first one at the church and this is the only one we get to do at the cathedral.' For the moment she ignored the fact that her haughty sister was a come-drenched whore. Jesus Christ. The guy on the right had a *big* penis. 'He has to – I mean, he needs to do this.'

'Of course,' gushed Michele. 'I understand. You know, I know just the girl. She'll stand in for Lucille. She's *very* friendly, you'll like her. She has been on my staff for ages – and you know, it's just so lucky for Lucille that Becky always wanted to get married in a cathedral.'

Michele patted Pamela's hand and pulled her up the stairs. 'Please let me introduce you two. Now just remember to tell your mother not to worry – minor stomach flu, that's all. Lucille is – being tended to . . .'

'In the basement? She'll never believe it. Lucille hates basements.'

'Tell her she has a headache and she doesn't want any sound. She has to have complete silence.'

'That's pretty clever,' said Pamela. The guy with the largest cock casually glanced in her direction. Pamela looked away, blushing. 'She'll believe that.'

'So, this is the young lady?' Pastor Baines beamed. He was fat and jolly with sparkling black eyes and a double chin.

'No,' said Martha. 'She's a stand-in. Lucille got sick.'

Pastor Baines turned to her. 'I am very sorry to hear that. I hope she will be fine soon,' he slowly enunciated.

'Oh, it's just a minor stomach flu. She'll be all right.'

'Very good then. Everything will be all right. Shall we?'

Why was the man talking to her like she was some violent retard?

The stand-in whispered something to James. She was certainly well dressed for the rehearsal, thought Martha. The woman was actually wearing a wedding gown, although a most revealing one. That slit went up past mid-thigh and the cleavage ... Well, that cleavage could not possibly be natural. Of course James wore his tuxedo.

'I think I ...' said James. He looked lost.

The stand-in grabbed his arm. She had long pink nails. The woman was engaged – she wore a diamond ring with a very large stone, princess cut. It looked like Lucille's. Could she have loaned her ring to this woman for the ceremony? Martha thought that was going a touch too far for the sake of realism. Perhaps it was a fake? The woman did not look like upper class – she had too much makeup on, platinum-blonde hair and those long pink nails. She pulled James off to the side and whispered something to him. Why was that woman talking to her prospective son-in-law? She was determined to get to the bottom of this.

'Let's give them some privacy,' said one of the groomsmen. 'Let them talk.'

Martha fought to place him. He was a mutual friend of James's and Robert Waverly's. 'Scott?'

'Yes – how're you doing, Mrs White? How is your blood pressure?'

Was he a doctor too? 'Doing fine, fine ... That woman is on the wedding planner's staff. She's talking to James ...'

'Well, she must know how it goes better than he does. She must have done hundreds of these.'

She had to admit that he had a point.

The stand-in straightened James's bow tie. She whispered to him some more.

Scott offered her his arm. 'Look, they're taking their places.'

Yes, she was pretty sure that he was a doctor. She took his arm gratefully and he lead her to her seat in the front pew.

'I spoke to the wedding planner,' said Scott. 'She said they wanted the rehearsal to be as realistic as possible. "Lucille" will marry James. It'll look like the real thing.'

Martha rolled her eyes. 'Yes, sure. I hope we can wrap this up soon. I can't really get into the spirit of things without Lucille here.'

Pastor Baines took his place at the altar. He avoided the eyes of the unfortunate creature in the front row. Doctor Waverly had assured him that she was not dangerous as long as her delusions about her daughter went unquestioned. Still, it was a sad, sad thing that the woman couldn't even enjoy what should be her proudest moment.

At least Doctor Waverly's friend, Martha White's personal physician, was sitting next to her. He would keep her occupied during the ceremony. Privately, given the peculiar circumstances, Pastor Baines thought that it was a good idea to perform the ceremony in this manner. Everyone was pretending that it was just a rehearsal. The merciful fiction allowed the old lady to continue to function in a state resembling normality (except that she didn't acknowledge her own daughter, of course). Why, everyone in the wedding played along beautifully. Some in the wedding party hadn't even put on formal wear. Lucille White and James Ballantine would enter holy matrimony today under the arches of the cathedral and the annual grant from James's company would help hundreds of women like Martha White cope with their sad lives.

Epilogue

Whenever Trixie went more than twenty feet or so from the kitchen the waves of pleasure just cut off. She kept searching but couldn't find the remote. She was bored – not that she had the faculties to do anything more demanding than strut around being the blonde bimbo maid that she was.

There was really no point in leaving the kitchen in any case. She had a lot to do, decorating dishes of appetisers, cooking and cleaning. She really wanted to please Michele and Lucille – after all, they had promised to be here for the party. There was champagne in the refrigerator and plenty of food too, professionally catered for Robert's upcoming bachelor party – but of course she was not allowed to eat or drink from that batch.

She checked her uniform in the mirror. It was a proper maid's uniform with a tiny miniskirt and a top that showed off her new DD tits. She found it difficult to walk around with all this new weight – her breasts kept unbalancing her when she walked – but Becky-Lucille liked to rub her own tits up against them and that made her pussy so wet nothing else mattered. Maybe she could go over to Gordon and ask him nicely for a sandwich – or a long hot dog. She giggled as she imagined his expression. Michele would like it; she seemed to enjoy sending her over to Gordon for all kinds of things on a regular basis. Irene didn't seem to be around much any more.

* * *

James drank some more coffee. God, he had a splitting headache! He lifted his eyes to stare at the hazy cloud of numbers on the screen. They all seemed to melt together. What the hell?

He shook his weary head. He was so tired! He had been at work for 48 hours straight. He needed to demonstrate his commitment to the company, of course – it was nearly bonus time and he had already spent the money, plus some. Becky – or as she insisted on being called in public, Lucille – demanded to be kept in the style to which she had become accustomed, and he could not possibly blame her. He felt himself get hard simply thinking about his wife.

Why, she had even insisted on coming along with him to the company's team-building function at Lake Tahoe. Barely any of the wives had attended the event. She'd insisted on spending time with him during the executive functions, getting to know the other top people at the company. She'd told him in no uncertain terms how grateful he should be for allowing him the pleasure of her presence. He'd only raised objections once, when he had been specifically told not to bring anyone to a top management-only meeting.

She had been petulant.

'Honey, I'm sorry, there is nothing I can do about it,' he had sighed. 'Jackson told us not to bring the spouses.'

'But I want to go!' she had whined. She'd strutted closer and sat in his lap, covering his head in her cascading avalanche of platinum-blonde curls. She'd unzipped his fly and begun to tease his cock with her fingers. 'Pweeeease, Jimmy!'

As always, she'd got her way.

She even got to meet Jackson. Strangely enough, the CEO did not object to her presence after he had met her at the reception. In fact, he insisted on giving James the responsibility of overseeing the new Saudi project – unfortunately, Becky had to remain behind for its entire duration. Women were not allowed in the Saudi facility at all. Jackson promised to keep an eye on her to make sure she had everything she needed while he was away.

* * *

235

Kitty looked through her shoes with a critical eye. She picked out a pair of shiny metallic six-inch stilettos to go with the latex cocktail dress she had selected to wear during the show. After all, she wanted to look her best – her instructions were that Robert's colleagues at the clinic should be blown away. She was extra careful. Whenever she did a show with Fifi she made sure she looked damned hot. In any case she didn't want to be upstaged by her sister's hot new tits – they were even bigger than Trixie's. The girl was just willing to do anything to get attention, the little slut.

So Kitty was determined to blow them away.

She giggled and covered her lips with her hand. If some of them played their cards right, they would be blown to be sure . . .

Scott and Michele were standing in front of Hot Summer's, by the curb. They were concluding a brief conversation in front of the fire-engine-red Austin Healey roadster.

'You know, they were no good for them anyway,' said Scott. 'No good at all.'

Michele smiled. 'You're so right. Why talk about it? Tina and Heather are waiting for you upstairs, Scott.'

Scott nodded slowly. He opened his mouth to say something but just then Heather came out of the scented darkness and pulled him inside.

In the champagne room, Tina took her customary place on Scott's knee. She rubbed up against him until she was sure she had his undivided attention. 'I've been sooo bad!' she sobbed. 'I've been such a slut!'

Heather sniffed. 'Don't believe her, she's a lying whore.' She flung herself down on the sofa next to him and peeled off her glittering teddy, freeing her luscious tits. She grabbed Scott's hand and pressed it in that awesome valley and then pushed her breasts together, trapping his hand. She giggled and tossed her long black hair. Her voice became a seductive purr. 'Play with me first!'

At the curb in front of Hot Summer's, Michele got in her new car. She turned the ignition and revved the engine. She closed her eyes and caressed the dashboard, twice tapping her shiny red nails on the polished walnut. She spoke slowly, savouring each word. 'Everyone got the toy that made them happy. Everyone. And mine is the most beautiful toy in the world.'

nexus

The leading publisher of fetish and adult fiction

TELL US WHAT YOU THINK!

Readers' ideas and opinions matter to us so please take a few minutes to fill in the questionnaire below.

1. Sex: Are you male ☐ female ☐ a couple ☐?

2. Age: Under 21 ☐ 21–30 ☐ 31–40 ☐ 41–50 ☐ 51–60 ☐ over 60 ☐

3. Where do you buy your Nexus books from?

☐ A chain book shop. If so, which one(s)?

_____

☐ An independent book shop. If so, which one(s)?

_____

☐ A used book shop/charity shop
☐ Online book store. If so, which one(s)?

_____

4. How did you find out about Nexus books?

☐ Browsing in a book shop
☐ A review in a magazine
☐ Online
☐ Recommendation
☐ Other _____

5. In terms of settings, which do you prefer? (Tick as many as you like.)

☐ Down to earth and as realistic as possible
☐ Historical settings. If so, which period do you prefer?

_____

☐ Fantasy settings – barbarian worlds
☐ Completely escapist/surreal fantasy

☐ Institutional or secret academy
☐ Futuristic/sci fi
☐ Escapist but still believable
☐ Any settings you dislike?

_____

☐ Where would you like to see an adult novel set?

_____

6. In terms of storylines, would you prefer:
☐ Simple stories that concentrate on adult interests?
☐ More plot and character-driven stories with less explicit adult activity?
☐ We value your ideas, so give us your opinion of this book:

_____

_____

_____

7. In terms of your adult interests, what do you like to read about? (Tick as many as you like.)
☐ Traditional corporal punishment (CP)
☐ Modern corporal punishment
☐ Spanking
☐ Restraint/bondage
☐ Rope bondage
☐ Latex/rubber
☐ Leather
☐ Female domination and male submission
☐ Female domination and female submission
☐ Male domination and female submission
☐ Willing captivity
☐ Uniforms
☐ Lingerie/underwear/hosiery/footwear (boots and high heels)
☐ Sex rituals
☐ Vanilla sex
☐ Swinging
☐ Cross-dressing/TV

☐ Enforced feminisation

☐ Others – tell us what you don't see enough of in adult fiction:

_____

_____

_____

8. Would you prefer books with a more specialised approach to your interests, i.e. a novel specifically about uniforms? If so, which subject(s) would you like to read a Nexus novel about?

_____

_____

_____

9. Would you like to read true stories in Nexus books? For instance, the true story of a submissive woman, or a male slave? Tell us which true revelations you would most like to read about:

_____

_____

_____

10. What do you like best about Nexus books?

_____

_____

11. What do you like least about Nexus books?

_____

_____

12. Which are your favourite titles?

_____

_____

13. Who are your favourite authors?

_____

_____

14. **Which covers do you prefer? Those featuring:**
    (Tick as many as you like.)

☐ Fetish outfits
☐ More nudity
☐ Two models
☐ Unusual models or settings
☐ Classic erotic photography
☐ More contemporary images and poses
☐ A blank/non-erotic cover
☐ What would your ideal cover look like?

_____

15. **Describe your ideal Nexus novel in the space provided:**

_____
_____
_____
_____

16. **Which celebrity would feature in one of your Nexus-style fantasies?**
    We'll post the best suggestions on our website – anonymously!

_____

THANKS FOR YOUR TIME

Now simply write the title of this book in the space below and cut out the
questionnaire pages. Post to: Nexus, Marketing Dept., Thames Wharf Studios,
Rainville Rd, London W6 9HA

Book title: _____

nexus

NEXUS NEW BOOKS

To be published in September 2007

BEING A GIRL
Chloë Thurlow

When Milly is late for a vital interview on a sweltering day, casting agent Jean-Luc Cartier pours her some water and holds the glass to her lips. When the water soaks her blouse he instructs her to take it off. Milly is embarrassed but curious. As she strips off her clothes, more than her shapely body is revealed; her deepest nature is slowly uncovered.

Jean-Luc puts her over his knee. He spanks her bottom and her virgin orgasm awakens her to the mysteries of discipline. Milly at 18 is at the beginning of an erotic journey from convent school to a black magic coven in the heart of Cambridge academia, to the secret world of fetishism and bondage on the dark side of the movie camera.

£6.99   ISBN 978 0 352 34139 6

To be published in October 2007

LUST CALL
Ray Gordon

Attractive, blonde Sarah lives happily with her husband in a state of suburban bliss. Until she receives a salacious email from a man called 'Brian', who knows intimate details about her. It suggests she is being watched. More mails arrive admiring her sexy outfits. Her bemusement soon turns to curiosity and she begins a correspondence with Brian. Convinced the writer is her husband, she begins to follow the requests in the emails and engages in sexual games with her husband. Hooked on the game, the requests become more extreme and she engages in affairs with other men. It is only then that she becomes aware that the identity behind Brian is not her husband. A stranger has transformed her from a loyal loving wife, to an insatiable adulterer.

Swamped by an overwhelming desire not only to discover who Brian is, but to find gratification from outrageous sexual acts, she begins to seduce the men she suspects are Brian. Time after time she attempts to solve the mystery of Brian, but fails, while slipping further and further into shame and depravity. And all the time, he watches, until . . . finally, he is revealed.

£6.99   ISBN 978 0 352 34143 3

CUCKOLD
Amber Leigh

A little knowledge is a dangerous thing. But that's all Edwin Miller wants. He has a good job, a pleasant home, and is married to the beautiful and loving Des. All he needs to make his life complete is the answer to one question:

Has his wife made him a cuckold?

Not sure if the idea is the sum of his fears, or the revelation of his true desire, Edwin struggles to uncover the truth. But the answer could mean his life is never the same again.

£6.99   ISBN 978 0 352 34140 2